I WILL ALWAYS LOVE YOU (MAYBE)

DANA HAWKINS

Storm

Ebook ISBN: 978-1-83700-063-0
Paperback ISBN: 978-1-83700-065-4

Cover design by Rachel Lawston
Cover illustration © Rachel Lawston

Published by Storm Publishing.
For further information, visit:
www.stormpublishing.co

ALSO BY DANA HAWKINS

Not in the Plan
In Walked Trouble
So Not My Type
The Ex Effect
Any Girl But You

*To my dad. I miss you every single day.
And to Kona. You are so much more than the "family dog." Thank
you for all the joy you've brought us over the years. We are so lucky
to have you as our fur baby.*

CONTENT WARNING

Although my book contains sparkles, I deal with a couple of heavier issues, including dealing with an unexpected death of a spouse and a dog going through surgery (the dog is fine! I promise). Please proceed with caution.

ONE

COLBY

Dog moms are a little bit like human moms—most everyone thinks their little one is a special snowflake. And I'm no exception. But my golden retriever, Kona, really *is* different. I'm not a violent person at all, unless of course a ref makes a terrible call during a nail-biter Minnesota Lynx WNBA game. But if anyone dare disagree that Kona is the best dog floated down to me from dog heaven, I might be tempted to throw down.

"Right, girl? Would Mama kick some butt for you?" I ask, bending down to rub the soft spot behind Kona's ears, which over the years has become as much of a calming mechanism for me as for her. And my poor girl; along with her upcoming CCL (ACL for us humans) surgery, she might have to get a fur replacement behind those ears, too.

Alongside me, Kona's paws crunch through the freshly fallen snow. Snapping twigs and branches are the only other sounds in my forested plot. The northern Minnesota winter air is dry and crisp, laced with the scents of pine trees and fresh snow. Sitting just outside of Duluth, I live in a pocket of what's considered some of the cleanest and most pristine air in the country—which is part of why I moved here six years ago, at a time when I felt like I couldn't breathe.

Minnesota offered me a fresh start, a place to shed my past, to help me move on. As a native Floridian, though, perhaps I should have done a little more research on exactly *how* cold and *how* much snow this place got before I settled on buying a secluded cabin in the woods.

Kona's sniffing the snow and trees, following the scent of whatever wildlife may have roamed my property last night. Despite the limp in her leg, she's happy. I swear if I could bottle up some of this doggie joy and sell it on eBay or something, I'd be a millionaire. How my girl can be in pain *and* happy at the same time, I'll never know. A few weeks ago, I tweaked my back from chopping wood and was in a funk for a week. Kona's been dealing with a torn ligament and still looks like she'd lick to death anyone who may come our way.

Five years ago when I took in Kona, everyone warned me that she'd probably, eventually, need this surgery. They said that golden retrievers are likely to develop arthritis, hip issues, ear infections, and a bunch of other things that I absolutely didn't listen to. I didn't need to, because there was no way I was keeping the dog. My former in-laws had to practically force me, kicking and screaming (not actually kicking, but yes, definite screaming), to foster the puppy until they found her the proper home. I needed something to love, they said. Something to take care of, a *purpose*. I disagreed but caved and said I'd take her for a month and not a second longer.

And then this dog that peed everywhere, and chewed the wood frame on my bedroom door, and disrupted my sleep for months, became my everything. Literally, my everything. I took up crocheting so I could make her blankets, I cook her all fresh organic food, I bring her everywhere with me. I even refuse to reframe the door, keeping her puppy chomps as a memory piece, probably the way a human mom keeps the little notches on the wall where they measured the child's height. Kona's not classified as an emotional support dog, but I swear she could be.

"Okay, girl, stay." I pop open my Jeep's tailgate and lug out the ramp. "Pretty soon, you'll be able to hop up there just like me in my college days when I used to hop up on stage and belt out a karaoke song to win free beer. What? I never told you that story?"

Do I know it's a little weird that I talk to my dog this much? Sure. Probably. I've never even had so much as a hamster before this, so I'm not really sure of the standard protocol of human–dog relationships. But besides wandering into town and chatting with the owner of Zoey's Bakery during my once-a-week cupcake run, thanking the cashier for ringing up my groceries, or the few times I bump into a delivery driver who's dropping off a package, Kona is my only interaction.

And I don't mean that figuratively.

I live alone, purposely. When my wife unexpectedly died six years ago, ripped from my arms in a snap, it changed everything in me—including the want or need to get close to anyone. The heartache was indescribable. The emptiness so sudden, so stark, so drastic, that weeks passed before I realized she was actually gone. A darkness invaded me. The kind that burns into your skin, etches into your soul, leaves you lifeless and steals your breath.

Everything changes in a moment like that. The way you sleep, eat, live... all gone. The person I was no longer exists, she died along with my wife. And the person I am now has a five-layer steel protective shield around her heart.

Kona waddles up the ramp and nestles into her blanket. Guilt flushes through me that she probably thinks we're going to Zoey's Bakery for doggie treats or into town on some fun adventure, but really, I'm taking her in for a procedure. A *routine* procedure, the vet said.

But I know a little something about routine procedures.

"It's gonna be okay, girl. Don't you worry about a thing," I say to Kona, but I know I'm saying it to myself. My pulse quickens, and I quickly pet her behind the ears. The slam of the tailgate echoes against the trees, and I rest my forehead on the window for just a moment, trying to regulate my breathing.

We bump down the long windy gravel drive with a layer of

fresh snow, and before I reach the edge, I skitter to a stop as a family of deer hop along. One turns and looks at me with large brown doe-eyes, and I swear it's looking into my soul. *Amelia?* I see signs like this, or what I think are signs, from my wife all the time. A butterfly resting on my arm. A deer peering at me. A peek of a rainbow through parted clouds. But, then sometimes, I think it is what it is—part of nature that means nothing.

Signs. For years, we missed the signs. Us, the doctors. No one knew, they said. No one could have known, they said. Amelia would joke that she was out of shape when she got fatigued or ran out of breath too quickly. We'd laugh about the days as teens when we could tear around the soccer field, but once we hit our late twenties, we were done and needed more rest.

You couldn't have known...

On the country road heading towards Spring Harbors, my lifted tires easily plow through the snow. I flip on the radio, look at Kona, try to take in the serene surroundings, but it's useless. No matter what I do, I cannot distract myself from what happened six years ago. The thoughts of that day invade me, stick into my skin like a webbed thorn. The doctors did all the pre-op tests. Amelia was a young, healthy, thirty-year-old woman with a torn rotator cuff. That morning, we'd gotten dressed, and she complained that she couldn't have her skinny vanilla latte before the surgery. At the hospital, she snapped a selfie in her hospital gown, told me I had to film her after surgery so she could see what she was like coming out of anesthesia, and made me promise that before we left the hospital I'd steal the wheelchair and whip her around in circles like we were at the teacup ride at Disney World.

I teased her that I was going to hop over to Disney World while she was in surgery. Which of course, I would've never done because one, Amelia would've killed me, and two, Disney World is not my thing at all. I used to joke that if anyone ever questioned my love for my wife, all they had to do was look at the yearly photos of me at Disney wearing the most embarrassing—and tight—red-and-white Minnie Mouse ears. But Amelia loved it, so it was a small sacrifice.

When I pull up to the red light, I adjust my rearview mirror to look at Kona. She's so content, resting on top of her blankie. Ugh. Maybe we don't have to do this today. I mean, she looks happy. Why would you put an animal through surgery when they're *happy*? Selfishly, I've already held out longer than I probably should've getting her this surgery. Putting Kona under the knife felt extreme. I'd talked to the vet in Spring Harbors, got a second opinion, then a third. I read every article on canine pain meds, physical therapy, light therapy, vitamins. I increased the fresh salmon and eggs in her diet, kept her walks to a minimum, but nothing changed.

Routine surgery.

Shaky, unsteady breaths release with each mile. When we finally pull up to the clinic, my hands are so fatigued from gripping the steering wheel that they start to tingle. "Ready, girl?" I say, shaking out my grip. But *I'm* not ready. Maybe I can reschedule. Get a fourth or fifth opinion. Is there some sort of acupuncture they can give dogs? Could I sacrifice something to the gods? I mean, really, how often do I use my pinkie?

I pop open the tailgate and give her a rub behind the ears. "Okay, girl, we got this," I say to my unsuspecting, innocent dog as I lower and adjust the ramp. "You be brave and I'll be brave, and in a few hours this nightmare will end. And you're going to feel so much better, okay? There is nothing to worry about."

The leash feels so natural in my hand, the leather band worn down to a soft, smooth surface. My heartbeat locks in my throat. If something happens today, do I just spend the rest of my life walking alone? With nothing in my hand, with no purpose?

I ease Kona down the ramp, and she wobbles on one leg. *Sweet girl.* So trusting, so happy, so totally unsuspecting of what's going to come. Each step closer to the entrance, my heartbeat thumps harder, and a deep sickliness settles in my stomach. The sharp cool breeze springs tears to my eyes, layering on the fear-laced tears already present. I pull in air, singeing my nostrils, try to wave off the nausea, and march through the doors.

Inside, I do a perimeter sweep like I'm a special agent and Kona is my principal client. The place smells clean, like the last time we were here, a faint scent of lemon antiseptic and floor cleaner. It's bright and airy, with a small waiting area with hard black benches. A dog is in the corner, some black lab mix, and I pause. Are they friendly? Properly leashed? A man sits on the bench with a cat in a carrier on the floor, and a woman at the counter has something rattling in a shoebox.

I exhale. So far, so good.

"Hey there, beautiful!"

A cheery voice cuts across the room, and I peek at the woman who it belongs to. Soft pink hair, less cotton-candy and more pink-kissed; rose sleeve tattoos poking out from under her scrubs; a hoop nose ring; and lovely, warm, chocolate brown eyes.

"I'm talking to the dog, not you," she says, then pulls her pink-glossed lips into a smile. "And that sounded a thousand times worse than what I intended. Apologies. I'm only on coffee number four and it's normally twelve by now, so I can't be fully held responsible for my words or actions."

For the first time today, I crack a small grin.

The woman doesn't remember me, and that's okay. But I remember her. *Josie*. A year or so ago, I briefly met her on the sidewalk as she walked with Zoey, the owner of Zoey's Bakery. Her hair was a little different, brown back then, more of a shag and less of the messy bun length it is now. But even with new hair, someone like her is pretty memorable.

Sure, I don't talk to hardly anyone, so it's not that out of the ordinary that I'd remember one interaction from a year ago. But even if I was crowned the town's resident social butterfly, I'm pretty sure I would've remembered her. Besides the high apple cheekbones and wide smile, she had a sort of... sparkle. One that seemed to sprinkle around her and floated to me and somehow captured me in that moment. And despite the fact that we only chatted for a few minutes, I very much went home and thought of her one too many times over those next few weeks.

With Kona panting at my side, I clear the slight nerves from my throat. "I'm here to check in Kona for her appointment."

Josie's short, bright, hot pink nails dash across the keyboard as her eyes scan the monitor. "Looks like we have a routine CCL scheduled for today."

My chest pinches tight. *Routine.* That's what they said for Amelia. Only, nothing about that day was routine. Flashes of the hospital lights flicker at the edge of my vision. In a snap, I can smell the antiseptic, hear the shuffling of the nursing staff's hurried footsteps among the beeping of heart monitors. And then... I see the doctor sitting me down to deliver the news. The way his face dropped, the way he put out a hand when he asked me to sit down, the way his gaze flicked to the floor.

"Excuse me? Colby?" Josie says, a small crease forming between her brows.

The vet clinic narrows back into my vision. "I'm sorry, what?"

Josie stands, and the stiff fabric of the pink scrubs with miniature rainbow unicorns scrapes against itself. Safe to say she obviously has a signature color. "If you could sign here and here," she says, circling two spots on the paperwork.

I'm frozen. I hear her, I feel Kona next to me, I'm rubbing the back of her ears like they're a stress ball, and still, I'm motionless. Once I sign this, they'll take Kona away. My signature is the last and final article of defense. I don't know if I can do it.

My eyes search Josie's face, begging her to say a scientist discovered a last-minute pill that will heal dog ligaments without surgery. Or that the doctor made a discovery during the third consultation and the only thing Kona needs is a brace. My pulse is racing in my chest, my mouth turns dry.

A small dimple pops in the corner of Josie's cheek. Her smile is kind, *really* kind, and any other day I would maybe take comfort in it. But today, I can't. "Signature?" she says again.

The pen trembles in my hands. I hold my breath and scribble across the paper.

"Awesome." Josie tucks the papers back in a file, types a few more things, and clicks, like I didn't just sign for my dog to be put under, cut open, and potentially leave me for life. She moves from behind the counter, squats in front of Kona, and holds out her hand for Kona to sniff. "I'll take the leash."

My grip tightens around the final lifeline to my dog. "I want to go back there with her."

Josie frowns sympathetically. "I know, but we can't." She strokes Kona's fur, and behind her ear, like she knows exactly her favorite spots. "The handoff is here. But I promise she'll be given such good care."

Breathe. This vet clinic is probably doing five of these surgeries this week, did five last week, and will do five next week. I keep repeating this to myself, but my brain is fighting away the logic.

It was a freak occurrence, they said. We are so sorry, they said.

My shoulders stiffen and Kona looks at me, surely smelling my energy. A tremble starts in my chin. When I lower myself to kneel in front of her and scratch under her chin, I can barely look into those deep, unsuspecting, trusting eyes. "You be a good girl, okay?" My voice cracks and I clear my throat to cover it. "You're going to take a quick little nap, and everything will be better. I'll be right here waiting for you."

When I hand over the leash, the hot sting of tears rushes behind my eyes.

"We got it from here," Josie says with a reassuring grin, palming the leash. "We'll call you when it's time to pick her up."

Absolutely not. "I'm going to stay right here."

Josie squints, confused, and I can see why. This vet hospital is not like a doctor's office. There are no cushy chairs, no vending machines, no TV in the corner silently playing the news. "Really, it's probably best if you leave," she says. "This will be at least a five-hour—"

"I'm not leaving." My voice is firm, leaving no room for negotiation. I don't know their policy, but I won't back down. With Amelia, they told me to leave, and I did. I walked my ass down to Starbucks, drank a mocha, and brought my work laptop to catch up on some meaningless quarterly financial report, not knowing that my wife was across the street, fighting for her life.

I refuse to do that with Kona.

Josie's smile fades, but she nods. "Okay. Well, make yourself as comfortable as you can and let me know if you need anything." When I don't move, don't blink, probably don't even breathe, Josie places a warm hand on my forearm and gives it a little squeeze. "We're going to take really good care of her."

And an immediate assault of conflicting emotions barrel through me. Besides my family, my doctor, and my dentist, that touch was the first physical contact I've had since Amelia passed. The moment was so quick, a whisper really, but my arm is still tingling. But then, as I watch Kona hobble back with Josie, so trusting, so peaceful, my body sinks.

Kona probably thinks she's going to play or maybe get a treat. Sure, she's a little agitated being in this place with all the animal smells and new people, but an outsider would hardly be able to tell. I bring her with me almost everywhere, and she's acclimated to most places.

Routine surgery.

So I wait. One hour turns into two. My butt gets sore on the hard wooden bench. I read the back of every single product label on their shelf, I pace, I sit. For ten, maybe twenty minutes, I stare out the window at the soft dusting of snow, and feel the minutes click by like someone is strangling a noose on me, notch by notch. Everything in me is screaming when I step outside to pull in some cold, fresh air before coming back to start my pacing and sitting routine again.

Two and a half hours in, the anxiety has set in to the deepest part of my bones, it's in my core, and I'm going to puke. Something is very, very wrong. My heartbeat is pounding so hard that I can't hear the animals or any voices over it.

When a clinic staff comes from the back room and whispers to Josie, taking a hard glance at me, the world stops moving. I leap from my seat and bolt to the counter. I know exactly what they are going to say, and God help me, I don't think I can handle it.

TWO

JOSIE

I kind of hate myself for pretending that I didn't remember Colby from the moment she walked into our vet clinic a few hours ago. Now it's going to be weird, and I'll feel all unsettled and jittery for the rest of the day. Which, honestly, is a state I'm pretty used to.

What I should have said was that I'd actually thought of Colby more than a few times this last year after we'd met, and idly wondered if I'd run into her again. However—as to not be that freaky sort of intense person that I've been accused of being in the past—I'd withhold that I walked down that same sidewalk several times a week for a month or so, just to see if I'd bump into her.

Besides not wanting to come off like a stalker, I know *exactly* why I didn't say anything to Colby. And right now, I'm not trying to think about those reasons. I've spent the last year burying those thoughts and the last thing I want to do is dredge up the past and mess with my current inner harmony.

This town is not that big, and a woman like Colby is extremely hard to forget. She has this incredible chestnut brown hair, so thick that I wonder if it gives her headaches being tied into that ponytail. And she has these eyes... huge, beautiful, amber brown eyes, accented by the type of deep black eyelashes that companies would pay good money to replicate. The type of eyes that feel like she's allowing you a glimpse into her soul, set perfectly on a heart-shaped face.

But way more than her obvious beauty, Colby carries a sort of introspectiveness, a stillness, that's rare and hard to explain. I picked up on it immediately when I met her last year and I saw it again today. It's like she's observing everything first, and she thinks, thoughtfully, before she speaks. Maybe I noticed it because it's so opposite of me—the one who laughs the loudest in the room, the one whose goal in life is to make people around me smile, the one as a child always scolded for being too loud, too obnoxious, *too much*. I've always been just a little too much for everyone, but I don't know how to be less. Back then, I wanted to dance and sing and audition for *Annie*. Community theater, drama, debate team... I joined everything in the hopes of being seen. And I've been chasing this same urge my entire life.

Whereas Colby seems like the type who's content to sit in a coffee shop, read a book, and observe quietly in the corner.

However, had I not remembered Colby, I certainly would've remembered that dog. I've always held a soft spot for goldens, and that Kona girl melted my heart the second I laid eyes on her last year on the sidewalk. Someday when I'm responsible enough, I'm going to adopt one.

At the desk, I check in a pet bunny for stitches, a cat for its wellness check, answer a call about a mobile vet for horse vaccines, and keep my eye on Colby. We've had patients sit here before, but never for this particular surgery. Five hours minimum. We're close to three hours in, and Colby hasn't even so much as pulled out her phone to doomscroll. I swear I want to introduce her to the magic of TMZ, or Reels. But she goes from pacing, to clasping her fingers behind her neck, to staring out the window, to asking me, yet again, if there are any updates. Every thirty minutes, like clockwork.

And just a few minutes ago, after a vet tech came and whispered about some breakroom drama—there's a yogurt stealer among us—Colby bolted to the front desk like someone popped off a gunshot. It took a little convincing to assure her that the conversation had nothing to do with Kona.

"Hey, how did the Bikram yoga go today?" Leo, the head receptionist, who also doubles as my cousin and best friend, says next to me as he clicks against the keyboard, responding to emails.

"Ugh," I say, scanning a vaccination record into the system. "Good until I sweated my damn thong off."

His nose scrunches and he tosses his blond fringe out of his face. "Gross."

The first ten minutes of hot yoga *were* great. My frozen limbs thawed in the studio. I breathed in the warm, humid air, stretched my limbs, attempted—and failed—to meditate. But shortly after, I was panting like a dog in heat. "Why did I think doing exercise in one-hundred-and-five-degree heat was a good thing?"

"Why do you think *any* of your ideas are a good thing?" he asks with a horrible, awful sparkle in his blue eyes.

Whatever. "Not all my ideas are bad."

"Fair. I did like when you took that Moroccan cooking class and brought me that tagine stuff. That shit was delicious." He reaches over me for the stapler. "But besides that, not sure your track record for ideas is batting you a thousand."

"Don't be a dick," I say with a scowl. "Besides, I don't get that reference because I don't watch basketball."

He rightfully groans at my terrible joke. Leo's not trying to be a jerk. But he's also not wrong. In fact, he's probably trying to help me not spend money on frivolous stuff. Since moving back to town a year ago, I've tried *everything* to try and discover what fuels me. Cooking classes, online computer programming courses, yoga that made me melt, tennis, tai chi, swimming. I even tried gymnastics, which we will never, ever speak of again because for some reason I assumed my thirty-three-year-old body would still be as agile as when I was twelve, and let me tell you, it's not.

As if the universe knew it was time to judge me, my phone vibrates with a notification pop-up for drum classes tonight at six. I sigh and swipe the reminder off the screen. One of these days, something will stick. I'm sure of it. The thing that I need, that will make me feel whole, is waiting for me. So far, though, trying to find whatever that may be has been like trying to capture steam in my palm.

But... maybe drumming will be the one.

After Leo rings up a customer for flea medication, he nudges me with his elbow. "There's no shame in just going home and reading a book."

"That sounds miserable," I say. "Who reads?"

He lifts a brow. I chuckle, but I'm not totally kidding. Quiet, calm activities are not my thing. Maybe reading a book while skydiving or cross-country skiing, or anything where I don't have to be alone in my thoughts, might be something I could give a try.

Besides, Leo doesn't understand. He's twenty-five, beautiful, loves his family, his girlfriend, and quiet nights in with conversation and wine. We may share the same lineage, but we are built completely different.

The next hour flies by as I file and scan in lab results. Today is actually one of my days off, but sitting at home doing nothing sounded miserable, so I picked up this receptionist shift. Being a vet tech, I'm normally in the back with the doctor, so this feels like an entirely new change of pace. And today, it just so happens to give me a front-row seat to Colby.

Does she remember meeting me? It was such a quick moment last year, a blip really, but something about that interaction left a lasting impression. But if I'm being honest with myself—which is kind of a miserable thing to do—it might have been all the other events that led up to that moment on the sidewalk that contributed to that evening being so memorable.

I like to refer to that time as the Avalanche of the Misguided and Terrible Decisions Era. The year I spent making one bad decision after another, like some weird, tangled snowball that grew bigger and more powerful the further it rolled down my shame hill. Truly, the amount of things I screwed up in such a short amount of time is damn near impressive.

After a decade together, I left my girlfriend Zoey—who just so happens to be the only legitimate baker in town, which sucks on a whole different level as I now have to drive thirty miles to get a decent pastry—to find myself.

I'd been unfilled and unhappy in our relationship, in myself, in my life. So, I moved out of our place and into a small apartment in North Minneapolis, and worked at a vet clinic. That first year, I spent my time joining every organization, club, and singles event I could think of. I went out, on dates, met women, went home with women, danced, sang, *lived*. And then when that didn't fulfill me the way I thought it would, I spent the following year trying to win Zoey back.

So embarrassing.

Every month for a year, I sent her a letter, and she never responded. Determined to turn whatever life I had around, I decided to move back to Spring Harbors, sure that my destiny was to win Zoey back. Thank God, she had the sense to kindly turn me down. At that time, even after a few years apart, she knew me better than I knew myself. She knew that deep down I was lost. I probably still am, and getting back together wouldn't fix what is broken in me. But it just so happens that the night I met Colby was also the night I made a mortifying grand gesture to win back Zoey. Maybe it's a good thing that Colby doesn't remember me, because I really don't want to explain the circumstances around why I was on the sidewalk with Zoey the day we met.

As I type into the screen, I see Colby approaching the desk from the corner of my eye. She removes her hands from the front pocket of her hooded sweatshirt, and cracks her thumb knuckles. "Any updates?"

"No, sorry," I say and shake my head. *Just like the six other times I said no.* Obviously, she's nervous, and I can totally understand that. I'd rather have a nervous dog mom in here than ones that don't care at all. But unless the dog, God forbid, passes on the table, there will not be an update until it's all done. Although I haven't said those exact words, because I'm not heartless, I've alluded to it enough where I'm surprised it hasn't sunk in.

"I'm sure Kona is doing just fine." I keep my smile as bright and disarming as possible, even though this is getting annoying. "This is such a routine surgery."

Her nostrils flare at this and she stomps away. Literally, boots against the floor, stomping with a heavy thud. *What the hell?* I glance a side-eye at Leo. "What did I say?'" I whisper.

The clicking of the keyboard doesn't slow as he peeks at Colby and shrugs. A few moments pass when he stops, and cracks open a pop. "Emma and I are talking about heading to Mall of America this weekend. You wanna tag along?"

Leo's a dude, not always the most emotionally intelligent, and his invite is genuine. But that's exactly what I'd be doing—*tagging along*. Besides Leo, I have mostly a sprinkling of what I like to call *acquaint-ends*. Lots of people that I see, that I chat with, that I engage with at whatever activity that happens to be my flavor of the month. But none that I'd feel comfortable enough to ask to come with me for a day trip to the Mall of America, and certainly none that I would be comfortable enough sharing anything even remotely personal.

"No thanks. I'm trying pickleball this weekend." Yep, *pickleball*. I'm heading down to the local senior center, hand to God I'm not joking, to join some retirees in a fierce game of whatever the hell pickleball is. Yes, friends. This is where I'm at in my life. But living in a town of a few thousand people, the options for local activities are running low, and beggars cannot be choosers.

Today is busy. The lobby area is filled more than normal, which is never a great thing for a vet clinic. Not all animals are friendly or comfortable around other animals. Colby moves from the bench so someone can have her spot, which is kind and all, but now she's pacing like a caged zoo animal. I can't exactly kick her out of the place, but any more of her dark, anxious energy, and I'm pretty sure the dogs in the exam rooms are going to start howling.

The automatic door opens, bringing in a breeze and an elderly man, a cane in his left hand and a shar-pei attached to a leash on his right. The dog seems to have more control over the man than the other way around, and I leap from my chair to make sure that no catastrophes occur.

"Oh, hey there, sweet thing," I say as I approach the barking dog, using my calm voice and demeanor to sooth the canine's nerves. Too bad I can't have treats in my pocket to hand out, but we never know what the animals are in here for and the very last thing I want to do is mess up a lab or flare an allergic reaction. "Are you okay if I take the leash from you?" I ask the gentleman.

When his liver-spotted hand reaches over with the leash, I squat at the side of the dog and let him sniff my hand.

"Are you here for an appointment?" I ask, keeping my eyes focused on the man, who's trying to dig out a paper from his pocket while balancing on his cane. My attention goes to Colby, who's still pacing, then dashes to a cat that's meowing and pawing against the metal bars of its crate so much that the clanking sound screeches across the room. A dog barks fiercely in the corner, and then... *no, no, no.* The shar-pei cocks its leg and pees all over me. And not even a little spray. That leg is lifted like a missile and lands a direct hit right down my shin.

Are you kidding me?

I jump back, the liquid seeping into my bare leg, *so freaking gross*, right as the doors swing open again. In stumbles a very frantic mom, a barking chihuahua, and a toddler that gets loose from her grip and begins running, screaming, in a circle. "Ah, wait... one second..." I say to anyone who will listen as the shar-pei that just decimated my clothes starts barking at the chihuahua.

"Charlie! Stop!" the mom yells, over the growling shar-pei and barking chihuahua and ringing phones. I scramble backwards, hands up like I'm a soccer goalie. The kid launches one hell of an impressive temper tantrum on the floor in front of the products, kicking his legs like he's fighting a demon, and lands a foot on the stacked cans of wet cat food.

The crash of metal cans hitting the floor terrorizes the

eardrums of everyone in the place, and makes the dogs outbid each other in a ferocious barking contest. Leo leaps from the desk to help wrangle the humans, or dogs, or cans. I can feel the trickle of dog pee dripping down my leg and getting my sock soggy, which might even be a worse feeling than my leg being wet.

In less than two minutes, Leo and the mom have taken control of the situation, and I've escorted the shar-pei to a room. I return to the desk and start stuffing paper towels in my socks to soak up as much urine as I can, when Colby marches over to the desk.

"Please, it's been five hours," Colby says as she tugs on her ponytail. "Can I have an update?" I hear the desperation in her voice, I really do, but for God's sake this is the seventh, maybe eighth time she's come up to the desk. I have pee seeping into my shoes, I haven't eaten for a few hours, the phones are ringing off the hook, the lobby is jam-packed. And I'm sorry, but she is not the only person in the world needing an update. The doctor is good here, but strict, and only comes out when ready to address the caretaker; otherwise, they'd be cornered in the lobby for half the day.

The quietness, stillness, that I thought Colby had before is quickly shifting. I'm beginning to think that she's just the type of woman who is used to demanding things and getting her way, and does not take kindly to people telling her no.

My patience is hovering slightly above zero, and I think if she asks again, I might lose my shit. "Seriously?" I say, a little harsher than needed, but *my God*. This is probably why we tell people to leave and come back when their animals are ready to be picked up. Colby's beautiful brown eyes narrow at me with a deep fire. "I have pee all over me. We are crazy busy. There are products all over the floor that are both a human and animal trip hazard, and I told you before, *there is no update*." The constant ringing of the phone is piercing my ears. "I'll let you know when she's done. Please, can you go outside or something? Maybe go grab yourself a coffee or pastry or something at the coffee shop?"

Her mouth drops open, her huge eyes going even wider. "I

absolutely will not go outside or go grab a coffee. I have every right to be here, to check on the health of my animal."

Jesus. This feels a little reminiscent of me—dramatic, over-the-top, and a bit attention-seeking. Did Colby grow up in a home with six siblings, an absentee father and overworked, exhausted single mother, too? Tightness spreads in my jaw, but I breathe it out. "Your dog is receiving excellent care. Our veterinarian is one of the best in the state."

Her gaze pins me, and she crosses her arms across her hooded sweatshirt. "I need you to go check. Now."

The firmness in her voice almost makes me recoil. It's absolutely reminiscent of my college days when I worked at a dive bar in Duluth and people snapped their fingers to get me to come to the table. Heat rises in my chest, crawls up my neck, and is most likely going to turn my face as pink as my hair. "Look," I say, matching her steeliness and exhaling through the disrespect she's throwing my way. "I can appreciate that you're nervous, but we have a strict policy. We wait for the doctor to update us, otherwise we'd be constantly agitating and interrupting the animals—"

"There's no way you can't just go peek at the chart, or crack open the door, or *something.*"

And now, I straight-up bristle. I don't go into wherever her place of business is and tell her how to manage her job. Nor do I want to be on the receiving end of the doctor's wrath—who is amazing with animals but isn't as fond of humans—by breaking her rules.

Colby strums her fingers against her arms. "So?"

"For God's sake, I've said this like ten times," I say, tightening my spine. "The. Doctor. Will. Let. Us. Know. When. They're. Done."

If this were a cartoon, I'm pretty sure this is when smoke would have billowed from Colby's ears. She plants her hands on the counter, seething. "Do you not have a heart? I just need a fucking update!"

Is it coincidence, or did all animals stop barking, the phone stop ringing, and the place go eerily silent? I look around the room, the people stare back at me, and my cheeks are now definitely burning. I pull my lips into my mouth and anchor them between my teeth before I really say something to escalate. How *dare* she.

And then... one of on-duty vet techs comes out and whispers to me that Kona is ready. Although this is normally my favorite part of my job—bringing animals back out to meet their owners—I practically stomp back to the recovery area and burst into the room. But one toe in, my body softens.

Oh, sweet thing with her shaved leg. Yes, I see dogs with a half-shaved leg post-surgery all of the time. But they always look so chilly with their missing fur. Couple that with the stitches running across the skin, and a plastic cone hanging from a drooping head filled with anesthesia disorientation, and you'd have to be totally heartless to not feel something.

Some people here at the clinic have gained a level of desensitization. I have not.

The vet tech on duty, doctor, and I have a quick logistics chat, then I grab the leather leash. "Come on, girl," I say to Kona, "I think your mama is very anxious to see you." With notes in one hand, and the leash in the other, I push through the door to the lobby and walk slowly with Kona as she tenderly puts weight on her leg as she trails slightly behind me.

In the lobby, Colby glances up at me and Kona and leaps from her seat. She drops on the floor next to the dog as she hugs Kona. "Oh, baby girl... are you okay?" A half-choked sob sounding like a strangled hiccup escapes her throat. Tears slide down her cheeks and drip from her chin as she swaps back and forth between hugging Kona and checking her wound.

My heart positively melts. Colby obviously adores this dog. We all have different reactions to when our loved ones are in surgery. And even though I could've done without the drama for today—which is saying a lot since I normally thrive on drama—I can see how worried Colby was.

Colby swipes her eyes with the back of her hand and her chin trembles. "She's okay?"

And I *see* it—the heartbreak, the fear, the red in her eyes that highlights the beautiful soft amber within the brown. There's so much pain there, so much worry, and a deep urge consumes me to take it all away.

"She was a champ," I say, crouching to meet her and Kona at eye level. "A really good girl, and everything went perfect. The doctor will meet you in the consulting room in a minute to talk about follow-up care, and I can schedule some post-op appointments for you."

Colby is looking at me, a little, but her focus is almost entirely on her dog. I speak a little more, but it's like Colby can't hear me, at all. She's cooing in Kona's ears, swiping away tears, taking full, shaky breaths. Is it crossing a line to give her a hug? I don't normally hug customers, but she looks so broken. I *know* broken. I've seen broken, and this is it. Instead of crossing that line, however, I settle for a hand on her shoulder and hold out a tissue. "Colby? The doctor has some follow-up notes."

Finally, she blinks up at me, and the anger she had before is gone. She gratefully accepts my tissue and wipes her nose and face. "Thank you," she says as she rises. Her gaze sweeps the floor, and she tucks a loose tendril that fell from her pony behind her ear. "I'm so sorry about before... the way I spoke to you... I, ah... I guess I was nervous."

There's more there. I can see there's more, and why, why, why is there desperation to know more, to ask more, to somehow help and take it away? I don't even know this woman, not really anyway, and yet in a snap, I'm falling into a laughable, predictable pattern. But I almost don't care. I want to know what *the more* is.

The doctor escorts Colby to the room, and through the window I see her nod, run the corner of her palm across her cheeks to catch a few more fallen tears, and never remove her hand from behind Kona's ears. After several minutes, she steps out from the room and grabs the paperwork.

She glances at me through phenomenal, dark, long lashes. Her mouth opens, then closes, when her gaze sweeps the floor. "I'm sorry again," she says, then turns and slowly moves to the door with Kona trudging at her side.

Something about watching them leave tugs on my heart in a way that it shouldn't. I work in a vet clinic. I see all kinds of injured or sick animals, and upset owners, but in all my years, nothing has produced this *level* of tug. But I'm not an idiot. I know this tug is for Colby. I also know my pattern, my need for a thrill, to seek out the next great thing. So, therefore, I need to plant my plump ass right here, in this office chair, and go back to logging notes.

The words on the screen blur, and I close my eyes. *Don't do it. Don't do it, don't effing do it.* A few hard heartbeat thumps later, I leap from my chair, grab my jacket, and race to the front door.

THREE

COLBY

Outside of the clinic, I'm barely able to catch my breath. Reality, painful memories, and intense relief flood my system. My hand hasn't left my dazed dog, the smooth fur behind her ear providing me the comfort I'm craving right now. *I thought this would be like last time...* My lips quiver, and I clamp my mouth closed. For the rest of the day, I need to pull it together. Kona cannot see me fall apart. She'll have this intrinsic need to make me feel better, but right now, she needs to focus on resting. Kona is all I have, but sometimes I forget I'm all she has, too.

At my lifted Jeep, the relief I felt just a moment ago crashes and burns. The ramp I use to get Kona into the Jeep, which looked so accommodating before surgery, now looks like the summit at Mount Everest. I chew on the inside of my cheek as I try to coax Kona up the ramp. "Oh, girl, I know this is scary. We got this. Can you walk a little?" I nudge, offer treats, beg, and nothing.

Okay, okay. I got this. I mean, what the hell do other people do? I plant my waterproof hiking boots into the snow, steady myself, and grab under her belly to lift. *Jesus.* I work out a lot, I chop wood, I shovel constantly, but ninety pounds of dead weight when I'm trying to be as gentle as possible is not working.

Shit.

A few soft snowflakes flutter down, and I blink the moisture from my eyelids. "Come on, girl. You've got to do this. I need to get you home so you can rest and feel better. Okay? Can you work with me here?"

No reaction. My pulse thuds against my ears and a sickly helplessness weaves its way through my stomach. What am I supposed to do? Leave her here and run to the hardwood store to see if they have a makeshift lift? How did I not think about this?

Right before I'm about to break out into a heaping pile of panicked tears, yet again, the front doors open and I hear, "Colby!"

Josie's dashing across the parking lot as she zips up her bright pink jacket and snugs a floppy knit beanie over her head. When she reaches me, she stops and says nothing. Not a single word for several long, super odd moments. "I, um, I just wanted to say I'm really glad that Kona's doing better."

I tilt my head. The way Josie ran out here, I thought I left Kona's pain medication back there or something. Red infuses her cheeks, maybe from the cold air, maybe from something else, and I give her an apologetic grin. "I'm *so sorry* for how I acted." Shame trickles into my system and settles uncomfortably. God, I cannot believe I swore at her in the middle of her workplace. I'm not that person. I'm the type of person who would never send back food at a restaurant even if it's totally wrong. The type who only leaves five-star reviews for books or products, the one that holds doors open, the one who lets a person with fewer groceries budge ahead in line at the grocery store. I am *so* not the person who yells at someone trying their hardest in the middle of a chaotic shift with freaking pee running down their leg, and yet I did it. No matter how anxious I was, there is never an excuse to treat someone the way I did.

"It's okay," Josie says. "Sometimes I forget that I see this every single day and am sort of desensitized. To me it's a work shift. But to the animal parents, it's terrifying." She rubs the top of Kona's fur and looks at the Jeep and the ramp. "Do you need some help?"

Everything in me wants to say no. Relying on anyone, in any

capacity, sets you up for failure when that person is no longer there. Once you rely on someone for one thing, it creates an avalanche of dependencies, and it's a crutch I can't afford.

But Kona. She needs to get home, the sporadic snow flutters are accumulating, and my extremities are so cold that any moment now they're going to uncomfortably tingle. I *hate* saying yes, but I sigh, and do it anyway. "That'd be great, thanks."

We shuffle around each other as Josie explains how to lift the dog with the least amount of pressure on Kona. She's at Kona's chest, and I'm at Kona's hind legs, and as gently as possible, we heave Kona into the back seat. She nestles in the blanket with a heavy thud, her plastic cone scraping against the floor. My heart is ripping at the seams watching my dazed and confused dog, still under the anesthesia fog, look at us with hazy, unfocused eyes.

"Oof, thank you," I say, shutting the bottom tailgate. "I don't know what I would've done had you not come out here."

"It's no problem at all." Josie looks through the tailgate window at Kona. "Poor thing. I'm sure she's so confused right now." She twists her mouth. "Don't you just wish that we could logically explain everything happening to them?"

"More than just about anything." Maybe all of this would've been easier if I could have reasoned with Kona. Let her know what was happening, that sedation is scary and will feel funny, and that after this is all done, we will go home and she can curl into one of her dog beds scattered throughout our home.

Josie shoves her hands in her jacket pockets but makes no motion to leave. And even though I'm exhausted and really do want to get home and get Kona settled, I also want to keep talking. Which is an absolute freak occurrence.

Six years ago, I moved to this sleepy Minnesota town for solitude. And thus far have not only achieved but surpassed my goal for minimal communication. And now... I can't force my feet to move.

"Okay, well, you have all the notes, but call us if you have any questions," Josie says, dusting off snow from her arms. "You can ask for me, and if I'm in with a patient, I promise I'll call back as quickly as possible. Even if I have dog urine soaking through my pant legs."

I cringe. "That looked... gross."

"Sure was." She laughs, and *my God*. What a smile. The kind that makes me momentarily forget the stress of this entire afternoon. It's so bright that if the sun were out, I feel like it would ricochet a smattering of stars like a toothpaste commercial. There's a tiny little gap in her front teeth, an imperfection that makes her smile even more perfect, and a fanning of smile lines that crease up her cheek.

"Do you have someone at home to help you get Kona down?" she asks.

Crap. *Someone at home?* No. I don't have a someone, anywhere. Not a relative I could call that lives in the state, not a friend, not even a neighbor. My face must have shown the horror of realizing, yet again, that I'm totally unprepared.

This is not like me. Kona's surgery threw me off. My house is prepped like I'm waiting for the air-raid sirens to go off and might need to shelter in place for months. Kona's vitamins, vaccinations, my work are all on a precise, perfect schedule. But I didn't think of how I would transfer the most important being in my life from the Jeep into my home? "Oh, um, no."

Josie tilts her head. "Maybe like a neighbor or something? Family?"

Outside of obligatory twice-monthly calls to my parents, who live out of state, the person I talk to most is Zoey who owns the bakery. But not even enough where I'd classify us as friends. She's more someone who knows the name of my dog, what my usual order is, and I know that she dates a woman named Quinn who owns a Christmas tree farm. But even though I talk to her the most, it's still not nearly enough to ask for help.

However, saying out loud to Josie that I have literally no one is more isolating and embarrassing than I thought it would be. The solitude that I sought out, that I craved, that I convinced myself I needed for healing, I've officially achieved. Because do I have someone? No. I had Amelia. And then she was gone. "I, um, actually... I live outside of town, kind of secluded. The nearest house is a few miles from my place."

"Wow." Josie checks her watch and shifts her weight in between her feet. "I'm sure your girl is anxious to get home." We both look at a dazed Kona lying on the blanket inside the tailgate. "I'm going to be off shift in about an hour. If you want to wait here, or drive around or something, I can totally help you."

Wait, what? My head flinches back like she snapped a twig in front of my face. "No... no, you don't have to do that. Don't you have somewhere to be?"

Josie swipes off a few snowflakes from her cheeks. "Well, I was going to try a drumming class tonight, but I also didn't expect to get peed on. And it's been such a chaotic day that this is exactly what I need to end on a good note." She smiles and holds out her phone. "For real. Here. Want to put your contact info in my phone?"

I'm not surprised that her phone case is pink and glittery, and when I hand her mine, I think her hand dips with the weight of the industrial-level case protector. I thank her a million times over and we say a quick goodbye. Josie tears back into the clinic, and I hop in the Jeep.

And then I panic. As the tires push through the slushy grounds, I drive around until Kona's muffled groans quiet, and snoring fills the Jeep. *Someone's coming to my house.* I keep a tidy-enough house, but what if today I missed something? What if my underwear is flung on the bathroom floor, or the garbage stinks, or I didn't make my bed? Will it have one of those dog smells that non-dog owners will pick up on? No one has ever been to my place, and I have nothing to gauge what a potential reaction will be.

But not only do I have a someone coming to my place, I have a *woman* coming to my place. A nice one. A *cute* one. My pulse quickens.

On Main Street, I slow to the red light and push out a breath. Kona is snoozing loudly in the back, which is not surprising. The combination of her being like an infant that's soothed by a car ride, the pain medication, and her favorite nap place being in the Jeep is the perfect cocktail since I need to kill an hour before Josie comes over.

Josie's coming to my place.

A few blocks past the light, I thank my lucky stars that a parking spot just opened up in front of Zoey's Bakery. I leave the Jeep running as I step onto the sidewalk and cup my eyes to peer in the back window. Good. Kona is completely out cold.

The bell jingles against the door handle as I open it, and I walk inside to the warm, brightly lit bakery. Normally, the soft pinks and whites of Zoey's Bakery, along with the sweet fog of chocolate, cinnamon, and dough, bring me a little bit of comfort. It's hard for me to warm up to places, and even harder for me to find places that I like that also allow dogs. Zoey's is both of those things, but today, I know it's not going to give me any reprieve.

"Hey, Colby," Zoey says, as she wipes her flour-dusted hand on her apron. "Where's Kona?"

I nod my head towards the Jeep. "Sleeping, thankfully. She just had surgery on her leg, and we're on our way home."

"Oh, that was today? I knew it was coming up, but wasn't sure which exact date." Zoey pushes her glasses up her nose and slides open the display case. "How did she do?"

"*She* did great."

Zoey hovers tongs over my usual chocolate and raspberry cupcake. "And how did you do?"

Terrible. I know we only left there fifteen minutes ago, but the fear-laced adrenaline that rushed through my veins is still bubbling right below the surface. My stomach is so twisted that the cupcake that Zoey's holding, which normally makes me salivate like a puppy with a jerky stick, looks damn near unappetizing. "I was a nervous wreck, honestly. But... it ended up being okay."

Zoey doesn't know about Amelia. No one in this town knows about my past and couldn't possibly draw the parallels I did between Amelia's surgery and Kona's. But still, she gives me a kind, sympathetic nod and points to the cupcake. "The usual?"

"Um, two, this time." I take a step back and scan the display case. The desserts here are actually quite beautiful, but I've never taken the time to really look. Cupcakes with edible flowers, desserts that look like a pink-bowed gift, macaroons with edible glitter. Does Josie like cookies? Pastries? Cupcakes? I scratch the back of my neck, my fatigued brain swirling with too many decisions I need to make. "And maybe... some cookies?"

The tongs stop midair and Zoey's eyebrows shoot up sky-high. "Two, huh? *And* cookies?" I know she wants to ask. The week after I moved to Minnesota, I discovered Zoey's Bakery. I've stopped in here at least once a week for six years and have only ever had one dessert, and it's always been the chocolate and raspberry cupcake. A heat creeps up my neck and lands on my cheeks, and I don't even know why. This really is not a blush-inducing moment, and yet, here I am, flaming pink. "You probably won't remember this, but last year, I ran into you and a friend on the sidewalk."

"Quinn?" Zoey asks, referring to her girlfriend, as she puts the food in a small box.

"No," I say as I dig out my credit card from my wallet. "Josie."

Zoey stops mid-cookie shuffle and stares with the blankest of blank faces, so much so that a nervous smile flushes my lips. "*Josie?*" she asks, still frozen.

"Yeah, Josie," I say as I slide over to the register. "I assume you already know this since you're friends and all, but Josie works at the vet clinic where Kona had her surgery. Anyway, she offered to come to my place and help me lift Kona out of the Jeep because her leg is too hurt for the ramp."

"Wow. Josie, huh?" She finally puts all the pastries in the box and slaps a piece of tape to close it up.

I wish I knew Zoey a little better so I could decode whatever this look is that she's giving me. Not happy, not sad, not upset. More contemplative? Or curious? Sure, I only saw Zoey and Josie together last year for a brief moment, and I have no idea how close they are, but it's obvious they know each other.

"Well, yes, she certainly loves animals," Zoey says and rings up the order. "There isn't anyone else you can ask?"

Second time in a day that someone has asked me this, and it doesn't really feel any better than the first time I was asked. I shouldn't be sheepish at this question. This is how I designed my life, and what I want.

I think.

"No, just me and Kona and whatever goblins come out in the forest at night."

"And Josie's coming to *your* house to help you?"

I nod. I mean, yes, I already know it's weird that the woman from the vet office is helping me, but Zoey seems *really* weirded out by it. Am I that detached from how healthy, functioning adults operate in society? Perhaps. But I'm already nervous enough, and this isn't helping. "I can say hi to her from you if you'd like?" I say, with some sort of misguided peace offering to defuse whatever is happening right now.

A moment passes on Zoey's face when she smiles. "Oh, ah, sure. That's... nice of you."

Okay, well, now, it's confirmed—I'm giving off some funky vibes based on this weird encounter. And it shouldn't shock me. I've been off this whole week. And today, I swore at Josie at the vet clinic, broke down and sobbed into my dog's fur, clung to her like she had just returned from deployment, and had flashbacks to the worst day of my life.

Back in the Jeep, Kona is still snoring loudly. I run my gloved palm against the steering wheel as I sit and think. *I'm having a woman to my house.* And it's fine. I know it's fine. But there's a feeling in me that creeping in, threatening to invade my every cell.

Because right now, even though it's technically fine, everything feels very, very wrong.

FOUR

JOSIE

Have I ever offered house service before to a customer? Nope. After over a decade in this profession, this is a new one. Although I've thought someday I might join a mobile vet place, I'm not *actually* part of one, and as I toss my bag into the back seat of the car and take off toward Colby's house, I'm questioning my impulsive offer.

It's fine, right? I'm just doing a good deed, helping out someone in distress, giving that good old white-glove service that my manager keeps droning on about, and nothing more. I would have done this for anyone.

Right?

The sadness gutted me. While watching Colby with her dog, the way she looked so broken and distraught, something in me flickered. I don't think there is anyone in my life that would care about me so deeply like that if I were to have leg surgery. Sure, I have my brothers and sisters, and my mom. But ever since my dad left when I was twelve, my mother spent years in a perpetual state of exhaustion. And the moment the last one of us left the house, she's spent years making up for lost "me" time. Not that I blame her. Being a single parent for six of us killed something in her. The fire, the joy I saw when I was younger—when my dad was still there—left along with his suitcase. And the rest of the family sort of... scattered. My siblings spread themselves across the country and moved on with their lives and families. We do our obligatory Thanksgiving dinner when possible, but other than that, I keep tabs on everyone via social media. My siblings don't call and check in, don't ask how I'm doing after all my life changes, don't wonder if I've found whatever it is that I need.

And here, Colby broke down for her *dog*.

I turn at the last light in town and head up the county roads towards Colby's place, keeping one eye on the navigation and one on the snowy road. In the quiet, on drives like this, is when the thoughts start filling my brain. I know deep down I would not have made a house call for "just anyone." It's *Colby*. And I need to be very, very careful how I tread these waters.

From the moment I met Colby last year, something deeply intriguing had affected me, and now, that same feeling stirs beneath the surface. Those soulful, haunting eyes carry something huge, something much deeper and more profound than I think I can understand. But there's this urge in me to know more, to burrow myself a little bit into her world, and start unraveling these pieces.

And... her lips, all right. There, I admitted it. Her lips are freaking phenomenal. They're soft, and a Cupid's bow shape, and a deep plum color, and... I shake my head.

Nope. Not doing this. Definitely not going to do this, not now, not again. My MO for these last two years has been the same—fall quick, take no prisoners, deep regret later. I'm looking for something that doesn't exist in the arms of these women, and I need to stop.

Snow-covered pine trees and bare-branched oaks and cedars fly past my window. The navigation system says I'm going to the right place, but I'm not sure if this is actually the right place. I haven't even seen another vehicle for the last five miles. I'm not that far out of town, maybe only ten minutes or so, halfway in between Spring Harbors and Quinn Lee's Christmas tree farm, but

I feel like I'm literally in the middle of Pine Tree Island, a white wasteland on a single lane road with nothing but me, the air, and whatever deer are contemplating jumping in front of my car. Thank God there's no corn field and a gravesite, or I may have pulled right back around.

One mailbox and a reflective marker in the shape of a waving dog sitting at the edge of a cleared patch is the only indication that I'm most likely at the right place. My small sedan chugs up the narrow, windy hill as I grip the steering wheel and hope I don't slide into a tree.

The property is absolutely beautiful. Dusk is settling in, but it's still light enough to see the tall snowflake-dusted pine trees and large rolling hills. I feel like someone lifted my car and plunked me in the middle of a forest nestled inside a snow globe. At the top of the hill, Colby's Jeep comes into focus. Behind it, what I assume is Colby's house. *"Whoa..."*

My God, I feel like I'm a character in a Thomas Kinkade painting. Warm, glowing, lantern-style lights adorn a pathway leading up to a log-cabin-style home. Huge, rustic cedar logs for the siding, a small wrap-around porch filled with firewood, a matching shed off to the left.

Colby is snugged into her boots and jacket outside of her Jeep, with the tailgate popped open. She's rubbing Kona's head, and waves to me as I pull to a stop.

God, she's pretty.

"Hey," she says, her cheeks rosy with the cold air. "Did you have any problems finding this place?"

"No problems at all. Google Maps for the win," I say, as I tug on my mittens. Northern Minnesota is God's land, one of the most beautiful places in the country, but I never take the time to come out to places like this, or Lake Superior, or Black Beach, to appreciate the natural landscape. I make a quick mental note to add to my list of excursions some sort of nature walk or activity. "It's so picturesque out here. I love it."

"Thank you," Colby says with a soft grin. "When I bought this place, that was exactly what I told the realtor I was looking for—quiet and picturesque. I wanted it to look and feel like a cabin and make me believe the rest of the world was a million miles away."

We cannot be more different. For as long as I remember, I've searched for constant stimulation. Hobbies, friends, jobs, working long shifts, sports... I've done it all. Being alone with my thoughts is a nightmare. But even without this compulsion, there is no chance in hell I'd ever live out here alone. With my luck, a lightning strike during a thunderstorm would zap electricity into a scarecrow and bring it to life Stephen King-style or something. Or an axe murderer would pop up and plant his dirty palms into my window. *No thanks.* Although in Spring Harbors, the scarecrow is probably a more likely scenario. Last summer, the weekly police blotter—which is one of my favorite things to read in our local newspaper—touted the biggest scandal this town has seen in the last five years. Twin fourteen-year-olds stole their grandma's car, hit a bunch of mailboxes on a county road, and went on a two-mile-long high-speed chase until they pulled over for the police.

"Okay, we ready for this?" I ask, looking at Kona, who's resting on her chin in the terrible cone of shame, glancing up at me through the hard plastic with weary eyes.

"I think so. I'm ready to get this girl into the house and settled." Colby and I shuffle around each other to scoop Kona in our arms and rest her gently on the earth. She slowly sniffs the ground and limps in a circle until she finds a spot to go to the bathroom. Her body is moving exactly as expected post-surgery, but Colby's brows are creased with worry.

"Good girl," Colby says as she pats Kona's head, then glances over to me. "I've never been so relieved in all my life that I live in a place without any stairs."

She guides Kona through the snow, fussing. The dog's poor shaved leg looking like it's freezing in the crisp air. Should I stay? Leave? When exactly is the point when my helpfulness becomes creepy and overwhelming? "First surgery?"

Ugh. Why did I ask this when I already know the answer since

I'd looked at Kona's chart today? But I don't want to leave. I want to stay, and talk, and learn more, and ask more questions that I might already know the answer to, and this, my friends, is a huge fucking problem.

"Yeah. It's just more than what I thought it would be," Colby says as she inches toward the front door with a reluctant Kona trailing behind. "I feel like I know my dog better than myself, but I just... I didn't expect all of this, you know? I didn't realize how disorientated she'd get from the meds."

I should go. Right now. Leave her be, leave the dog be. Maybe I can still make my drumming class, or catch a movie at a theater, or see if Leo wants to grab dinner. "Do you want me to stay and help for a little while?" *So much for that plan...*

The worried crease on Colby's forehead smooths. "I can't ask you to do that. You've already gone above and beyond."

"Ah." I wave away the words. And sure, I don't know Colby, not really, but her eyes are so expectant that there's no way she doesn't want me to stay. She's probably just like all the locals in this area who consider hard work next to godliness and asking for help is akin to dancing with the devil. But besides the fact that I really don't want to leave, I'm also dying to see the inside of her place. "It's really no problem."

Colby nibbles on her smile, and we both spend the next few moments coaxing Kona inside. Colby offers her a treat, which Kona completely ignores, but finally, Kona moves inside, knocking the cone into the door frame in the process. The hard plastic scrapes against the wood, the floor, and the poor dog is so confused and agitated that I want to hug her.

At the door, we both tug off our boots, and Colby moves to the doggie bed next to the couch. She sits next to it and pats the cushion. "Come on, girl, you got this. Come lie down."

While Colby tries to get Kona to lie down, I take a moment to scan the house. It's both exactly how I thought it would be, and also better. Cozy, lived-in, *loved.* A completely open space, with hardwood floors and various throw rugs. From where I'm standing, I can see the dining area, kitchen, and living room. Next to the tan couch and cedar coffee table, there's a huge wicker basket of chunky knitted blankets. A sitting chair with an ottoman, lamp, and more blankets rest in the corner next to the floor-to-ceiling window. A huge brick fireplace is against the wall in front of the couch, a few shotguns are attached in a case on the wall, and a pile of wood rests next to it. The place smells warm and homey, a mix of fresh chopped wood and a little bit of vanilla.

Someday, maybe, I'll do something like this—make my place a home. Put up some paintings, buy a few plants, maybe get some throw pillows for my couch. Being on my fourth apartment in three years is not boding well for my inner Martha Stewart, but I swear she's in there somewhere, begging to be unleashed.

Colby is at the floor, sitting crisscross in her leggings and oversized hooded sweatshirt, talking to Kona in a low, sweet voice. My gaze travels the sweep of her neck, the line at her jaw, her profile with the cutest nose. *Okay, seriously. Stop.*

What in the hell is wrong with me?

She unwinds her long, chestnut-colored hair from the ponytail holder and shakes it loose, letting it cascade down her shoulders. It's beautiful, thick, luscious, and I picture my fingers gripping it. *Enough.* I need to leave. I absolutely need to leave before I say or do something stupid and spend the rest of the week cowering with embarrassment. I'm standing awkwardly at the door, waiting for my cue to leave. When Kona slumps all the way down, and closes her eyes, I take it.

"Looks like she's all good and settled," I say and shove my foot into a boot.

Colby wraps her hair back on top of her head and sighs. "Thank God. Ugh, that stupid cone. I hate that she has to wear it. I wish I could just tell her not to lick her wound." When she glances at me shoving my other foot into a boot, her smile drops. A moment passes when she swallows. "You don't have to leave so soon."

I really, really do. I feel this thing, the low hum of an electric current, and it's not rational. It's too quick, too unjustified, too predictable. And the worst part of this—but my only saving grace—is that I don't think it's reciprocal. Colby is giving no indication that she has a similar tingle of energy running through her the way I do. So, I should go. Because if I stay... I know what happens when I stay.

"Do you want some tea?" she says, already rising from the floor. "I just bought some great cinnamon-spiced loose tea from a shop in Duluth over the holiday."

My shoulders slump, but not in defeat or disappointment of staying. More in frustration in myself that my pattern continues. "Tea sounds amazing."

The way Colby's eyes light up takes away my hesitation. Perhaps I can shove all this one-sided sexual tension far away, and focus on creating a friendship. Having a friend might be really good for me. And just because I'm having tea in this incredible cabin, with the warm lights glowing from the smattering of lamps, with an absolutely stunning woman, doesn't mean I have to screw it up with anything *more* than a cup of tea.

Tea is sometimes just goddamn tea.

"Oh, I almost forgot," Colby says, moving to the door, and stuffing her feet back into her boots. "I have something for you in the Jeep. I'll be right back."

She has something in the Jeep for me? Now, I'm intrigued. As Colby runs outside to get whatever this mysterious package is, my starched pink scrubs shuffle against my skin as I move over to Kona and sit on the couch with her at my feet.

Ten minutes later, after Colby returned from outside and beelined for the kitchen, and I checked my emails and replied to a text from Leo, a fresh cinnamon scent fills the air. Colby comes into the room, holding two mugs in one hand and a plate of goodies in the other. I leap to help her before settling back down on what's got to be the most comfortable couch in existence. I pull the mug to my nose and take a deep inhale. "Yum, this smells amazing."

"It's so good," Colby says, moving to the fireplace. "About ten years ago or so, I went on vacation to the UK, and there was this tiny café in Cornwall that served the best cinnamon and apple tea. I've been sort of obsessed with finding that same flavor here. This isn't it, but it's a close second."

With the ease of someone who's done this a million times, she stuffs a few newspapers in between a couple of logs, swipes a match, and gets the fire going before I even take a second sip.

"I bet everything over there just tasted better, huh?" I say, lifting the mug to my mouth. Mmmm. She's not wrong. I'm normally a coffee gal, but this is delicious.

Colby chuckles as she returns to the couch. "Yes, it really did. But... I've gotta admit, Zoey's Bakery could be a really strong contender." She nudges the plate of cookies and cupcakes towards me. "That place is my favorite. Pretty sure everyone who lives in this town shares the same sentiment. But you live here, so you'd obviously know that."

God, this is *so* awkward. Not the chuckle, which is cute and disarming. But the whole situation with Zoey. Where exactly is the line between calling out something deeply personal too quickly to someone I basically just met, and holding out too long where it gets weird that you didn't mention it sooner?

"Are you two friends?" Colby asks as she sinks her teeth into the chocolate and raspberry cupcake. "You probably don't remember this, but I saw you guys together last year on the sidewalk on Main Street. We actually chatted for a minute. I mean, it was no big deal at all. I just... I don't talk to many people, so it was pretty memorable for me, but you talk to like a million people a week, so..."

A blush creeps across my cheeks. She *does* remember me. "I totally remember you," I say. *You're very hard to forget.* "I was going to say something when you walked into the clinic, but you were so worried about Kona, and I didn't want to make it all about me."

"Oh, you remember? No, I get that," Colby says, wrapping her pretty mouth around the mug, and I think she's hiding a smile. But I also think a lot of things, read into things, tend to get overly emotional about things... "So do you hang out with Zoey often?"

I bite the inside of my cheek. "Um, no. We don't." Oh God, okay. I have to call this out, right? It would be weird if I don't. And unless I want to fake some sort of emergency and leave, which I really don't want to do, I need to tell her. "Zoey's, ah, she's my ex-girlfriend. We're cordial, of course, and anytime I've seen her in town, I'll wave or say hi, but no. We're not friends."

Colby slowly lowers her mug, and a long moment stretches between us. "You and Zoey dated?"

"We did," I say and take another long sip of the warm cinnamon drink. "For like... a decade."

Eyebrows shoot up. "*What?!*" Colby crisscrosses her legs and rests her elbows on her knees. "You and Zoey from the bakery dated for a *decade*? I have so many questions."

I giggle at her wide-eyed, surprised look. The town is small enough, a couple thousand people at most, but most of the time it feels even more close-knit than that. And as celebratory and affirming as this town is, there's not a ton of queer people around here. I'm surprised that when Zoey and I split three years ago, it didn't make the front pages. "How do you *not* know this? Pretty sure it was the hottest gossip in town that year. Might have even trickled into the hottest gossip the following year."

Colby shrugs and tugs the sleeves of her sweatshirt to the middle of her palms. "I don't talk to a lot of people."

"But didn't you say you've been here for like six years?"

"I *really* don't talk to people."

Hmmm. Yet more that I want to unpack, but not sure if now's the time. I take a bite into the dessert, and yep, I'm immediately thrown back to when Zoey and I were together. Zoey was the type of person who when she set her mind to something, it stuck. She loved baking and dreamed of opening a bakery. So, she followed through, and here we are—Zoey's Bakery is heading into her eighth year of occupancy.

And yes, back then, I was so proud of her, and wanted her to follow her dreams. But I wanted so many other different things, too. I wanted to sell our belongings and backpack around Europe. I wanted to skydive off the Empire State Building, and go skiing in the Alps, and try new things, find something that gave me that spark, that zing, that I craved. But Zoey wanted to be here, in this life, in this town. She's such a nice woman, and we had a lot of great years. But during our relationship, our communication was often just slightly off.

Colby and I polish off the tea and treats, chat about my job as a vet tech, how much I like the clinic, and talk about no matter how much my cousin Leo sometimes likes to get under my skin, it's been nice to reconnect with him since moving back here last year. When I glance at my watch, I can't believe over two hours have passed. I don't even *remember* the last time I sat and talked with anyone for two hours.

"I really should get going before that dog that peed on me earlier today has its DNA seep into my skin." I grin and help gather the plates and mugs and follow Colby to the kitchen. "Thank God for always having backup scrubs in my bag, but my body is begging for me to get in the shower."

Colby scrunches her nose. "No doubt. You might have to do an extra loofah routine to really get it out," she says and sets the plate in the sink. "Can we all just be thankful it wasn't cat pee?"

I laugh. "So true."

At the door, Colby thanks me again as I tug on my boots, then reaches for my jacket hanging next to hers at the door. She's quiet as I get ready, standing with a flushed face, and the amber in her eyes glints under the flicker of the fireplace.

Oof. She's really beautiful. She mentioned that she has no one at home, no one to call to help with Kona, but how does someone who's so sweet and obviously caring have no one? Traumatic breakup of her own, I wonder?

Once I zip up and turn to leave, Colby reaches over and pulls me into a very surprising hug. A deep, hearty, heavy hug, and I can't help but melt as I catch the scent of something soft and subtle on her neck, maybe lavender and sage. She has impossibly firm, strong arms, which carry a warmth to them that I haven't felt in a very, very long time.

What's happening here? I hug and touch people all the time. My dance troupe, friends I hang out with, Leo, the list goes on. I probably hug someone at least once a week. But this feels different. A spark flickers, igniting an electric charge, and when she pulls back, pink blooms across her face, and something in her eyes shifts.

I *see* it. Whatever just happened, she feels it, too.

And I fucking bolt.

FIVE
COLBY

During my recording sessions, there's a little bit of a ritual that takes place. The moment my large, noise-cancelling headphones grip my ears, my brain flips a switch. Under the cushioning of the headphones, in front of the microphone, in my sound-filtering room, is where I feel the most connected to my past. The most alive version of myself, or at least who I was before all this happened, reignites.

But still, it's not *me*, me. It's Amelia.

After Amelia died, I was restless, missing her so much I could hardly breathe, and in a state of denial. I was desperate to do something to keep her memory alive. Back in the day, on the weekends, Amelia and I would scour the love-advice forums, read the expert opinions, and debate if their response sucked. After her death, to both pass the time and keep connected, I'd read those same relationship-advice columns, and picture how Amelia would respond. Thus, the inception of the podcast show began—a place that I could relive our weekend routine while channeling her energy.

Honestly, I didn't think it would go anywhere. I made a couple of episodes a week, threw it online, and within a year it took on a life of its own. Maybe it's a spirit wink from Amelia, who somehow got it on a few influencers' radars. Maybe it's good luck and good timing. Or maybe people were just like us and loved listening to these types of shows, and this one struck a chord with the audience.

As part of the recording ritual, I first record my digital journal entry for Amelia. I glance at Kona sleeping away at my feet, take a breath, and hit record.

"Good morning, Amelia. I know it's been a few days, and I have a ton of things to catch you up on. So, my girl Kona is hurting. The procedure was so incredibly scary, and I wished you could've been there with me," I say and rock back on the office chair. "When I took her into the clinic, I *saw* you. I mean, not you, obviously, but in a snap, I was right back to that hospital room. I was sitting on your bed pre-surgery, teasing you for generously tearing your rotator cuff so I could finally pitch that season in the softball league. I swear, it's like I could see you giggling back at me, convincing me I didn't suck as bad as I did, I could hear the doctor give us instructions for post-op, I could smell that almond scent of yours in your hair when I kissed your forehead. I swear, *I was right fucking there*, not in this Minnesota small-town vet clinic."

After Amelia died, my family, her family, our close friends, literally everyone single person I encountered, tried to force me into counseling. When I refused, the secondary option was practically dragging me to support groups. But I didn't want to engage. Even if someone had been through what I had, it was different; they couldn't possibly understand. No one truly could understand this level of shattering pain.

And maybe it makes me sound like a selfish asshole, but the very last thing I wanted to do was to sit around and hear *other* people talk about their pain. I had more than enough of my own and no interest in piling more onto my already suffocating grief. After six months of near solitude, even more than I have now, they all staged a version of an intervention. My mom and dad, Amelia's parents, and two of our former close friends, sat me down at the tensest dinner of all time, and tried to shake some sense into me.

You need to journal, meditate, go to a priest, see a counselor, do *something*, they said.

But what I actually needed was to move far away from Florida, from everything that reminded me of Amelia, to a place that was so vastly different from the life Amelia and I had shared. Because then I could forget.

It didn't work, of course. I never forgot. So begrudgingly, I started voice journaling. I record myself talking to Amelia, telling her about my day, about Kona, lamenting on about the Minnesota weather. It took a while. Months probably, maybe more, before it felt completely natural.

"But something kind of crazy happened..." I continue. "I think I met a friend? Well, maybe not friend since I basically screamed at her right in the middle of where she was working. But a good person. She came over here that night and helped me with Kona, and when she left, I gave her a hug." There's an underlying thread of guilt in my voice, even though I can hear Amelia absolving me. But Josie's cute. *Really* cute. Smooth skin, great smile, that messy pink hair. And three nights ago, when she was here, I felt a bit of an awakening. Something in me stirred. Something I thought was dormant and buried, sparked alive.

"At your funeral, so many people hugged me, touched me, and I just couldn't. I equated the hugs with the loss, and I never wanted to hug anyone again. And I haven't. Not once. But then I hugged Josie, and I don't know... It felt nice. Different somehow. Can there be hope attached to a hug? Is that too new age, and all 'the universe is speaking to you' or whatever crap that you used to talk about? You know, when I'd nod and smile, and pretend I understood what reading auras and seven chakras meant?" I sip from my coffee and move closer to the microphone. "And later that night we had a few text message exchanges."

I glance down at my phone, where Josie's texts from that night now live, asking how Kona was. She'd then followed up a few moments later saying that dog moms deserve bubble baths.

I'm not delusional or tiptoeing on the edge of sanity—I know my wife is dead, that she's not here, and that my journaling is just a way I process things. But still, something prevents me from talking about all the *other* text messages we exchanged. Dozens and dozens of messages in the last three days. All in, it's literally the most human contact I've had in years.

I scroll through them now to reread, starting with the one I sent after Josie told me to take a bath. That night, I'd hovered my thumbs above the screen for way too many moments when I pulled the plug and popped off a message.

COLBY

I'm really sorry if I made it weird about you and Zoey. I obviously had no idea.

JOSIE

Do you know what the worst part is about Zoey being my ex?

COLBY

What?

JOSIE

She really is a fantastic baker, and I can't go there. Obviously. So, I'm stuck eating crusty dusty doughnuts from the gas station, or the subpar overpriced ones at the grocery store.

COLBY

I'm not an entrepreneur or anything, but I can sense a good business deal when one presents itself. Give me your order, I'll buy them for you and only mark them up 50%. And they still won't be overpriced.

JOSIE

You drive a hard bargain, but it's a deal. I'll meet you in the alley off Main and 4th wearing a green fedora and going by the name of Trixie. Code word: baby goat

COLBY

Hmmm. I take it back. Potential prison time and sacrificing my reputation by whispering "baby goats" in an alley is not worth a 50% markup. It just upped to 100%.

I stretch my back, adjust my headphones, and fire up my laptop, ready to start recording my show. But maybe rereading a few more messages can't hurt...

JOSIE

how did the girl do last night?

COLBY

Pretty good. She was super out of it for a long time but took the pain meds fine.

JOSIE

and how did Mom do?

COLBY

Terrible. 😕 How do parents of infants do this? Between the pain meds schedule, and my constant waking up to check and see if she's breathing, to waking up every time she moves, I am tired as hell.

JOSIE

Please put this on number 169 of why I never want children. I'm like a pink-haired Hulk if I don't get enough sleep.

COLBY

The Hulk. Like the 300-pound green man? Not sure that analogy sticks, but who am I to judge?

JOSIE

Hmm. How about I'm like one of those super peppy tradwife influencers, but after the cameras are off, I scream at my family and force them to eat day-old tuna salad with fake mayo and generic mustard.

COLBY

This is oddly specific. I think there's some things to unpack here.

Okay, okay. I do need to get to work. Sure, I work on my own time and make my own schedule, but the moment I get lax on that, things might go downhill. Besides, Kona is sleeping so hard that I need to take advantage of this time, and my energy level, while I still have it.

I check my watch. It's Josie's break time, so maybe one quick exchange.

COLBY

did you see the "storm watch" on the weather channel?

When the three dots immediately pop up, my heartbeat increases. I stare at the phone in my palms until the message appears.

JOSIE

No. But this is Minnesota. Don't let it freak you out. There are snowstorm watches, thunderstorm watches, tornado watches, like a gazillion times a year.

it's so disappointing. Like just hit us already with something good. Such a tease.

how did you acclimate to the weather out here when you moved?

COLBY

I never quite understood the joy of multi-thermal layered underwear before, but here we are.

I also didn't realize there were so many variations of gloves. Wool, insulated, leather, knit, windproof, waterproof, ones that you can tie onto a capsizing ship and it will save the entire crew... I mean, how do you all keep it straight?

JOSIE

and here I have my ski ones, my mittens, and my "it's not cold enough to need gloves" ones.

I grin at the message, set my phone down, and pull up my

laptop. As I scroll through the topic for today, my phone beeps. I should set it on silent, but...

> **JOSIE**
>
> OMG I have to tell you. This morning, a man brought in his parrot, which we can't even treat 'cause it needs a special doctor, and the parrot kept saying "Mikey's an asshole. Mikey's an asshole."
>
> I died! I don't know who this Mikey is, but I'm determined to find out
>
> break's up, gotta run. I'll text you later.

And I sigh. Okay, day three of feeling human again after so many years, and I want to hold on to this a little more. I take one last peek at Kona near my feet and click back on the microphone.

After leaving Florida, after Amelia, everything that I once knew changed. The MBA I'd received was meaningless. The company where I'd worked since my college internship and risen to senior management before turning thirty meant nothing to me. How could I sit there and review and analyze ROIs and quarterly forecasts and budgets when my world just collapsed? The numbers, which I'd once loved, blended together. They no longer made sense in the way that they once had. Who gave a shit about audit standards when my wife just fucking died?

When Amelia and I got our life insurance policy right after we were married, we joked about who was going to off the other one to cash in. The amount was high, *so* high, but we were in our twenties, the premium was cheap, and we took it knowing we'd never use it because people our age don't die.

So, after Amelia passed, I cashed out and left the finance world with its numbers and annual budget planning, and didn't work for a year until I stumbled into something that gave me a little bit of life. And today, I'm so close to recording my one thousandth episode, which is mind-blowing. Something that started as an outlet, a way to get me talking, a way to channel Amelia, has amassed a following I never dreamed possible—close to two hundred thousand monthly listeners.

And not a single person in the world knows it's me.

There's so much freedom in having a dual personality like this. A stage name, a pen name, a cloak of anonymity. I can say whatever I want without the repercussions of anyone knowing it's me. I close my eyes and think of Amelia's grinning face. Once I picture her fully and conjure her personality, I take a full breath, exhale through my nose, and hit record.

"Hey, everyone! Welcome to the *Love 'Em or Leave 'Em* podcast, where we do a deep dive into all things love, including if it's time to stay together, or break it off. I am your host, Ruby Reanne—the woman who's not a therapist, not a doctor, not educated whatsoever in the study of human relationships, and one hundred percent not even remotely qualified to be giving you *any* sort of advice. My only credentials are being in a fabulous marriage of fifteen years and counting, and miraculously holding on to a beautiful, incredible wife who puts up with exactly zero of my shit. With that all being said, I am *so* excited about today's show! So, saddle up there, cowboys and cowgirls, and yep, I just dropped that phrase and have no idea where that came from. And as we all know, I purposedly do limited editing on this show, but I'm at a solid regret-level eight for using that term and knowing I won't cut it in post-production. We don't have to be perfect, friends, we just have to be good enough."

I tap into the laptop and pull up the questions. Hundreds of communications come into me a week—from voicemails to DMs and emails, and on the website, I have a listener submission section. Depending on how much I ramble, any one show might only get through a handful of questions, so I really need to pick and choose. I, of course, pre-read the questions, but to maintain authenticity, while swallowing back the irony that I'm deceiving the audience about my identity, I try not to think of the answer ahead of time and instead do my WWAS—What Would Amelia Say.

Sure, my listeners have grown to know and love me. And I've

never pretended to be a doctor, or therapist, or anything. The only thing I've pretended is that I'm currently married. And yet, I know it's a lie. Deep down, I realize there is a level of deception taking place. But I think with the entertainment value, along with the hopefully helpful advice I give, it outweighs the bad.

At least, that's what I tell myself on the hard days when my conscience eats at me.

"Okay, everyone, this email comes from Brooke. The email says, 'Hey, Ruby, I have a problem. My husband is so upset and angry over a situation, and I think he's completely blowing it out of proportion. We've been watching a Netflix show together for the last six seasons, and it just came out with the final season last week when I was on a work trip. We watch together, every night. And while I was stuck in the hotel room, I watched it at night to pass the time. I wasn't going to say anything and still watch with him. But when I got home from the convention, we go to watch it, and he noticed on my profile that it was already watched. He confronted me, and I told him the truth. He was so mad that he slept on the couch that night. Honestly, I really don't see what the big deal is. Please tell me he's being totally unreasonable. Sincerely, Brooke.'"

I hit pause on the recording, take a sip of coffee, and peek at Kona, who looks so uncomfortable as she sleeps in the cone. Amelia and I did this, too. Our shared streaming shows. After she was done teaching her second graders for the day, and I was done drafting whatever report was needed at work, we'd do our nightly routine—dinner, walks, maybe softball or grocery shopping, then we'd snuggle in and watch an episode or two of our show. And I would have never done what this woman who emailed me did, but the listeners love anecdotal experiences—real or fiction—so I give it to them.

"Thank you, Brooke, for your email. I mean, the choice is obvious here. This is divorce-court material. Any judge in their right mind would not even go fifty-fifty but just award one hundred percent to you for him being unreasonable," I say with a chuckle. "But before you seek out the Harvey Specter divorce lawyer in your town—*anyone catch that reference out there?*—I want to offer up a tiny bit of perspective. I did this once, years ago because I learned my lesson, to Amelia. It was the final season of *Suits*—again, the Harvey Specter reference, people—and Amelia had left to visit her parents. Honestly, I knew it was kind of wrong, but it was *Suits*! The original Meghan Markle show before she became the princess or duchess or whatever, you know? It was like a year before the streaming service had the last season, and we'd waited *so* long and I just had to find out what happened with Harvey and Donna. So, I snuck in an episode. And a few things happened. One, I felt really shitty. I *like* watching shows with my wife, and I missed having that moment where we paused the show and looked at each other with wide eyes, or added our commentary, or threw a pillow at the TV when Louis did something wrong. And two, when Amelia found out, she was really, really hurt. I took something that she, *we*, value, and ruined it for us. Looking back on it now, I see that it was really selfish. I denied us the ability to bond..."

As I continue on, I think of Amelia, of course, but also Josie. Which is an utter surprise. Does she stream shows? Is she a horror kind of gal, or humor only? Does she like Disney, or Netflix, or does she do basic cable-style watching? I try to blink away the thoughts of Josie, as to not mess with the Amelia-energy I need in order to record, but she is simmering below the surface.

For the next two hours, I spend the rest of the episode answering a few questions, taking a break to grab more water, reviewing the sound quality halfway in between, and look again at my sweet girl on the studio floor. She's sleeping so peacefully that I don't want to wake her up, but I'm feeling the need for some doggie snuggles. I slide off the office chair and nuzzle up next to her, spreading my palm on her soft belly as it rises and falls.

I peek at her stitches, my poor girl, and lean in closer.

Wait. Shit. I press my hand against her leg. Oh. Oh no.

No... no... no... My heart thuds against my chest. Oh God, this is not good. I dash up from Kona, grab my phone, frantically scroll through my contact list, and hit dial.

SIX

JOSIE

I swing the stethoscope around my neck and gently close the exam door behind me, when Leo rounds the corner and juts his thumb over his shoulder toward the front desk. "Hey, can you take a call? There's a woman on the phone freaking out and wants to talk to you."

Colby? I quickly pull out my phone from my pocket—which is always set on silent at work as to not scare any skittish animals—and tap it on. For the last few days, we've had dozens of text messages, giving me a delicious lust buzz that I haven't had in a long time. I've been checking my phone religiously in between patients to see if a new one popped up. But a few hours ago, we got in a rush, and I haven't looked at my phone.

And shit... Yep, I've missed five calls. I rush up to the front desk and grab the clinic phone. "Hey, it's Josie."

"Something's wrong with Kona," Colby says, her voice panicked and breathless. "I was in the room and laid by her, and her leg is on fire. It's so hot and red, and I don't know what I should do, and I can't bring her in there because I can't lift her and I'm not sure if she's in a ton of pain, or if I should put ice on it..."

"It's okay, it's okay. This happens sometimes post-op," I say, using my calmest medical voice. "It probably got a little infected, which is unfortunate, but totally normal. She needs some antibiotics."

My heart pinches, thinking of Colby alone in that place, filled with worry, pacing back and forth while trying to reach me. "I'll have the vet write a prescription and you can come get it. We always have this kind of medication in stock, so Kona won't have to wait."

A moment passes before Colby speaks. "I don't think I can leave her. I just... I don't want to leave her."

I am pretty sure that I have never met another human who loves their dog as much as Colby loves hers. Outside, fat fluffy flakes are falling, and the wind is picking up a few additional flurries, but the "storm watch" that the news and my social media is blowing up with seems to be just that—a watch. "I totally get it. No worries." I flick my wrist to check the time. "I'll be off work in an hour and will bring them to you. Does that work?"

A loud, audible sigh releases from the phone. "I really don't know what to say. Truly. You are such a lifesaver, and obviously, since I can't leave Kona to buy meds, I can't leave her to buy you cupcakes, either."

I smile and hate how much my heart is skipping with the idea of seeing Colby again so soon. It's been three days since I've been to her place, and the fuel I'm getting from our text message exchanges alone is running dry, no matter how many times I make an excuse to send a message. "I don't need cupcakes," I say, giving Leo a little scowl, who's darting some serious "WTF?" glances my way. "I'll be good just knowing you guys are okay. I really don't want to think of Kona in any pain."

I'm not doing this, I'm not doing this. The whole insta-love thing feels so much like my MO that I'm pretty sure it's part of my DNA at this point. I'm pretty sure if you pulled up my picture on Wikipedia it would say "serial lover" underneath it. So embarrassing. So *predictable.*

After being with Zoey for a decade, when we split, I dated several women and I fell hard for every single one, almost immediately. We'd sleep together, I'd think I was in love, it would be an amazing honeymoon period for a few weeks, until a sickly realization seeped into me that, yep, I did it again. I'd go through a few weeks of mourning that I'd reverted back to old behaviors, vow to take up some hobby other than the need to find love, and then find myself doing it again. Even the year I spent trying to win my ex back, I was dating and trying to fill a void.

But four months ago, I stopped, cold turkey. No more women until I figure out what it is that I'm searching for, and until I'm ready to be a partner. A *good* partner. Someone who is reliable and stable and has their shit together. Which I already know I do not. So, yes. I can be friends with Colby. Friends is good, healthy, wonderful even. But absolutely no more. And if my insides don't get this message soon, I'm going to have to badger them into submission.

On the way out to Colby's home, the wipers squeak against the falling, fluttery snow. My gym bag is next to me on the passenger seat, all prepped with the clothes I was going to wear tonight while going to a YMCA in a neighboring city to try a barre class. I was really excited for the class, but spending time with Colby and Kona sounds way more enticing.

The setting sun is beautiful, a gold-and-fuchsia stream pushing through the pine trees, casting a glittered glow on the setting snow. I crack open my window and pull in some crisp, dry air as I make my way up the windy hill.

When I pull up, Colby is outside, shoveling off snow from the patio. She scrapes off a final chunk and tosses the snow over to the side with a heavy plop, and rests the shovel against the side of the house. Christ, I am a walking cliché, but is there anything hotter than watching a beautiful woman do some outdoorsy manual labor?

And that will be the final indecent thought I allow myself for the rest of the night. Switching to friend mode... now.

"Hey, you," I say as I step out of the car, holding a bag of supplies. "You doing okay?"

Colby nods with her mouth twisted down, and I see the worry from all the way over here. It's the same face I saw for hours at the clinic, and to the deepest part of me, I want to hug her again and take away her fear.

"I'm just really scared for her," she says, clapping off the snow from her gloves. "I hate seeing her like this. She can't tell me what's going on, I can't reason with her. I just... I feel so helpless. It's the absolute worst."

"She's going to be okay. This is totally normal, but I know it can be scary as hell when it happens." At the outdoor mat, I stomp the snow off my tennis shoes and step into the house, and *whoa*. A gush of something hearty and savory, with onions and beef, fills the air. My stomach immediately growls, and I definitely regret not finishing my leftover Thai takeout for lunch.

Colby takes off her jacket, and *oh... okay*. Swapping out her oversized hooded sweatshirt for a snug, white Henley makes my mouth water more than it should. Rounded shoulders, full breasts, taut stomach. *Dear God.* I had no idea all that was under there.

Cool, cool. Focus on the dog.

"Oh, sweet girl, what do we have going on here?" I say as I peer down and look at Kona's inflamed, red skin. Colby's crouching next to me, close, enough where I get a small whiff of that soft lavender scent. I shift away. "Can you grab Kona a high-value snack? Something that we can give her to take this antibiotic. And a few towels."

"Yes. Be right back." Colby hurries out of the room, thankfully, because I need to pull it together. I'm around her for exactly two minutes and getting some thoughts, and I should not be having *thoughts*.

I grab a few things out of my bag and line them up on the cedar coffee table, when Colby returns with several towels and a cheese stick. As I work on laying out the items, Colby stuffs the pill in the cheese, then gives it to Kona.

"This really isn't too bad," I say, looking at the area surrounding Kona's stitches. "But I'm going to clean it a bit. Just so you know, you really shouldn't do this on your own. Some people do hydrogen peroxide, soap, all sorts of things, and it makes it so much worse. The last thing we want is to make her infection worse by doing some sort of funky home remedy." I dig out the sterile saline solution, gauze, and tug on latex gloves. "If you can just comfort her and keep her steady, we should be able to do this pretty quickly."

Colby removes Kona's cone and rests the dog's head in her lap. She strokes her head and the top of her ears. We work together silently, with the exception of a small tune that Colby's humming to Kona. I'm not even sure Colby knows she's humming, but as I peek at her from my peripherals, a warmth fills me. The love inside this woman is so obvious, so massive, that my heart swells.

After I flush the wound, I soak the gauze in the sterile solution, and with the most tender touch I can manage, clean the infected area. Kona is an absolute champ and barely moves during the procedure. Once finished, Colby reattaches the cone while I clean up all the supplies.

At the farmhouse-style deep kitchen sink, I peek out the window at the woods in the backyard, at least as far as I can see, as I wash my hands. Endless amounts of trees span through the dark and falling snow. It's so pristine, the outside holding a sense of calm that I really don't see anywhere else. I stare for a bit longer when Colby moves into the kitchen, hands me a towel, and digs out a wooden spoon from the drawer.

"I'm starting to wonder if there is another phrase that I can use besides *thank you*," she says as she lifts the lid to a large pot on the stove and leans in to smell the hearty steam. "I seriously owe you, and I don't know how to repay you. Do you accept Venmo? Flowers? My left kidney if you may ever need it?"

I rub the towel in my hands, and grin. I get it, I really do. If someone were to do these things for me, I'd probably feel the same. And it's impossible to explain in enough depth where the person will actually grasp it, that doing things like this—helping, being there, supporting—makes me feel good. It lifts my spirit in a way that it needs to be lifted, so much so that I often wonder if helping others is more of a selfish act than selfless.

"Seriously, Colby. It's no problem at all," I say as Colby tugs up her sleeves and stirs the stew. God, those forearms. Strong, tight, rigid muscles... Seriously, so much for my pact to not allow any indecent thoughts to ransack my brain. "I should probably get going." *I don't want to go.*

A slight frown appears as she taps the spoon against the pot and puts the lid back on. "Do you have somewhere to be tonight? Some extreme sport class?"

"Actually, I was going to try barre tonight, but I'm not going to make it in time."

Colby's face falls. "I'm so sorry."

Oh, dang. I didn't mean to make her feel bad. "Don't be sorry," I say as I reach out and touch her forearm, and dammit. I shouldn't have done that. Her skin is warm, and smooth, and I immediately pull back. "I'm not sorry at all. It's nice to see you, and I love seeing Kona." I toss the paper towel in the trash under the sink and lean against the butcher's block countertop. "Ever since I was little, I've always wanted a golden. They're my favorite."

"So why don't you have one?" Colby asks as she reaches for two water bottles in the fridge and hands me one.

Such an innocent question that would take me hours to answer and a solid few months in therapy to really dive into the deeper reasons. I work with animals in my everyday life. I love animals, all of them, and taking care of them daily brings me more joy than I could ever explain. But I don't feel responsible, or settled enough, to be the type of owner a dog would need. "I'm gone too much during the day and wouldn't want to leave them."

This is not a lie, obviously. But it's not the entire truth, either.

"That absolutely makes sense. The few times when I leave Kona, I hate it," Colby says, cracking the top open on the water bottle. "Codependency for the win."

I sip back some water and wipe a few droplets from my lip.

"When I was younger, we had a dog, Lucky Charms. He was this feisty but sweet border collie mix, and God, I loved him so much."

"Was he with your family for a long time?" she asks.

It's a fair question. Yes, and no, is the best answer. I think I was around eight or nine when we got him. I remember begging my dad for months that I wanted a dog, and one day he picked me up early from school and took me to the shelter. I'll never forget strolling by the cages and pleading with my dad that we should bring all of them home. He'd smiled at me, in his kind fatherly way that I always loved, and said we couldn't bring them all home. But we could bring one. So I picked the fluffiest dog out and my dad let me name him. And it seemed perfectly reasonable at the time to name him after my favorite cereal.

That memory is stamped in my brain forever. A core memory that hurts as much as it brings a sliver of joy. Just like I'll never forget strolling the aisles with my dad, I'll also never forget the look my mom gave us when we came home from the shelter, the arguing that broke out between my mom and dad, the hushed whispers and slammed doors. I was too little to understand why Mom wasn't happy we "surprised" her by bringing home a dog. I didn't get the extra burden it put on her and my dad, the other mouth to feed, the other entity that had to be cared for. And three years later, when my dad left all of us kids but took the dog with him, my heart split into pieces.

But Colby is probably not wanting to know this whole sob story, or the way that I blamed myself, thinking my dad left because I made him get me a dog, so I shrug. "Lucky Charms was with us for... a few years."

A long silence follows, and she doesn't ask any more questions. She lifts herself from leaning against the counter and stirs the pot one more time. "Do you have dinner plans tonight? If not, I'd love for you to stay. I made stew."

My mouth is already watering. "Like real stew? Not the stuff from the can?"

A quick chortle leaves her mouth. "Definitely not from the can."

I want to stay so bad, which means that I should be responsible, politely decline, and leave. "I'd love to," I say and hand her a couple of colorful bowls resting on the floating shelf next to the sink. "I don't even remember the last time I've had a home-cooked meal."

Colby fills up the bowls with the stew, hands me a spoon, and I follow her to the two-seater table in the corner by another window. When she pulls up the chair, she tucks a loose piece of hair behind her ear, and a soft grin flushes her face. "Well, I'm glad that I could give you one."

The look on her face is sheepish, expectant, warm, and my tummy flutters. Right now, sitting here in the golden light, the fluffy snowflakes falling outside, the crackle of the fire across the room, feels just like a date.

And I hate how much I love it.

SEVEN
COLBY

A woman is at my house, right now, *for dinner*. I am having a woman over for dinner. Not that it was planned, of course. This stew is my favorite, and during the winter I make it on a constant rotation. And I always make enough to last for a week. I love to cook, but sometimes it feels wasted. When I was married, this was sort of my thing. I'd take a few cooking classes and spend a chunk of time on the weekends decompressing by making me and Amelia fancy meals. It's been six years since I've cooked for a woman, and I think I'm going to pass out from holding my breath as I watch Josie take her first bite.

"*Mmmm.*" She rolls her eyes and moans. "Colby, this is *phenomenal.*" She scoops up another bite, blows on top to cool it off, and swallows it down. "Seriously, so good."

Please don't blush. "Yeah? You think so?" I ask with a lifted brow.

Josie waves her hand. "Nope. Don't do it. This is not the time for the humblebrag thing. You know it's good. There's no way in hell you don't know it's delicious."

Do I have a sort of cooking praise kink? Is that a thing? Because everything in me warms at her words. Feeding someone, knowing they love it, watching them enjoy it, is almost as good as eating it myself. "Well, I do think it's good, but honestly, I haven't cooked for anyone in so many years that it's hard to know."

Josie cuts a slice of rustic bread from the board in front of us, and hands me a piece. "Why not?"

Well, I walked directly into that one, but I don't want to talk about Amelia. Not yet, not now. I dunk the bread into the stew, and chew. Finally, I shrug. "Life of a single person, I guess."

"Ah," she says and doesn't push. Thankfully.

I glance at Kona snuggled on the dog bed at the edge of the couch, still sleeping. "Man, she really isn't feeling good. Normally, when I sit down to eat, she is right at my leg, panting and drooling. A solid number of yoga pants have been destroyed for the evening by her saliva."

Josie peeks over at Kona with a nod. "In two days, those antibiotics will kick in and she'll feel so much better. Soon enough you'll have a solid drool puddle at your toes."

As we continue eating, a few things happen. One, Josie tells me stories about her workday, she goes into more detail about the parrot who wouldn't stop swearing, and talks about holding a baby goat. Two, I talk about when I moved to Minnesota and discovered my love of snowmobiling, snowshoeing, and cross-country skiing. Also that I absolutely did not love snowboarding, which I tried once, and only once, and thanked the universe that I didn't break my face. Three, I become so comfortable with her that I forget this is only the second time she's been in my house.

When we finish, I move to the stove. While I pour the stew into containers for the week, and Josie washes dishes, we *laugh*. I actually fucking laugh. Of course, it started because Josie didn't know how the kitchen hose worked and accidently sprayed herself in the face, but it was a genuine laugh, sparking something alive in me, and I realized how much time has passed since my body did that activity.

Right now is a natural time for Josie to leave. We had dinner, Kona is settled, our bellies are full. But she is not making any movement for the door, and I don't want her to go. I snap the lid on the final container, shove it in the fridge, and eye the chilled wine on the lower shelf. "Do you want to have a glass of wine?"

Josie slings the dish towel back on the hanging rack. A moment passes where she tugs her lower lip between her teeth, and I wonder if I've gone too far when she nods. "Sure."

I bite back a smile. And then I breathe through the nerves. *It's just wine. Like dessert.* No biggie, no hidden message, no reason to be freaking the hell out right now. My trembling hands struggle to uncork the bottle, but thankfully, Josie is back on the couch, pink scrubs and all, sitting near Kona.

Not only do the scrubs not look all that comfortable, they also look a little chilly. I have the urge to offer her a sweater, but she pulls one of the knitted blankets from the wicker basket and tucks it over her legs.

"Here you go," I say as I hand her a glass. The fireplace is roaring, but I add another log, so I don't have to keep getting up. And perhaps to buy myself a few more moments to pull my nerves together.

It's just a glass of wine. Yes, yes, it's just wine, and Josie is just a person, but she's also pretty damn amazing. She's funny, and generous, and kind. She's come out to my house now, *twice* for God's sake, out of the kindness of her big, beautiful heart. And her text messages to me, showing she's thinking about me, making me smile, are drops in this empty bucket of mine.

And... she's beautiful. I can't get over it. Those warm, chocolate brown eyes. That pretty mouth. The soft pink-and-blond hair that looks like angel feathers. She's got this skin, pale and flushed that looks so soft, so inviting, that I have the tiniest urge to swipe my thumb across her cheek, just once, to confirm it's as silky as it looks.

I settle into the couch next to her and tug the other half of the blanket over me. "I still can't get over that you and Zoey were together." I twirl the wine in my glass and take a small sip of the crisp apple-flavored pinot. "If it's not too forward, can I ask what happened to you guys? You both are really nice, good people. I'm surprised it didn't work out."

"Well, thank you for that. She is a really nice person. It's just..." Josie tucks her legs under herself, and shifts towards me. "You know, sometimes people spend so much time being polite, caring, giving, that you lose yourself a bit. Zoey is a people pleaser. You've probably noticed that from being in her shop. And it's a lovely quality. But in a relationship, it's not always the best. She said yes to anything, whatever I wanted, and I made all the decisions. After a while, I think she lost herself in our relationship, and at the same time, I realized that neither of us were fully invested, you know? I didn't push enough for her to tell me her needs. She didn't advocate. We were, I guess, complacent. Going through the motions of what a relationship looked like without being fully into the relationship. If that makes sense."

The wine is smooth, tart, and I continue to take small sips as Josie keeps talking about Zoey. I respect the hell out of her that she's not bashing an ex. It's a frequent theme on my show, and back when I had a group of friends, ex-bashing was often the main topic of conversation. But Josie talks about how the issues really ran deeper than being polite, and it took until Zoey proposed for Josie to be slapped with the reality that this was not where she wanted to be. And she knew Zoey didn't want that, either.

Through the fireplace crackles in the background, Josie tilts her wine glass to her lips. "I lead with my heart, not my head, in so many situations," Josie says, swirling the wine. "And my relationship with Zoey was no exception. And to be totally honest, I don't always make the best decisions."

This tone piques my ears. "What do you mean?"

A fresh blush of crimson moves through her cheeks, nearly matching the pink of her scrubs. "God, this is so embarrassing." She sets the half-drunk glass on the table and scoots back into the couch. "This sounds really dumb, so you have to hear me out, and reserve any and all judgment for after I leave."

"This is the safest, most judgment-free zone this side of Lake Superior," I say, grinning at her sheepish tone. "Promise."

Josie tugs her bottom lip into her mouth. "God, this is so terrible." She plops an elbow on the back of the couch and rests the side of her head in her palm. "Have you heard of the podcast *Love 'Em or Leave 'Em with Ruby Reanne?*"

I choke on the wine in my throat, then quickly follow it with more wine. *Shit.* She just brought up my podcast. No one in the entire world knows I'm Ruby. Not my family, not my former in-laws, not even my bank that handles my ad-dollar transactions. And I'm *never* going to tell anyone it's me. "Oh, yep. I've heard of it."

Josie rakes her fingernails through her pink hair, and nibbles on her lip. "So, for like two years or so, I was kind of obsessed with the show. I went back and listened to every episode ever made, never missed a new episode, had an alert set up in case Ruby did any bonus episodes, subscribed to her show, the whole nine yards." She flicks at the stem of her glass with a soft ting, and takes a breath. "A few months before Zoey and I broke up, there was this one episode, and it just resonated with me so hard. The caller talked about feeling lost in a relationship, how they didn't think they were the best version of themselves, how they didn't know if they were with the right person or not. You've listened to the show, so you get the format."

You get the format. A thread tugs in my stomach and is knotting. Josie sighs, and inside those beautiful brown doe eyes, I see her struggle with this story. I almost want to tell her to stop, that I don't need to hear any more, but that would be so deeply unfair to stifle someone's vulnerability. At the same time, I can't tell her who I am and what I do, and this is so unethical.

I think. Is it unethical? My insides cringe, and I brace myself to hear more.

"Anyway, so Ruby told this story about when her wife was in the hospital overnight for surgery," Josie continues. "And Ruby walked into the recovery room, and the heart monitor ticked higher, you know, with a faster pulse. And I swear it was the sweetest thing I'd ever heard. And it started me thinking that I wasn't sure if either Zoey or I were in a hospital room, the machine would kick up higher. I thought it would all just stay flat. No high or low heartbeat, just stagnant. Does that make sense?"

I'm going to be sick. Yes, I know the episode Josie's referring to, or at least one of the several episodes I used this story on. After Amelia passed, I had a fantasy in my head and played out the scenario of how I wished it would've gone with Amelia. So many nights, I replayed this image—Amelia knocked out after her surgery, me tiptoeing into the room with the doctor, and the monitor beeps increasing. I pictured the doctor making a joke about knowing it's true love that while unconscious, your loved one's heart flutters with your presence.

But it was a lie. By the time I got to Amelia's room, there was no heartbeat at all.

"Anyway, I just wasn't sure if I'd ever walk into a room and Zoey's heart would kick up for me, or vice versa," Josie says, reaching back for her glass of wine. She studies my face for a long time, which I can only assume has taken on some ashen look of horror. A self-deflecting giggle flies from Josie's mouth. "Ah! You think I've lost it, don't you? It's okay, you can totally say it. I mean, who listens to a podcast like that and starts applying these stories to their own life? Not only that, who listens to a podcast and starts *changing* their life? I fully recognize how completely bananas this sounds."

Oh God, seriously what do I say to this? Tell her that I have some inside knowledge that this story was made up? Tell her that the entire podcast is fictional, that there is no Ruby, there is no Amelia, that none of this is real? That Ruby is a personification of my dead wife, a way for me to live in a fantasy world, to escape before reality crashes into me. "I... can absolutely see how a story like that would resonate with you. Who knows if that was even a true story or not? Maybe it was an analogy or something?"

Josie twists her mouth. "Maybe, but I think the foundation of the podcast is that she uses real-life stories. I'd be surprised if someone would just make something like that up." As hot red flames burst in my chest, Josie takes another small sip of wine. "But there's more."

Oh God...

"So I move to Minneapolis, determined to find myself, what makes me happy, discover who I am outside of being with Zoey. I mean, we'd been together since we were like twenty years old. Essentially my entire adult life. But in Minneapolis, I'm still not finding what I need. So, what do I do? This is so embarrassing, but I freaking write Ruby Reanne, the podcast host, like some sort of lunatic. Can you believe it?"

It's so hot in here that I'm going to pass out. I remove the blanket off my lap and tug up the sleeves of my Henley. "No way," I say, swallowing back the feeling of sickliness weaving in my throat. "Did she read your stuff on the air?" *Please for everything holy let it be one of the thousands of emails I have to let go.*

"Oh yeah, she sure did," Josie says with a sheepish grin. "In my letter to Ruby, I said how I thought I made this huge mistake and left the person I thought I was supposed to be with. And Ruby was all like 'you need to fight for her, tell her what you think, it's true love, do something bold,' blah, blah, blah, bullshit. And so I did. That's actually what I was doing the night *we* met on the sidewalk last year. Me following the advice from the podcast to be 'bold' and 'brave.' I took Zoey to dinner and told her I wanted her back, and obviously, she said no. I was so fucking humiliated."

The deep-seated need to defend my fictional character grinds into me. "I mean, Ruby didn't have all the information, so she probably did the best she could." I instinctively reach down and comfort stroke Kona's fur. "Doesn't she say at the beginning of every show that she's not a doctor or therapist?"

"Yeah, but she also talks a lot about her perfect marriage and how to achieve it," Josie says as she weaves her fingertips into the edge of the blanket. "I swear it's like watching those cooking influencers online, and then finding out they are a complete fraud and just had it all catered in."

Ouch.

Josie unravels her fingers from the blanket and moves the glass back to her lips. "Whatever. That Ruby woman sucks anyway. I stopped listening after that. Honestly, I hope the show goes off the air."

She laughs.

I don't.

"Oh God! That's probably really weird. I promise I'm not a stalker or anything, and this entire situation is just so ridiculous. It's just a show, and I was just a fan." Her smile fades for a moment and she looks into the flickering flames at the fireplace. "But it really hit me, you know. It's like yet another person in my life that has somehow let me down and led me astray."

The urge to flee from this room is heavy. I know I won't say anything to Josie. I won't point out that she is probably projecting some of her anger onto someone else, and it's not fair. But at the same time, I get it.

I don't feel the need to out my identity. My show is my safe space. I'm anonymous for a reason, and I don't owe an explanation to anyone for the reasons why. But still, it settles in my stomach, low and uncomfortable, that I might have contributed to someone's pain.

A long moment passes between us, when Josie crosses her arms and looks at me with a lifted brow. "So tell me, Colby, did you break up with your last person because of a podcast?"

Another round of red fills my body. I hadn't planned on talking about Amelia. I don't talk about Amelia, at least the *real* Amelia and what happened. But Josie is the first friend I've made in years, she's so easy to talk to, and she was just so vulnerable that it feels wrong not to share.

"No," I say and swallow the pressure in my throat. "My wife died."

EIGHT

JOSIE

My mouth feels impossibly dry as I stare at Colby's downcast eyes. The flames from the fireplace cast a golden hue across her room, Kona is nestled at her feet, a half-drunk glass of wine sits on the coffee table, and I am at a complete and total loss of words.

Colby's wife *died*? "Oh my gosh. Colby. I'm so sorry." I have a million questions. When? How? What happened? I have no idea if it's appropriate to ask anything at all, or what might be triggering, or what might cause tears. But I can't just leave it hanging in the air. "How long ago?"

Colby pulls her lips in between her teeth, and I immediately regret saying anything besides *I'm sorry*. "You don't have to tell me anything," I say. "I'm just so sorry."

A long moment stretches where Colby hooks a finger into her collar, and tugs. "I, um, haven't talked about this for a very long time." As if on cue, like the dog doesn't want to talk about it, either, Kona moves away from us and trudges down the hall. A few moments later, I hear the thump of a dog finding a new resting place in a bedroom. "It was six years ago, a few weeks after her thirtieth birthday party."

"Oh my God, that's so young." I'm desperate to know more, but I'm not sure how much Colby wants to share. Her mouth is opening and closing, she's fidgeting in her seat, and biting at the edge of her pinkie nail. At any moment, she looks like she's either going to cry, or bolt upright. "Can you tell me something you loved about her?"

A lightness overtakes the fidgets, and Colby leans back into the couch. "She was a terrible singer."

A slow grin pushes through. "*That's* what you loved about her?"

Colby peeks through her dark eyelashes at me with a smile. "Well, not that exactly. More like she was a terrible singer, but she absolutely did not give a shit. In church, at a bar, in the car, during karaoke, she couldn't care less that dogs started howling and people covered their ears."

A quick chuckle escapes. "I kind of love that. Unashamed, huh?"

"Totally. That was just who she was. She was so carefree and funny. But had a terrible eye for recognizing things. No lie, during our relationship, she probably approached ten different people convinced they were celebrities. She thought this woman at the grocery store was Meryl Streep. Like Meryl would just be casually strolling the aisles at a Whole Foods in Orlando. But it happened a lot, and these poor people. Harry Styles, Selena Gomez, Keanu Reeves. Like she practically tried to convince these people that they were the celebrities as they slowly backed away from her." Colby chuckles and presses her palm into her forehead. "It was so unbelievably, perfectly awkward."

Oh, the love that is coming through Colby is something I crave. Maybe someday I will have someone talk about me like this, with their eyes lighting up, flickering with nostalgia and life. I smile at her wide grin as she stirs in her seat.

"But then the one time, the *one freaking time* that we were actually in a place and I saw Jodie Foster—and almost passed out on the spot—I tried to drag her with me, and she convinced *me* that I was the delusional one. Sure enough, later on that day, a mutual friend snapped a selfie with Jodie and I'm still bitter about it."

This is so damn cute. And understandable. I would have been pissed had I given up the opportunity to take a selfie with Jodie Foster. "Okay, so besides a terrible eye for spotting celebrities, tell me more about her."

Through another full log on the fire, after each of us polished off a glass of wine, through a mug of cinnamon tea with a few cookies, Colby tells me all about her wife. That she was a teacher in Florida, that she loved Disney World, that her parents were also teachers and Colby fell into a once-a-year tradition of wearing an apple-and-alphabet T-shirt to family gatherings so she fit in. She talked about the summer trips they used to take, the love of the ocean and how Amelia loved drinking piña coladas and dancing wherever they were, regardless if there was a dancefloor.

Each word Colby says seems to unlock something, and the words cascade out, like a plugged geyser that has just been released. She talks. She talks *so* much that I barely have to pepper in any questions, and something about it is so comforting, so lovely, and I can feel the tug of a bond forming between us.

We've polished off the cookies, drunk two more mugs of tea, and now I'm sitting sideways with my back against the couch armrest and my knees hugged against my chest. Colby has her legs splayed out, facing me, and it feels so comfortable to have her toes tucked by my thigh, like we've done this a million times.

"We played on this softball league for a few years, and she was the pitcher. I always joked that I wanted to pitch, but really I don't think I could've handled the pressure. Community league or not, those players are competitive as hell." The smile drains from Colby's face and my heart pinches. "During one game, she tore her rotator cuff. We actually didn't even realize it. She thought she just strained a muscle, but after a few weeks it was still bothering her. So, we finally went in to get checked out."

She sucks in her cheeks and is no longer looking at me. I wish I could see inside her brain, flip through the mental images she's clearly flipping through. She picks at the cuffs of her sleeves, with short, slow breaths. I rest my hand at her ankle, patting it and encouraging her to tell me more if she wants. And then she tells me everything. How her wife went in for surgery, and she went to a coffee shop to do some work for her job. How she had no idea that her wife was back on the surgery table, dying. "Cardiomyopathy is what they called it."

"Oh... no," I say. I know what this is. It happens in the animal world, too.

"It's a disease in the heart muscle that makes it hard to pump blood. And it's really dangerous to go under anesthesia, but no one knew she had it." Colby tugs on her ponytail and takes a sharp breath. "So, this routine, basic surgery that was supposed to last a couple hours, ended up taking her life."

Even though I know what it is, I don't interrupt her as she explains it to me. The trembling in her lips makes me want to pull her into me, hug her until the trembles disappear, take away this pain she still so clearly has. And then... the lightbulb goes off and I press my palm against my mouth. "Oh my God. So when you brought Kona in for the routine surgery..."

I don't need to finish. She just nods, and I see it all. The fear. What I thought was an overreaction. The pain. The relief.

"Yeah. It brought up every emotion from that time, all these feelings that I thought were buried. But I guess they're not." A couple of tears blink from Colby's eyes and she swipes them away with a flick of her pinkie. "Sorry."

"No, no, don't do that. Do not apologize for feeling all of this. You obviously loved her so much. You have every right to cry. Anytime, anyplace." I unfold myself and inch closer, trying to catch her gaze, trying to make her see the comfort I want to give. "Thank you so much for sharing this with me. I can't even imagine how difficult that was to tell me all of that."

Colby finally glances at me through those impossibly dark eyelashes. The flicker of the fireplace flames highlights the warm tones in her brown eyes, and casts a golden hue against her skin. My urge to comfort her overtakes any good sense in maintaining a comfortable boundary. I tug her hand into my palm and squeeze.

I don't let go.

And neither does she.

She licks the corner of her lip, her eyes filled with weary exhaustion, and years of being so tired that it's probably seeped into her bones. "Sometimes I don't want to hurt anymore, you know?"

"I absolutely know," I say, swiping my thumb against her soft, porcelain skin. "I'd want to stop hurting, too."

Colby releases a sigh and flips her hands so we're intertwined. Not tight, not heavy, just sort of light, absentminded distraction. "Sometimes I just want to forget. I want to forget so fucking bad that it hurts."

The moment is so raw and devastating, and also beautiful someway. I feel it nipping at my soul. We both look at our hands clasped, and the moment seems to carry on for minutes. And then I lift her hand to my mouth and kiss her inner wrist. Just one brush of my lips, something to show I care, that I'm hearing and absorbing her story. Something in her gaze shifts.

She pulls my hand to her face and leans into it like I'm the support she needs, like I'm the one holding her up in this moment, and my insides melt. I cup her cheek, brushing my thumbs against the soft, silken, skin.

I honestly don't know who leans in first. Me? Her? But our mouths meet, with soft tastes of cinnamon tea and dessert. It's startling at first, like a shock you'd get in a staticky house. She's hesitant, I'm hesitant, and it's a bit awkward and clunky.

"I just want to forget..." she whispers into my mouth.

And I want to stop chasing.

I shouldn't do this. I shouldn't do this. I shouldn't do this. But, oh God, I *want* to do this. My skin is on fire; the need to touch, be touched, to stop running, seeps into me. Colby's soft, perfect tongue slips into my mouth, and I grip the back of her head.

I shouldn't do this...

But fuck it. Right now, I don't care.

Hands and heavy breaths fill the air. Her mouth on me, on my neck, tugging at my shirt. Palms, and hands, and fingers dragging across skin. Moans and flutters and *hunger*. So much hunger.

Scrubs off, bras off, fingers dipping, mouths moving. There's licking and sucking, and oh hell… everything feels incredible. I don't want to chase, and she doesn't want to think, and no one fucking cares, and this all feels so goddamn good.

The wind and snow slap against the window, the flames in the fireplace burn bright, and tentative hands turn into desperate hands. We move, messy, unhinged, tangled. The blanket is kicked off, naked bodies swivel, soft lips and gentle mouths swap for a rushed, frantic, frenetic need to burn off energy, to burn off memories, to allow for a moment of reprieve.

Right now, I no longer care about consequences.

NINE

JOSIE

Sharp, crisp air hits my bare shoulder, and I blink my eyes open into the space. It takes only a moment in my sleepy haze to realize where I am. I bolt upright and drag the blanket across my body.

Oh, no. No, no, no, nooooo. *Shit.*

What have I done?

The evening before comes back to me in a flash. A terrible, yet phenomenally hot, flash. The sex was great. Oh God, it was so unbelievably great. Hot, frantic, urgent, messy. But—I did it again. I chased something and made a terrible, impulsive decision. I let my heart and body make decisions that my mind knows are wrong, and the need to connect made me do something very, very stupid.

And clearly Colby thinks the same thing because she is no longer curled next to me on the couch where everything happened. Nope. I'm alone. Covered up with an extra blanket, a fresh water bottle on the coffee table next to me, a pile of folded blankets beside it, but definitely alone.

I'm gonna cry.

It's been forever since I connected with someone, like this, and made a friend, and the first thing I do is sleep with her? What the hell is wrong with me? But... oh... those lips, those fingers, the way she moved. My chest flushes with the desperate need to do it again, and the guilt of what I've just done. Yes, I'm sexually open and free and a firm believer that any consenting adults should do whatever they want, but this is so much more. This is me going back on my promise to myself to find what I'm seeking and not numb myself with sex. And I've failed, again. *With Colby.*

I scoop my clothes off the floor, tug the blanket around my naked body, and tiptoe down the hall to use the bathroom and get dressed as quick as humanly possible. Colby's bedroom door is shut. Thank God. The very last thing I want to do right now is face her and everything I've done.

Well, I fucked this one up good. Whatever budding friendship was happening here, whatever flicker of something potentially brewing, I ruined because of my need for *something*. And as hot as the sex was last night, as luscious as her lips were, as good as everything felt, I still didn't find what I was looking for. This constant, endless, unfulfilled ache in me is as present today as it has ever been.

The hardwood floors in this place are so creaky, and I'm praying to whatever entity out there that may exist that neither Kona nor Colby wake up. Flames fan my cheeks. I absolutely cannot have this moment right now. I throw on my jacket, stuff my feet in my tennis shoes, and quietly step outside.

You've got to be kidding me.

It appears that while I was having multiple orgasms last night the storm of the century was getting busy outside. The area is covered in a blanket of white. *Covered.* It looks like someone just plopped us in the deepest part of the Arctic Circle and any moment a polar bear is going to rise from the hills and give chase. It's barely dawn, just the tiniest murky ray of light is peeking over the horizon, but I think even if we were in full sun, I'd have trouble spotting my car.

The wind is whistling, whipping more flurries into my face; the snowflakes are thick and fat as they slam down. I shield my face against them as I run to where my car is buried. As the car warms, I take a deep breath, push the back of my head into the seat, and close my eyes.

"*Shit.*" I allow myself a few more moments of wallowing, before I reach in the back to grab the snow brush. Once I'm home, I'll allow myself a proper cry and a few moments of verbal self-flagellation. But now is not the time. Now is the time to break free from this place and run as fast as I can to the safety and serenity of my own bedroom.

Outside, the long brush swooshes across the roof, the windshield, the hood, and massive mounds of heavy snow plop to the ground. My feet are buried up to my midcalf, icy cold wetness soaks into my leg, and why, *why*, did I not change into the boots I have buried in my trunk? Let's add a solid case of frostbite to my terrible decisions for the last twelve hours.

"It's okay, it's okay, I got this..." I say, trying to fake to myself that I do, in fact, got this. Which I'm pretty sure I don't. My legs are freezing, the scrubs offering as much protection against the snow and wind as a piece of tissue paper. I frantically brush off the last of it and scurry back into the car.

Oh... heat. Glorious, glorious heat. I tug off my mittens, rub my palms together, and then press them onto my exposed cheeks. God, it's cold out there. The prickly sting of cold skin from damp pants clinging to my legs sends shivers through me, and I quickly tug them up and blow the warm air vents at them.

My heart pounds against my chest. I need to leave. I need to get the hell out of here and take a shower and have a good cry, and seriously, why is there so much damn snow? Even on max speed, sitting in Colby's driveway, my wipers can barely keep up.

I blow out a deep, ragged breath and slowly ease down the driveway. The car pushes through the thick, heavy snow. "Come on, come on," I say, and someone tell me why I thought a tiny little sedan was a good vehicle when I live in Northern Minnesota. I lean as close to the windshield as I can to try and get better visibility, and pray that I don't make a sudden stop and face-plant into the glass. The wipers squeak against the windshield as they drag the heavy accumulation to the side.

Visibility is so low it's disorientating. Thank God Colby doesn't live on a cliff where I could go over the side. I can't tell where the gravel drive ends, but if I follow the tree line, I should be good. All moisture in my mouth has zapped away, and my body quickly starts overheating. I throw my hat to the side, grip a solid ten and two on the steering wheel, and inch my way towards freedom.

A small dip in the road, along with the howling wind, edges my car into a small snowbank and I stick. "No..." My teeth grit. No, I am *not* stuck. I can't be stuck. There is no way the universe would be cruel enough to let my car get stuck on Colby's property after everything that happened last night. I press on the gas, and tires spin. I put it into reverse. Spin. Neutral, then drive, spin.

This is not happening. I swipe the beads of sweat lining my forehead and put my car into park. Every swear word that I know, and a few that I picked up from my seventeen-year-old nephew, comes flying out of my mouth. "*Think, Josie.*"

There's no chance in a frozen hell that I'm going to stay here. I refuse to let my walk-of-shame nightmare turn into a stuck-in-shame nightmare.

I'm not giving up. I grab my gloves and hat, pop out of the truck, put on my boots, and grab my mini shovel.

I have an idea.

TEN

COLBY

The bright cedarwood ceiling in my bedroom is staring back at me, judging me. I heard Josie get up and tiptoe around the house. And as quietly as I'm sure she tried to be, even Kona, under her pain meds and antibiotic fog, heard her. Not that Josie was loud, at all, but living in total solitude for six years, then having another body here is jarring for anyone. I calmed Kona from wanting to go inspect and calmed myself for not wanting to face what I'd done.

I pinch the bridge of my nose and sigh. I heard Josie shut the front door, heard her start the car, can hear her now out there, scraping something as her car runs. And the kind, honorable, decent thing to do would be to go outside, help her with whatever she's doing, and bring her a hot coffee.

But instead, I'm lying in my bed like a chump. My stomach knots, my heart aches, and my brain is fatigued from not shutting off the entire night. "Ugh." I shimmy down the bed and tug the comforter over my face.

Last night was good. Amazing, actually. A tension release, a *memory* release, and something in me stirred to life. Last night, after so many years, I felt feminine and sexy and wanted. After all these years, I had no idea how good it would feel to orgasm with someone else, and not alone. Being touched, touching, kissing, everything felt wonderful. My skin is still flushed with desire, a sort of lust hangover, and I both want to totally forget what happened, and run out there and do it again in the cushioning snow.

I had no idea how much I'd been missing touch over the years, and Josie filled that void. It was so messy and hot and frantic, clear that both of us were needing something in that moment, but I'm not sure either of us found what we needed.

But right now, I'm consumed by the guilt of my actions. There's this tug in me, this deep pull, where I want to hug Josie, and make sure she is okay, and I want her to hug me and ask if I'm okay. I want to run into the recording booth and record a journal entry to Amelia to get that final approval even though I already know, to the deepest part of my core, that she'd be okay.

So, really. I should be fine. But am I? I don't think so.

After Josie fell asleep last night, I immediately slithered off the couch, scooped up my clothes, and ran back to my room. Honestly, I wanted to sneak out the moment it was over, and what does that make me? God, I'm a horrible human. But then I felt so terrible that I left her out there, alone, on the couch. When I put on my pajamas and tiptoed down the hall, I watched her for a moment. So peaceful. So beautiful. And I needed to make sure she was okay. So I stuffed a pillow under her head, brought her water, covered her up, and tried to stop myself from crying.

The bed squeaks as I toss to one side, then the other, then finally sit up and rest my head against the headboard. What am I doing? This is not good. I shouldn't want to cry after sex. But I also shouldn't want to do it again, especially if I'd almost broken down from it last night, right? Am I losing my mind? Have all these years of solitude finally taken the mental toll that my family warmed me about? Right now, I don't feel like I've cheated on Amelia, but I don't feel good about any of it. I was desperate to not think for a bit and it worked. *My God*, did it work, but is that healthy?

A low, dull ache spreads in my chest. Did I use Josie to stop myself from thinking about Amelia?

Last night was too frantic, too urgent, too messy. Sex has

always been such an intimate thing for me, and here it was just sort of frenzied and hot. *Oh God, so freaking hot.* Her smell, her taste... It still lingers, and I want more. I want to do it again. But also, don't.

My head pounds with a low but fierce headache. Each of us only had a single glass of wine so I know it's not from that, but the thuds are spreading, like a jackhammering wildfire, up my neck and through my temples.

A fierce rev of tires jars me upright. "What the hell?" Is she stuck? Josie's from Minnesota, for God's sake. She should know as good as anyone if she actually gets traction with how fast her tires sound like they're spinning, she's going to go flying directly into a snowbank or a tree.

I leap out of bed, rush through my house to grab my jacket and boots, and fly through the front door. *Jesus.* It must've snowed over a foot last night. It's so blustery, the snow so thick and swirly that I have to blink through the storm to see Josie a hundred feet or so away. I tug on my hat and gloves as I stomp through the thick, heavy accumulation to reach her.

The revving of the car stopped, thankfully, and I see her behind the car, kicking at the tires, pushing, using a mini shovel to dig around the car, and pushing again. The grunts and swear words are almost as loud as the wind, and I can't help but crack a smile.

"You know... you can ask for help rather than saying words that will make the neighborhood children cry," I say as I approach. "Pretty sure you even rattled some demons awake with that language."

Josie turns to me with pink cheeks and a deeply sheepish look. From last night, from right now, I'm not sure.

"You don't have any neighbors," she says with a grin.

"Good point." I walk the perimeter of the car and take a deep breath. She's definitely stuck. And based on the amount of snow she's spun from her tires, she was as desperate to get out of here as I was desperate for her to leave.

And again, the guilt consumes me. Did I make her feel unwelcome? Did she not have a good time? Was it because I went and slept in my bed last night? It was just so overwhelming, and I probably didn't handle it the best. But the very last thing I wanted was for her to feel like she *had* to leave.

I could help push Josie out of here, maybe even attach my winch to my Jeep to pull her out, but it would be useless. I live completely off the path of the snowplows. Even if they did plow the county street, which is highly doubtful since we are the last to be done, the snow is coming down so fast and furious it wouldn't be safe. We could shovel until our arms burn off, but the half-mile gravel drive on my property would take us until May to complete.

Josie's stuck.

Holy shit. *I'm* stuck with Josie.

She scratches at the back of her neck. "Don't suppose you have a plow, huh?"

Not one that will get her through this mess, although right now with the wind hitting my face and buckets of snow being dumped from the sky, I don't want to explain the difference between a Bobcat-style one, and a straight blade one that I can attach to my Jeep. "Sadly, no. Although every year I think I should probably get one, but I never do." Panic rushes her face with these words, and I offer her the most comforting smile I can manage. "But what I do have is backup emergency food that will keep me alive for a year."

And based on how heavy the snow is right now, we might go through all of it. I breathe through the shaky nerves, and try not to stare at those lips that are pinked with the air, or think of the way she tasted in my mouth, or think about how mortifying it is that she's going to come back inside and we will no doubt need to have the most awkward conversation of my entire adult life.

"Hey, I really need to bring Kona out here to use the bathroom, and you look like you're freezing." I cringe at the wet streaks on her thin scrubs. "Why don't we go back inside so you can warm up, I can take Kona out, and then we can have some coffee?"

Although her body is shivering, her face looks like she wants to be anywhere *but* inside and warming up. We stand silently for way too long, when finally, her throat seems to roll with a heavy swallow. "Sure, thanks." She turns off the car, grabs a duffel bag from the back, and pats the bag with her palm. "Backup gym clothes."

"Do you have a backup set of drumsticks, too?" I ask, lifting a brow. "Never know how long we'll be stuck."

The corner of her lip twitches into a tiny grin. "Unfortunately, I left those at home. I do however have a pickleball set in my trunk. You know, for emergencies."

We shuffle back up the hill through the wind and snow, and by the time we reach the house, both of our pants are soaked. I can't believe I let her stand out there this whole time, while I was in my bed contemplating every bad decision of my life. Would she have come back to the house? Frozen to death? Slept in her car? I shake my head as I grab the leash for Kona and bring her outside as Josie stomps her feet at the door and drops her bag.

When Kona and I return, Josie is still standing in the doorway. Her shoes are off, but her feet and legs are dripping wet. "Josie... Seriously, you're freezing. Why didn't you go change?"

"I didn't want to get your place all wet," she says with a shrug.

"Seriously? I have a dog and live on my own. You're good, okay? Please don't worry about getting my floors wet." And not that I am going to call this out at all, but it's not like we didn't get all sort of stuff on the couch last night. The very last thing I'm worried about is my floorboards. I hang my jacket on the hook behind the door, and release Kona from the leash so she can go to her spot by the couch. "Why don't you go take a hot shower, okay? I have towels in the closet, a toothbrush and toothpaste in the drawer, and just dig for whatever else you might need."

She's avoiding my gaze, most definitely, but making an excuse like she's inspecting her arms, then her feet, then her bag. "Awesome, thanks."

When I hear the shower water turn on, I move down the hall into my recording booth. I need to chat with Amelia, to process everything, to get last night off my chest. There are too many conflicting emotions running through my head, a push and a pull that is making me dizzy.

Today, I leave off my headphones so I can hear when the water shuts off, and I hit record. "Hey. Well, some intense shit happened last night, and I don't even know where to begin. Josie slept over. At first, we talked about her life, and then the conversation moved towards you. I told her *so much* about you. What you were like, the missing celebrity face recognition chip in your brain, and all about the day you died. And she listened." I take a deep breath and confirm that the shower water is still running. "We talked for hours, and ugh. It was amazing. She's really cool. You'd love her. She reminds me a bit of you, actually, but also totally different, if that makes sense. She has that life to her, that spunk, this pink hair that I'd never be cool enough to pull off, but it's like so effortless for her..." I purge everything I've thought about this morning when I woke up, from when I went to bed, to how I'm sick to my stomach that I may have used her, to this unsettling knowingness that I need to have a tough and awkward conversation with Josie soon. Oddly enough, I leave out the fact that Josie and I actually slept together. I'm not ready to share those details with Amelia quite yet.

When the shower water turns off, I end the recording and rest my head against the desk. Like it or not, I'm stuck here with Josie for the foreseeable future, and I need to deal with what I've done.

Starting now.

ELEVEN

JOSIE

There are few things in life more rejuvenating than being frozen to the bone and then stepping into a long, hot, glorious shower. I wash away the remnants of last night, the coldness of this morning, and take a moment to think of my next steps.

I dig in my bag for fresh clothes—which entails exactly one black sports bra, my backup underwear, and a pair of yoga-style biker shorts. When I put on the outfit and face the mirror, I shake my head. Well, this certainly doesn't leave a lot to the imagination. Not that Colby didn't see me naked last night, or touch me in every place, but it was so rushed and hurried, she didn't really see *all* of me.

The fresh coffee aroma fills the house, and I follow the scent to the kitchen. At the counter, Colby has switched into sweatpants and a flannel and is sipping from a mug while staring out the window.

"Hey, any chance you have a second cup," I say, adding a deflecting tone to my words.

"Of cour—" she starts and then stares at me. Her gaze travels, down my chest, down my naked belly, past my thighs. She quickly flicks her gaze back to the mugs and grabs one off the hook. "Of course. Cream or sugar?"

"No, black is awesome," I say, feeling both the need to cross my arms and cover myself, and the naughty desire to sit in front of Colby and watch her squirm a little more. Okay, seriously. Something is very, very wrong with me. "You don't happen to have an extra sweatshirt or something I could wear, do you? All I had in my bag was this for barre class, which is practically clothing optional."

She chuckles and hands me a mug. "For sure. Let me grab you some things." A moment later, she returns with sweatpants, a sweatshirt, and socks. As I tug them on, I'm grateful that she wears her clothes loose. We're not that different in size, but my God, she is muscular and fit, where I'm more soft and curvy. But the clothes feel intimate somehow, like I'm wearing something unfamiliar, foreign. Not bad, just different. They smell like her delicate soft lavender and sage scent, and I resist the urge to bring it to my nose and pull in a deep breath.

"So, do you want the good news first, or the bad?" Colby says as she leans against the counter, mug to her lips.

"Oh God, this game is always a lose-lose," I say, blowing into my mug. "Let's do the bad news first."

"The storm of the century that Minnesotans always talk about, but it never actually comes... Well, it's here. And it's going to get worse." She sets her mug down and casually peels a banana like she didn't just drop the worst news imaginable. "They're expecting the next five days at least to be like this."

Five days! Everything in me feels itchy and impatient. My neck, my head, my arms. I cannot be stuck with Colby for five days. I cannot be stuck *anywhere* for five days, much less a secluded cabin in the middle of bum-fuck nowhere with nothing to do but sit with a woman in an open-plan space who I happened to tongue rail last night. I'll absolutely lose my shit.

Yep, this is karma creeping up and bitch-slapping me. This is exactly what I get for doing what I promised to myself I wouldn't. Ugh... If a crater could swallow me whole right now, that'd be amazing.

I push out a weak smile even though the air feels like it's locked in my throat. "Wow. That's... ah, wow. That's a lot of days to be stuck somewhere." What an idiotic statement, but I have no other words. The room feels fuzzy, blinking in and out of focus. I need to sit before I tilt over completely.

Colby sits on a chair at the table and I plop next to her. She gives my hand a quick pat, then pulls back like she's not sure if she should touch me. "Please don't worry," she says. "I wasn't kidding earlier when I said I have enough food to last a year. And if the power goes out, I have a stockpile of wood, and a forest filled with fallen trees that we can use, okay? We'll be good."

The physical survival is the very last thing that I'm worried about. Quiet, solitude, *sitting*, is mental warfare. It's my least favorite activity, the one I avoid at all costs, and not only do I have to do that, I have to do that with someone I just had sex with. I unzip the top of the hooded sweatshirt and fan my heated chest.

"Hey, are you okay?" Colby leans forward, her concerned eyes scanning me. "Maybe you should eat something. Your face is doing a very impressive routine right now and swapping between pale green and pink."

Maybe she's right. I grab a banana out of the fruit bowl and take a bite, but my mind absolutely will not settle. As much as I hate this, we have to address last night. And dammit, I need to apologize. Colby opened up, was super vulnerable, and did I take advantage of that because I wanted to do my escape artist routine? It's sick. *I'm* sick. Really. I do not like this version of myself at all, and Colby was caught in the crossfire.

"You said you had good news, too?" I say. Maybe I can just keep Colby talking. For five days, I will either hide in the shed and doomscroll until my eyes bleed or keep her talking so I don't have to own up to my terrible judgment.

"Yes," Colby says as she wraps her hair back up into a ponytail. "I have a fully functioning hot tub."

I crack a huge smile, my first one of the day. "You have a hot tub? How did you not lead with this? You always lead with 'I have a hot tub.'"

"There just didn't seem like an appropriate time to drop that on you," Colby says with a soft chuckle. "But anytime you want to use it, just let me know and I can help show you how."

I lean back in my chair. God, I love hot tubs, but hardly ever have a chance to use one. Sure, I can sit in one at the local YMCA among chatty strangers often with questionable body hair who don't understand the need to relax in silence. Maybe being stuck at Colby's place for a little bit won't be *so* bad. "I can't believe you didn't tell me last night that you had one."

Last night. As soon as the words slipped out, and the way that a white line flashes up Colby's neck like a shattered lightning bolt, I immediately want to suck them back in. Well, there. I did it. I dropped the bomb about last night, and now I have no choice but to actually call it out. I take a deep breath and open my mouth to apologize.

"I'm *so* sorry about last night, Josie," Colby says, her eyes focused on her fingers. "I should've never..."

"Wait, what?" *She's* sorry? What the hell does she have to be sorry about? Sure, it was mutual, consensual, *hot*, but I know my pattern, my MO, who I am, and still did it. "What are you talking about? *I'm* the one who should be apologizing to you."

Her gaze snaps back to me and she tilts her head. "Why would you apologize to me? You did absolutely nothing wrong. I, um—" Her throat bobs with a heavy, thick swallow. "It's, ah..." She stands from the table and leans against the counter, tugging at the fabric on her cuffs. "With everything that happened with Kona, it just brought up so many memories, so many awful, terrible memories, and I was looking for something to help me forget. Ugh... Please know that I really like you, a lot, and I'm so glad we've become friends, and I'm really worried that I completely screwed this up because I needed to be distracted. Nothing about what happened last night was fair to you."

The chair squeaks across the hardwood floor as I push it out and move toward Colby. I want to hug her but also tell her that she sucks, because no, it doesn't feel good to be used as a distraction.

But at the same time, I want to kneel in front of her and beg for forgiveness because I did the same damn thing. "Nothing here is screwed up, unless I did it."

Colby's eyes bore into mine like she's trying to read me, but confusion still crosses her face. "I don't think you get it."

I shake my head. "No, I don't think *you* get it." I inhale a quick breath. If we are going to spend the next five days together trapped in this home, now is the time to fully get everything out. "How about we move into the living room," I say through the tension tightening in my stomach. "I think there's some things we should talk about."

TWELVE

COLBY

Is it a little odd sitting on the couch, in nearly the same position as last night before I ravished Josie like some starving feral animal, to now be talking about the regret we feel from what we did? Most definitely. But here we are, two fresh mugs of coffee wrapped in our palms, a box of Honey Nut Cheerios resting in between us that we're digging into like a bag of chips, and an unbearable, weighty silence that I could chop with my axe.

The regret is so heavy in my body, as heavy as the snow that's coming down outside. A fierce tug-of-war of emotions starts inside me. This sickening feeling that I used Josie, this anger at myself for my impulsive decision, this softness I'm feeling by looking at Josie wearing my clothes. It's all too much and I need a moment alone to process. Which looks like it won't be happening anytime soon.

I've never seen Josie in anything besides scrubs and thank God she didn't say she was fine to prance around here in nothing but a sports bra and tiny shorts that accentuated her perfectly round ass. Ugh. This is not right. Josie is my friend. And I absolutely want to be nothing more than friends—with anyone—and thus, I need to stop thinking of the way she felt on my fingers last night.

"Josie," I say, clearing the anxiety from my throat. "I'm not looking for a relationship. Like at all. And I knew that last night when we did... what we did. And I should have said it upfront, right away, and not given you any sort of wrong impression that my feelings run deeper than friendship."

Josie's warm brown eyes peek at me over the mug, and she shakes her head. "Okay, this is what I'm talking about. Where there is an obvious disconnect." She tucks a leg under herself and sighs. "Can I ask you a super personal question?"

"I think we're past needing to ask permission," I say. "Please. Ask away."

"When was the last time you had casual sex? Like with someone you weren't in a relationship with?"

Kona hobbles over to us from where she was resting and nestles at my feet. I rub the top of her fur and think back to when I was in my late teens, and early twenties. "Oh gosh. I don't know. Fifteen years ago, at least. Before I met Amelia," I say. "I've only had casual sex with maybe two or three women at most."

Rose tattoos peek out when Josie tugs up the sleeve of the sweatshirt. "That's what I thought—that you haven't been with anyone since your wife. Last night when we were talking, and you told me everything about what happened with your wife... you were so emotionally vulnerable, and open, and trusting and ugh... Fuck, Colby, *this is what I do.*"

Huh? I feel my brows crease. Sure, I was in an emotionally vulnerable spot last night. I haven't talked about Amelia to anyone in years. I was raw, and exhausted, and needed to forget, but I absolutely knew what I was doing. "We didn't do anything that I didn't want to do."

Josie reaches into the cereal and palms a handful of Cheerios. She stares at her hands, then takes a breath. "You're not looking for a relationship. And honestly, neither am I. In fact, a few months ago I enforced a relationship hard stop for myself. But... this is my pattern, and I'm so angry at myself for doing this to you."

I still don't grasp what she's saying. But when I open my mouth to protest, she puts her hands up.

"One sec. Let me finish." She crunches through a few bites of the dry cereal and washes it back with coffee. "So, you haven't had casual sex in all those years. And you know exactly what you want, which is to stay single. But me... Ever since Zoey and I broke up, I fall headfirst, hard, madly in love, in a snap. I'm Queen Insta-love, and I know it and I *hate* it. It's like this twisted, sick, never-ending cycle and I've been trying to get out of it."

As Josie talks, my heart breaks a little bit for her. She tells me that she's been searching for something, something that's unnamed and out of reach, and she keeps thinking every woman she is with is "the one." She talks about looking for distractions, everywhere. Working extra hours, joining clubs, trying new activities, and when she sleeps with someone, she just knows that *this is it!*

"And then I told myself no more, that this pattern is completely unhealthy, and I need to stop," she says, running a hand through her pink hair. "And then the moment I'm alone with you..." She trails off.

This isn't her fault. As we sit here and talk, I realize that none of this is either one of our faults. We were both looking for something last night, some momentary reprieve in our lives to break the monotonous course of action, and we used sex to fulfill that need. "First, can I just say I really appreciate you sharing all of that with me?" I say, giving her a soft smile. "How about we both just agree that it was a mistake, and it will never happen again. Take a solid do-over?"

"A do-over. I like that," Josie says. "Like, let's rewind it, play back, and write an alternative ending. *Matrix*-style."

I chuckle. "Not sure that *The Matrix* is the best movie for this analogy, but it sounds good either way."

Josie leans in and gives me a hug. A warm, full, generous hug, and I melt into the touch. I rest my chin on her soft rounded shoulders, feel her body pressed against me, and release this guilt choke hold that's been with me since last night. "I'm going to take Kona out to go to the bathroom," I say, grabbing a scarf to wear over my coat. "Do you need to call your work or anything?"

"Today's my normal day off, but that's a good idea, anyway. I should probably check in and see how people are doing with the storm. I don't even know if they've managed to open."

Outside, the visibility is next to zero, and Josie's car rests at the edge of the turn that is buried under mounds of snow. The wind whips against my face, covering me with a blanket of snow, and I shake everything off, but it's useless. Kona is taking longer than normal, probably too freaked out to go to the bathroom with how loud the howl is in the wind, and a good twenty minutes must've passed before I step back into the house.

And when I do, a few things happen. I don't see Josie right away, which is a little odd since I have a completely open-plan home besides the bedroom, bathroom, and small hall. But then I hear her, on the phone with someone. There's a whisper, then a giggle, and then another whisper.

And something very unexpected happens. A touch of surprising jealousy flickers through me, a deep curiosity in who she is talking to, and—even as relieved as I am that we've laid out that last night was a one-time thing—a trickle of disappointment.

I'm sitting on the edge of the tub in Colby's guest bathroom, whispering into the phone with Leo. I don't even know why I'm whispering. It's not like I have anything to hide. But it's a little unnerving being in this quiet home that's so open that my naturally loud voice echoes against the walls. Colby is already putting me up during this storm. The best thing I can do is make myself as small as possible to not interrupt her routine.

"You're telling me that the woman who lingered around reception like the ghost of our great-grandma, the one who yelled at you... You're at *her* house. Stuck." Leo says all of this with the type of chuckle that makes me want to smash his face into a snowbank. "Like, how does this even happen?"

I'm bristling more than I should at this, because Leo, much like me, had no idea what Colby was going through when she was a borderline lunatic at the vet clinic. And it's not my place to tell him about the level of trauma and PTSD Colby was experiencing with bringing in Kona and relating it to when her wife died. "Your level of dickheadedness is at an all-time high," I hush under my breath. "But the dog got a post-op infection, she needed antibiotics—"

"Yeah, but you could've just dropped those off."

I could've. But I didn't. "Yeah, I know."

It takes a moment for the chuckling to stop. And when it does, Leo releases a heavy sigh. "You banged her, didn't you?"

Now I'm really bristling. And I refuse to answer. God, I hate that Leo knows me. I'm sure he can sense my blushed cheeks through the phone. My silence must give him everything I'm not saying, 'cause I hear another heavy sigh.

"As much as you think I'm judging you, I swear I'm not," he says with his voice much softer than before. "I worry about you, okay? A lot. More than I probably let on. I just don't want you to get hurt. That's all."

Damn him. I hate him right now as much as I love him. I appreciate that he doesn't want me to get hurt, but *I* don't want to get hurt. Nor do I want to hurt anyone else, and I absolutely know that one of these two outcomes is likely if I pursue what I did last night with Colby again. She is clearly not in the space for anything, and neither am I.

"Thanks," I say. "Really, everything was all good this morning. We're adults, we made an adult decision, and mutually decided to pause on anything more." Yes, of course, I know I'm not being completely truthful, but it's mortifying telling Leo what happened this morning with my failed great escape plan, and that I literally got my car stuck in a snowbank while trying to run from my sexcapade.

After I chat with Leo a bit longer, I hang up, plant my hands on the countertop in the bathroom and stare at my reflection. The cabin is so spacious, the land massive, and yet the overwhelming feeling of claustrophobia weaves its way through my body like a toxic smoke. A shaky, labored breath leaves my mouth. I splash some cool water on my face, drag a towel across my cheeks, and stretch. I've got to let this all go and deal with the fact that I'm stuck here with an amazing, beautiful woman, who is welcoming and accommodating. Really, with all the problems in the world, I'd rate this seriously low.

When I step out of the bathroom and meander down the hall, everything in me feels so uneasy. Where should I go? Just hang out with Colby in her space? Ask if she has a guest bedroom? Hide in the pantry? Colby is sitting on the rocking chair crocheting a blanket, and I decide to take a seat next to her on the couch.

"Hey," she says, glancing up at me and resting the hook and ball of yarn in her lap. There's a look on her face, one that I can't totally decode, but the energy is different. Not really dark, per se. But not as bright as before. "Everything okay?"

"Yeah, that was my cousin Leo," I say, tugging a blanket up and over my hips. "You met him, sort of, at the clinic. I just wanted him to know I was safe, but wouldn't be able to make it into work until the storm eases up."

And just like that, the energy in the room lightens. "Ah... That guy at reception was your cousin?"

"Yeah. He's the one that got me the job. And thankfully, for the most part, we get along. Otherwise, it would be so awkward at Thanksgiving, you know?" I grin. "He said the clinic is closed today because of the storm, and they don't know when they're going to open back up."

"I guess that's good for you, so you don't have to find someone to cover your shifts, huh?"

I nod as Colby picks back up the yarn. She wraps the yarn around a finger, puts a hook into it, and tugs it into a knot. "You like crocheting?" I ask, jutting my chin to the blanket. "I always thought I'd like to do that, but the couple times I tried, I lost patience."

A soft grin passes on her face. "We've got nothing but time. Want to try now?"

Another quiet activity. I don't know if I can do it. My body and brain feel the burning need to run. I'm tempted to see if Colby has a treadmill or row machine or something in one of the rooms. But that really feels imposing to start using her workout equipment along with her extra toothbrush and clothes, and the very last thing I want to do is overstay my already fragile welcome.

Colby lifts herself from the chair and drags a large wicker

basket in front of me. "Here," she says and opens the top. "Go ahead and pick a color."

Whoa. Inside the bin are dozens and dozens of all different colors and sizes of yarn. My fingers run over the fabric, some thick and heavy, some butter soft, others with frays, and a couple with sparkles which surprise me. Nothing about Colby screams sparkles. "Jesus. You really are prepped for the apocalypse, aren't you?"

"You want to know a secret?" Colby says, sinking back into the couch by me.

"Absolutely."

"Years ago, right after I turned twenty-one, I auditioned to be on the show *Survivor*."

My mouth drops open. "Stop!" I laugh. "Are you serious? I *love* that show. What happened?"

Colby shrugs and returns to looping her hook into the blanket. "I actually made it through the online application, went to the casting call, even had an interview. But I was cut as a possible contender pretty early on."

"Isn't there part of you that's relieved?" I ask as I pull out a soft blue skein of yarn. "All those bugs, and wild animals, and no freaking food. And no Wi-Fi? How are you gonna watch any Reels, or stream shows? That sounds pretty terrible, actually."

This elicits a solid giggle from Colby. "It does sound kind of awful when you put it like that. But I think deep down, there's a cavewoman in there that needs to be let out every once in a while. I've always had this sort of survivalist mentality. I think that's partly why I love being out here so much. In nature, chopping my own wood, those kinds of things."

A quick flash of Colby chopping wood stirs my insides, but I push that voice down, as low as it will go, and instead nod my head toward the rack in the corner holding several shotguns. "I did notice the shotguns the first day I was here."

"Those... Yeah. For protection, mostly. I don't hunt," she says.

"But I also don't want to be hunted, if you know what I mean. By a human or an animal."

This, I can definitely understand. I love animals and humans. But it doesn't mean we're safe from either one of them. After a bit, Colby shows me the basics of crocheting. She's patient, demonstrating on her hand how to do a single stitch, guiding me through how to work in a slipknot, talking to me about how to pinch the yarn so it doesn't slip off the hook and unravel. When I try a stupid amount of times to do my first stitch, everything in me heats with irritation. She scoots right up next to me, and that lavender sage scent seems to disarm me almost immediately.

"Here, like this," she says, over and over, coaxing me, encouraging me, never leaving my side.

For the next few hours, the wind fluctuates against brutalizing the windows, to settling down, and Colby and I slip into a comfortable silence. She makes us grilled cheese sandwiches and the stew from last night for lunch; after a few swear words, and one minor meltdown where I say that crocheting is not for me, I master my first few rows on a scarf.

The news plays in the background, mentioning that the storm should ease by tomorrow, and road crews will be hard at work to catch up. Images of plows barely keeping up with what's coming down, warnings to stay sheltered in place and leave the roads open for emergency vehicles only, and segments on indoor family activities fill the next hour.

"What will the clinic do if you're stuck here when they open up?" Colby says, handing me a glass of water and some orange slices that I never asked for.

I can't help but smile at the food. Even though I'm not hungry, it's nice. It's been so many years since I felt like anyone was taking care of me. Not that Colby's taking care of me. She's more hospitable than anything, but she's thinking about me, and there is something warm and fuzzy knowing that I'm in a person's thoughts.

"There are enough local staff that can hopefully cover if I can't make it in. But with the weather and limited staff, I think they'll reschedule the wellness exams and vaccinations and just stay open for more emergency and urgent care type of appointments." I tug on a long piece of thread and wrap it around my finger. "What about you? I know you work from home, but I actually don't know what you do for a living."

Colby looks down at the yarn and chews on the side of her lip. "Oh, nothing fancy like you, with saving animals' lives and all."

Am I being paranoid? Yes, we're crocheting, but it really feels like she's avoiding my gaze. "Oh... are you in the CIA?"

She chuckles and only peeks at me for a brief second. "Well, I wouldn't be a very good operative if I said yes, now would I?"

And then, nothing. No follow-up, no offer for additional information, literally nothing. Um... What's happening here? She doesn't say anything for the longest time, and each second that ticks by, the air is being siphoned from the room.

Is Colby unemployed? Her house is nice. *Really* nice. Maybe she comes from a wealthy family or something. Maybe she posts fetish videos online and I should mind my own damn business. Finally, the awkwardness reaches a peak level, and I can't take it. "I'm sorry. Is that super personal? I didn't mean to be so invasive."

Colby shakes her head. "No, not at all. I think I'm just not used to answering questions about myself." She drags out a new line of yarn and twists it around her finger. "I, um... Back in the day I used to work in finance. But after my wife died, I didn't want to do that anymore. So, I just do a sort of freelance digital editing thing."

I'm about to open my mouth to ask more questions, but Colby drops the blanket she's working on and lifts herself from the couch. "I'm going to go start dinner. Do you have any allergies?"

When I shake my head no, she gives me a soft smile and moves to the kitchen.

And as much as I want to think I'm being paranoid, as much as I tell my inner voice that I'm being sensitive, as much as I convince myself I'm overthinking, I cannot shake the feeling that I just did something very, *very* wrong.

FOURTEEN
COLBY

In a court of law, is lying by omission a crime? I should probably google this. In all fairness, though, I didn't omit *everything* when Josie asked about my job. I do, in fact, digitally edit my podcast. That's part of the gig. I just didn't tell her everything else. That's okay, right? No? Maybe?

I still can't get over what she said yesterday about the podcast and the negative effects on her love life. I never, ever meant to do anyone harm. Sure, I could just come out and tell her this, but no matter how close we've become this last week, I've still only known her for a week. Sure, during this time I've spoken to her more than I have any other human in six years—*combined*. But yet, I don't think this obligates me to tell Josie this secret that I hold so close to my heart—the one that is vaulted shut, the one that no human in the world knows—simply because she listened to my show and made a poor decision.

The clock shows it's after midnight and sleep is useless right now. I sneak past a snoring Kona to step out of my bedroom, walk the hall to the living room, and peek my head over the couch to see Josie sleeping soundly on it. Once she started yawning a few hours ago, I'd offered her my bed and said I could take the couch. She adamantly refused. I then apologized profusely for not having a guest bedroom. In theory this place has three bedrooms. Mine, the recording studio, and the third I use for storage. But honestly, since my parents don't travel, I never expected a guest, so it didn't seem practical to set it up as such.

I step into my office/recording studio and lock the door behind me—which feels weird. But it's a necessary precaution; I don't want Josie to come in and see my noise filters attached all over my room, or the microphone, or the several monitors, and wonder what it is I really do.

I slip on my headphones, leaving one ear popped open, and hit record. "Hey, Amelia," I say, whispering into the microphone even though the likelihood of my voice carrying is minimal.

I scratch at my neck and take a full breath. "Well, I slept with someone." I'm hit with a rush of sensations—my thighs warming from the memory, the ache in my gut from probably not being ready, the guilt. "And honestly, I don't know what to think, although I swear I can feel you right now, nudging me with your elbow, saying something like 'yeah ya did!' or 'hell yes' or some other words of encouragement. But I'm so conflicted. I know you would be okay with it. I know if you were right here, you'd tell me I should've moved on right away, that I'm wasting the best years of my life. You'd probably be supremely pissed and irritated that I've waited this long, but I don't know... It's just not easy for me to do this. Even if I did want to pursue something, Josie made it super clear that she's not in the right space for anything. So, we've got two people who regret what they did, and one of us that kind of wants to do it again."

I flush admitting this out loud, but it's true. Just because I'm feeling guilt and nerves doesn't mean the idea of sleeping with Josie again hasn't crossed my mind no less than five times today. "Ugh... So yeah, I'm not going to lie. Having a super cute, fun woman trapped with me for the next several days is not going to be easy if I keep looking at her mouth."

The guilt lingers that I used Josie to help me forget about Amelia. But she said this is her pattern that she's actively trying to break, so does this negate everything?

"That's not all," I say, tapping my fingers against the chair arm. "She listened to the podcast. And what are the chances that not only was she a listener, but she was a listener who wrote in and took my advice, and it totally backfired. And no, I didn't tell her it was me. No one knows! I'm not ready to tell anyone. But I feel like this lie is simmering beneath the surface, seeping into everything, but maybe I'm overthinking it? I mean, it's not like I held her at gunpoint or anything and told her to beg her ex to get back with her."

Right? I mean, how was I supposed to know? I do my show for entertainment. Even if I didn't, even if I was a real relationship guru, I could not possibly have had all the context in the world to offer different advice that didn't blow up in her face.

"Anyway, I'm just going to take it a day at a time, and hope that the first friend I've made since you died will stick with me."

I spend some more time talking to Amelia, until the time creeps toward 1:00 a.m. I'm still bright-eyed and can't sleep. But luckily, my last recorded episode needs edits, and it's probably a better use of my time to do this now than stare at my ceiling. I open the app I use to record my show, skip forward my typical intro, and read the question.

"Hey everyone, this next question comes to us from Marcus from Maryland. Marcus says, 'Hi, Ruby. A few years ago, I had an opportunity for career advancement, and me and my husband chatted about it for a long time. The job is demanding and high pressure—we knew this going in—but the money allows my husband to stay at home, which he wanted. It was a joint decision, but ultimately, we both felt that even with the increase of hours and moving us to a new town, it was worth it. But now I'm two years in, and I need to be totally honest. My hubby is driving me nuts.'"

I take a moment to edit out a way too long pause when I must've helped Kona, then dive back into the recording.

"'We don't have children or animals, which is a conscious decision, but now that he's not working, I have become his single, sole focus. And I love him. I really do. But I get close to ten texts a day from him, sometimes just funny Reels or GIFs. The second I get home, he wants my full attention. And I mean *full*. The rare occasions when there's a work happy hour that I should be at, he gets incredibly frustrated.

"'Prior to this, I had hobbies and "me" time, and now I spend every single second of any downtime being with him. Again, I feel like I need to keep saying this, but I really do love him. Last week, I had to miss his birthday dinner, and I felt terrible. But I had no choice. We had a huge launch, and work needed me. Let's just say, that did not go over well at all.

"'I've tried to talk to him about taking up a hobby or making some friends, but he just gets upset. I'm at a loss here what to do. I am desperate for downtime, desperate for a happy husband, and desperate to keep my job. Thanks, Marcus.'"

I press stop on the recording and crack open the door when I hear Kona shuffling down the hall. After I let her into the room, she slides in at my feet and almost immediately goes back to sleep. I return to the editing screen and press play.

"Hey, Marcus, thank you for this question, but *come on*, people, just once I need someone to send me an easy one. Like, help, my spouse snores, or my spouse hates cheese, or my spouse hates the movie *The Matrix*, which we all know are immediate grounds for divorce. Because sweet baby Jesus, ones like this are *tough*."

Five years into this show and I'm not sure if I will ever stop cringing at the way I sound. It's a weird dichotomy. I'm as authentic as I can be. The answers are what I *would* say. But it's also very clearly coming through the filter of Amelia's personality.

"So as you all know, Amelia is the highlight of my day, so I cannot ever imagine having this happen to me." My voice chuckles and I cringe again at the sound. "Okay, okay, I jest. I mean, not about the highlight of my day 'cause that's true. But also, we very, very much appreciate having alone time, our separate friend time, our own..." I listen to the rest of my answer, make sure that I didn't say something completely off the wall. But what I said still resonates—that it sounds like the husband is feeling lonely, that they have competing priorities, that Marcus themself sounded burned out, and that the emotional toll a high-pressure job takes on a relationship is real.

When I first took my Director of Finance job, I remember the stress, the need to prove myself, and the pulley system yanking me in all directions. But I also knew that my first priority was always my wife and making sure I was honoring her needs. And truthfully, at the time, I wasn't. Amelia and I definitely had some disagreements over that until I set solid boundaries at work. I type a quick note to add these thoughts to the episode notes.

"As simplistic as it is, and without knowing all the circumstances, I do have a few things to add. For your husband's birthday, I'm assuming you would've known this upfront, made alternative plans, and spoiled the hell out of him on that make-up day. So that aside, let's talk about these late nights and launches. If this is a once-a-quarter occurrence, that's one thing. But if these important work events are happening weekly, you really have to evaluate how much the extra income is worth to you. It's a very privileged place to say that money isn't everything, and I fully acknowledge that. But if you can find a job that maybe makes twenty percent less but has more flexible hours, and it means sacrificing a vacation or two, that's something to think about. For me, it comes down to this: When you pass away, the only person who will remember that you stayed at work instead of attending your husband's birthday dinner is your husband. You won't be given a bonus for that day, your VP won't acknowledge it. But he will never forget."

As I finish listening to and editing the episode, my eyes finally begin to droop. I slog back to my room, but before I get there, I make a quick pivot to check on Josie. She's still out cold, curled into a fetal position, her cheeks warm and rosy. The wind outside has slowed, no longer slamming into the house, and the only thing I hear is her soft breaths.

I shouldn't like it as much as I do.

FIFTEEN

JOSIE

The house is quiet when I wake up. I know it's only the third time I've woken up here, but I get the distinct feeling that both Kona and Colby stay up late and use the morning to catch up on sleep. In my daily life, I'm up early for work, go hard all day, push myself in some activity or lesson in the evening, and crash early.

Yesterday, Colby and I spent the entire day doing almost nothing except binge-watching *Fleabag* and *Killing Eve*, eating, watching the snow pile up even higher—which seems almost impossible—and snuggling with Kona. I'm not even sure when I fell asleep. My last memory is of being curled on the couch watching TV, legs tucked next to Colby's. When I woke up in the middle of the night, the lights were off except for a night-light Colby must've added, an extra blanket was on me, and Colby was back in her room.

I push my palm into my jaw to crack my neck, and cross the room to peek out the window. The wind has slowed from a howl to a whistle, and the snow shifted from brutal to gentle flutters. It's *so* quiet here. Colby's place reminds me a bit of when my dad used to take me camping and fishing. As the second to the last child, it always seemed like I was forgotten. I wasn't the baby needing extra help, and I wasn't the oldest paving the way for us younger kids.

But I think there was something in this birth order that helped build a special bond between me and my dad, who was also a middle child.

Whatever.

I need some fresh air. I tug on my boots, grab an extra flannel of Colby's hanging on the hook, and quietly step out on the porch. *My God*, there's a lot of snow. I've lived in Minnesota my entire life and am fully accustomed to accumulation, but this is a *ton*. In some places on the property, the wind blew the snow into piles that are as high as my hip. I pull in a deep, chilled breath of the crisp air, and start trudging into the shallower snow-covered areas with the sound of snow crunching beneath my feet echoing through the valley.

Soft snow flutters against my cheeks as I make my way down the pathway. There's an urge in me to run from this place. The quiet space and open air are a noose, suffocating me. I'm not bored, per se. Being lazy with someone else, doing nothing but watching shows and eating snacks, was actually pretty fun. My body seemed to be craving a bit of downtime, and that fulfilled my need.

But today, I'm restless. The yearslong need to chase is practically etched into my soul, and a day off is about all I can take. As I crunch through the snow, the sun hidden under a blanket of clouds muting the sky into a soft gray, I make sure to stay on the path and not venture out too far. The very last thing I need is to be lost in the woods in the middle of a snowstorm, especially since I made a severely amateur move and left my cell phone on the coffee table.

Ever since I was out of diapers, my dad used to take me on long walks in the woods. He'd give me all sorts of life lessons, everything from how to deal with bullies at school as well as my annoying brothers, to how to take time and enjoy nature. He'd spend hours teaching me about the berries that are poisonous or edible, how to track animals, how to not get lost.

A memory sharpens in my mind of us wandering through the deep, pristine woods in the Boundary Waters area. The bugs were as thick as a blanket that day, the industrial-size spray we'd brought not even making a dent in their numbers, but I was determined to see the water. I remember asking him what to do if something happened and we got separated.

"If you get lost, I'll find ya, kid, okay? Just stay put. I will *always* find you," he'd said as we kept hiking. "But if for some reason, if I'm not here..." His voice had trailed off. "Find the water. Travel by the water and you'll eventually find help."

Did he know then that in a few years' time he'd up and leave, breaking our family, splintering it in a way that it was never whole again? That as a kid, I had this twisted vision that if I walked long enough next to the Mississippi, I'd be able to find my dad, and convince him to come back?

As my heartbeat kicks up from trudging through the thick snow, I loosen my scarf to let in some cool air against my sweaty neck. God, I used to love the outdoors so much. My siblings never really appreciated it the way I did, and it became something for just me and my dad. Hours and hours were spent angling for fish, testing different types of bait from worms to leeches to corn, and pitching tents deep in the woods. At night, we'd sit around a makeshift fireplace, make s'mores, and keep ourselves silent while we tried to guess which sounds the animals in the forest were making.

As much as I don't want to give my father any credit for anything, my love of animals started during those times. Witnessing the magic of grazing deer, soft bouncy gray bunnies, and soaring eagles as a young child left a huge imprint in my soul.

But the even bigger imprint? The way my world collapsed when he left, disregarding me, our family, our mom, like we were meaningless. He stole so many things from me, one of them my love for nature.

Enough. He doesn't deserve an ounce more of my thoughts.

My skin cold but my body hot, I make my way back to Colby's house. When I arrive, I walk the perimeter until I reach the outdoor covered area with the hot tub. "Whoa..." I mutter and release a low whistle. A high-vaulted cedar gazebo with strings of lights, standing lanterns, a small circular propane fireplace table, and hanging plant baskets—which are obviously empty right now—adorn the space. *Beautiful.* There's a layer of snow on top of the cover, blown in from the unprotected sides, but underneath is glorious, warm, bubbling water.

I shouldn't...

With my forearm, I swipe a chunk of snow off the top and lift the cover. A billow of chlorine-scented steam arises. I close my eyes and pull in a deep breath of the heated, misted air.

"You know, you really can just go in there if you want to. You don't have to sneak out of the house in the dead of night," Colby says, peeking at me from the side of the house.

And the case is solved. I definitely would not survive being alone in the woods if I didn't hear either Colby or Kona stomp through the snow as they approached. A blush heats my cheeks, and I lower the cover back down. "This looks weird, huh?"

"What? You inhaling chemicals in my backyard? Nah. Happens all the time." Colby grins and nods towards the tub. "Do you want to go in?"

"More than just about anything in the world," I say. "But first, I need coffee."

I follow Kona and Colby back inside the house, and stomp off the snow from my boots and jacket. When I remove the coat, Colby cocks her head at her flannel that I'm wearing. "So sorry, hope it was okay to grab this. I didn't want to wake you, but I also didn't want to freeze to death."

A soft smile tugs at Colby's mouth. "No, it's totally fine. Help yourself to anything." She brings the coffee pot to the sink and holds it under the faucet. "It, um, it looks good on you."

The words are softer than expected and a blush moves through me. *She's just being nice. Do not read into anything. A compliment is a compliment.* I take a seat at the table, remove Kona's cone from her neck to wash, and monitor her to make sure she doesn't lick the wound as I clean it.

Soon a deep earthy aroma from the coffee fills the room. I step behind Colby to grab eggs, and while whisking, she hands me the pan and butter. Once we sit down at the table, and both bite into the eggs and toast, I glance out the large bay window to the falling snow. "I wonder when the snow's going to let up?"

"The news said it should taper off this afternoon," Colby says as she slides a bowl with eggs in it to Kona, who's begging at her feet. "But it'll still take a few days to get everything cleared."

"Another few days?" I choke out. Being out here is beautiful, being with Colby is kind of amazing, but I'm not sure if I can handle another few days of this. Even more so, I'm not sure *she* can handle another few days of this. Even though we've quickly picked up a routine, and seem to seamlessly move around each other, there's no way that I'm not a bother to her and her daily schedule.

"You okay?" she asks, adding a dash more pepper to her eggs. "I promise I'm okay with you being here. Honestly, it's nice having someone around."

The pinch in my chest lessens. "I thought you were a certified hermit."

"I thought so, too," she says with a chuckle. "Who knows, maybe I'm changing in my old age? I guess you *can* teach a dog owner new tricks."

"Um... I don't think that's how the phrase actually goes."

Colby grins as she adds some more creamer to her coffee and stirs. "Seriously, though, are you okay?"

Am I okay? I don't know. Something in my walk this morning sparked something in me. My brain feels more clear right now than it has for a long time, like the yearslong layer of fog that I've been under has fissured enough to let in a small piece of sunshine. I feel like I need another walk. Maybe two, maybe a hundred, but I want to capture this sliver of calming sensation that's swirling through me.

"Yeah. I'm good. I mean, I appreciate you putting up with me and everything." I hold the warm coffee cup against my palms. "I don't know what my problem is. It's like for so many years all I do is just *go, go, go* and to now just *sit, sit, sit*—even with the incredible company—I feel so restless. Like I should be out there doing some-thing, bettering myself, finding a hobby. I don't know. *Something*."

A playful smile appears on Colby. A moment passes when she lifts her brow, and says, "Well, I do actually have an idea... if you're up for it."

With that look, and that tone, my legs shouldn't be warming the way they are. But my physiological response has a mind of its own. Honestly, I've been kind of a rock with being around Colby and that phenomenally luscious mouth of hers, if I do say so myself, and have been only allowing a few naughty thoughts to seep in. "Oh yeah?" I say, matching her delicious tone. "What's that?"

I know we aren't ready to do anything *like that* again, but is there any other better way to pass the time?

No, no there's not.

"Well... it will certainly occupy us for a while and get out some of that energy you've been hanging on to," she says.

My eyes grow wide. My cheeks flush. My heartbeat thumps. I think I might love everything about this. "Okay, I'm in."

"Perfect," she says and lifts from the table. "Follow me."

SIXTEEN
JOSIE

So... admittedly, when Colby said *Follow me* with a cheeky grin, I had a brief panic that she really was going to lead me to the bedroom. Then my mouth started watering, anticipating what we might do in the bedroom. And then, I was simultaneously hit with half disappointment and half relief when she led me to the closet filled with winter gear.

"Make sure to bundle up," she says, handing me industrial-size gloves and snow pants.

"What exactly are we going to do?" I ask as I pull the snow pants on and scoop my arms under the suspenders.

"We're gonna go chop some wood."

Okay, the grin on her face is too cute to ignore. I think she was waiting for me to balk at this idea, or laugh, or ask if she was serious, but instead, I continue layering up and a few minutes later, after we both reassure Kona that we'll be back in not too long, we step outside and trudge through the pathway leading up to the shed. The snow has stopped falling almost completely now. Instead of the torrential downpour of flakes, it feels like someone is giving the clouds a good shake to get the rest out.

Colby tugs on the large barn doors, and the daylight illuminates the inside. It's surprisingly clean and organized—much different than the one I had in my childhood home—with garden tools, jackets, different axes, and saws. *And* an ATV and snowmobile.

How does Colby do all of this stuff on her own? There is something so deeply impressive—and admittedly pretty hot—about this woman being so fierce and independent that she hops on this ATV or snowmobile and tears through the woods, rather than hiring out or living somewhere with less maintenance.

Colby tosses some rope, a few different-sized axes, and a bag in the small trailer, throws a leg over the seat, and backs the ATV out of the shed. "Have you ever ridden on one?" she asks.

I shake my head. "I thought you aren't supposed to use an ATV in the snow?" I'm not worried... not really, anyway. I normally love things like this—trying something new that gets my heart pumping. But I'm also not a huge fan of being stranded in the middle of nowhere in the aftermath of a blizzard. I've seen enough survival-style shows in my day to know I'd be the first one voted off the island.

"Hey, I got you, okay? I'm not going to let anything happen."

She says this with such a mix of authority and empathy that I feel it in my stomach. Something in those words trigger something deep in me, and I know right now is not the time to process what it is, or why it's hitting me so hard. I *believe* her. She really won't let anything happen to me. For the first time in a long time, I feel safe.

Colby's beautiful eyes fill with concern when I don't say anything. She's probably thinking I'm skittish, but it's not that. It's that I have such an overwhelming urge to hug her and thank her for being here with me, that it's rendering me silent.

"Josie? You good? We're totally safe. This baby right here is rigged for the snow. Chains, snow tires, all the things. I'll go really slow, and we won't go too far. Still within walking distance if for some reason it can't make it back." She pats the back of her seat. "Hop on and hold on tight."

Through my smile, my pulse increases. I swing my legs around the seat and cozy in close. We have layers and layers of clothes between us, but I remember the way her firm body felt in my arms a few nights ago, and as much as I want to ignore it, I also want to remember it. She starts out slow, bumpy, and I tighten my hold around her stomach. The calm, cold breeze feels good against my cheeks. Invigorating, really, as we make our way on the windy path down to an area that has a pile of logs nestled up to a massive, fallen tree.

When we hop off, Colby grabs a large axe and hands me a smaller one. My snow pants shuffle against my legs as we move to the tree and a large stump. She grabs one of the logs and rests it on the stump.

"What can I do to help?" I ask.

"If you could hold on to the log while I'm chopping it, that'd be great," Colby says as she lightly swings the dangling axe. "Just make sure to tuck your fingers so, you know, I don't cut off a thumb or something."

All moisture zaps from my mouth. "Are you serious?"

"Nope," she says with a wide smile.

I slam my hand across my heart. "You almost gave me a heart attack. I'm all for a good adrenaline rush, but this is not what I had in mind."

And now Colby's smile grows even more. *Oof*, she has such a great smile. I've noticed being with her that even though she has a kind, gentle humor, overall, Colby's a pretty serious woman. And to see her face light up with a grin makes me feel like there's something in me, something special, that elicits this from her.

Colby tugs off her jacket, down to the flannel, hat, gloves. She palms the log again, balances it against the stump, then holds her hand out like she's pushing me away. "Stand back," she says and raises the axe high. With a hefty grunt, she slams the blade on the wood, and it splits on contact.

Holy shit, I'm pretty sure I've never seen anything hotter in my life. I don't care if right now I am a full-on walking stereotype—seeing her tucked in a stocking cap and flannel, the strength and precision it took to split it like that, the glorious sound of the cracked wood... *Yum.* No wonder her back muscles are so firm and tight. She tears the rest of the wood apart and throws it in the trailer.

None of this is lost on me that we don't *need* to be out here. Colby has what looks to be a year or two's supply of split logs lined outside of her house, and another one under tarps on the side of the shed. But I think she sensed that I needed to do something but crochet or watch TV, and this is her offering.

She's doing this. *For me.* And that urge to pull her into me, rest my head on her shoulder, thank her, consumes me again.

Colby tosses her grip on the handle to grab it from the middle and holds out the wooden edge. "Want to give it a try?"

I almost laugh. Sure, this morning I've been slowly getting back to my roots and appreciating nature a bit more. But chopping wood might be taking it too far. "Pretty sure I don't want to lose a limb today. Besides, I'm nowhere near as strong as you are."

"I think you're underestimating yourself."

Those words spark me with a bit of fuel. Leo has said this before. Zoey used to say this to me. Of course, it didn't have anything to do with chopping wood, but the sentiment is the same. Throughout my life, I *have* underestimated myself. Maybe now is time to flip that switch. I pull my lips in between my teeth and nod. The axe is heavy, much heavier than I thought, and drags my arm to the earth.

"You've never chopped wood before, right?" Colby asks as she tugs back on her jacket.

"No, not really. I mean, not like this," I say. "When I was younger, my dad used to take me camping and I'd 'chop wood,' but that basically consisted of me thinking I had magical superpowers and cracking wood chunks over my knee."

Yet another memory flashes of him, but I shake it away. I've given my dad enough of my mental energy today.

"Okay, so this is how you do it," she says. "Stand with your hands and legs shoulder width apart, raise your arms high, aim, and think of everything that has pissed you off this last week."

I laugh to cover up the terror ripping through me. I'm not normally a paranoid person, but visions of the axe slipping from my grip and flying into my head, or Colby's head for God's sake, or my stomach, or the blade cutting me... So many terrible scenarios. For the first time in my life, I'm regretting my horror-movie fascination as a child, which seemed to revolve around at least one head getting split open from an axe.

Okay, okay. I can do this. It's just a damn axe and a piece of wood. The cold air pierces my lungs as I pull in full breath. I raise the axe high above my head, aim it at the log that Colby placed upright, and heave. "*Owww!*" Shit, that hurts. Hitting the wood—in what I'm assuming is absolutely not the correct manner—sends an electric vibrating jolt up my arms, like when you jump off something high, land a little too hard, and it shocks your system.

Colby grits her teeth. "So, *perhaps*, I should've warned you that if you don't hit it right, you might get that jarring vibration. Sorry. I didn't want to freak you out."

She's one hundred percent right. Had she put that in my head, I think it would've been worse. Not only did I *not* crack the wood, but the axe blade is wedged, hard. I jiggle, I tug, I make some grunting noises that I don't recognize, and nothing. My heartbeat kicks against my chest. Did I ruin it all? Break it? Let's just add a new axe to the long list of things that I owe Colby. "Sorry, it's stuck." I try again for good measure, then give up. "What do we do?"

"Now you lift the whole thing at once and smash it again," she says with way too much calmness to her voice. "Do you want me to do it for you?"

As much as I'd love to see Colby chop wood again—because *seriously*—I shake my head. I've skydived before. I've swum in shark-infested waters. I've ice-skated on barely frozen lakes. I can certainly cut wood. But God, it's *really* heavy. And the idea of getting that electric jarring ransacking my nerves again doesn't sound pleasant.

"Good news is that you already split it a little, so you're making progress," Colby says as she tugs her hat a little lower on her ears. "You shouldn't get that shock again."

Okay, I've definitely got to do this. My belly fills with fire, and my eyes focus. This wood is *going down*. I can do this. I *will* do this. I flex my fingers, take another breath, lift the impossibly heavy axe with the wood attached to it, and slam the chopping block. One more time, and *crunch*. The satisfying sound of split wood is like some sort of super ear orgasm. It echoes through the land and bounces back to me. "I did it! Holy shit, I didn't think I would be able to."

"Yeah, you did," Colby says, with a smile that's wider than mine. "Will it sound super condescending if I say that I'm proud of you?"

Warmth fills me, and rushes to my cheeks. *Proud* of me. That's definitely something I haven't heard maybe since I was a little kid. I focus on grabbing the split wood and tossing it into the ATV trailer, wishing my smile weren't quite as big as it is right now. "Not condescending at all."

"For whatever it's worth, it took me a week of chopping before I could do this," Colby says, grabbing the axe resting against the chopping block. "And it took you like two tries. I'm both impressed and feel like crap, so... congrats, I guess?"

I laugh. "Well, if it makes you feel any better, I'm completely worn out and need a break."

In a very short amount of time, a rhythm builds between us, as if we've chopped wood together dozens of times. Colby chops about four pieces, then I do one. She sets up the logs for each of us, I carry the split wood to the trailer.

Colby's breath comes out in fogs against the cold air, but I see her face build with moisture. After an hour, both of us have our hats and scarves off, my chest is sticky with sweat, and the crystalized air feels good against my lungs. The sensation of stinging cold air against my hot body sparks my system, and the longer we're out here, the more refreshed, the more rejuvenated, I feel.

As I go in for my turn, I grab a bigger log than I've done so far.

Colby's eyebrows arch, but she doesn't say anything. A burn fills me. Pictures flood my mind. Of my dad. Of me bawling over missing Lucky Charms. Of my sobbing mother curled on the floor, or walking around exhausted and snippy, juggling bags of groceries and yelling at us to clean our rooms.

I don't think I can run from his memory for much longer. Over the years, I've buried it so deep I thought it disappeared. But it keeps wiggling itself from me, like it's trying to purge from my soul, but I'm not letting it escape.

The day he left is burned into me. Branded into my brain like a tattoo. I raise the axe. His truck filled with boxes, Lucky Charms in the cab, my mom screaming. I crash into the wood. His face as he looked at me, the way he pressed his hand to the window like he was going to wave, then dropped it and looked ahead like I was invisible. I grab another piece and slam the axe into the wood. The way the truck was louder than usual as he sped out of the neighborhood, the way I didn't understand what was happening, why my dad left, why he took my dog. My breath is heavy, sweat beads against me. I wiggle the axe free and raise it again. The way my mom walked me and my sister back inside but dropped to her knees once she hit the entryway. *Crack.*

The wood bursts in a loud, cleansing, cathartic crack. My chest heaves, breathless, my heartbeat thuds against my ear. I'm not even sure how much time has passed, but a gentle hand reaches over and tugs the axe from my grip.

"Getting rid of some demons?" Colby asks.

I flick away a few surprising tears. "Apparently," I say, pushing out a soft smile. "I think I have more pent-up anger issues than I let on."

Colby rests the axe against the chopping block, then digs out a few water bottles from her bag. "Want to talk about it?" she asks as she hands me a bottle.

Do I? Honestly, I don't know. I haven't talked about this in so long. I really thought I buried this, and that the situation doesn't affect me anymore, but it's obvious that it does. Colby stands next to me, letting the silence fall between us without pressing or prying. The clean air fills our lungs, and cools our skin, and I take several long moments to look at the snow-laden property as the fragmented memories settle.

I twist off the lid and drink some water. "Remember when I talked about my dog I had when I was little?"

Colby nods. "Lucky Charms, right?"

"*Whoa.*" Maybe it's not that odd that she'd remember, and maybe it is. But knowing that someone heard something I said a while ago, an offhand comment, and committed it to memory, makes me warm. "You have a good memory."

"I mean, you only told me like four days ago."

It's more than that, and I think she knows it, too. I cannot believe that I've only been here four days. There's a comfortability like I've been here a month. Like my job, my world, my life outside of this place is almost a distant memory. "Doesn't it feel like I've been here a month already?"

"Only in the best way," Colby says. "But yes, it feels longer."

Colby still doesn't pry, and I look out into the forest. The snowfall has almost totally stopped now. I'm not even sure if this is real snow, or just flakes falling from the trees at this point. Colby pulls out a Thermos from her bag, then points to a fallen tree a few yards from us.

We plop down on the tree trunk, the adrenaline from chopping slowing down now, and stare at the silent forest. The rustling pines, the crackling branches, and the sounds of nature fill the silence. Colby pours the warm tea into the cup, and we pass it back and forth. The sensations hit me. The sweaty bodies, the cold air, the warm tea heating my insides. Slowly, my body starts to melt.

"So, yeah, I had Lucky Charms for a few years. And God, I loved her *so* much. She was the sweetest dog in the world. She and Kona would be neck and neck over who would take home the trophy for most loveable dog, you know?" I sip the tea, and hand it back to her. "I think being in a family with six of us kids, I felt sort of invisible. And I wanted to be visible. And... I don't know. Lucky Charms did that for me. I was her person."

I think of the tattoos I've gotten over the years, and the different hair colors, the activities and lessons, all to help satisfy the craving I was seeking to get people to notice me. That somehow if they *saw* me, no matter what it was, it meant I was here, visible, alive. *Worthy.* "But when I was twelve, my father had an affair, and he left us to be with this new woman. All of us gone, discarded, just like that." I try to snap, but with gloves on the effect isn't there. "And he took Lucky Charms with him. It fucking broke my heart. *He* broke my heart. Lucky was my dog, and my dad was my person, and in a heartbeat, they were both just gone."

Colby inhales a sharp breath. "Oh, Josie. My God. I'm so sorry. I can't even begin to imagine how difficult that would've been, especially as a kid that probably couldn't process everything." Her gloved hand reaches out and settles on my knee. She leaves it there for a few moments, and even though I have on snow pants, and her hand is covered, I feel the warmth seep into my leg through multiple layers of fabric. "Do you still talk to him?"

"No," I say. "He tried, for a while. Sent birthday and Christmas money. Called a few times. He finally stopped when I was probably fourteen, fifteen?"

She pours a bit more tea into the cup and hands it back over. "Were you relieved or mad when he stopped?"

"Honestly, I don't know." It's so hard to think of my emotions back then, as an angry, sad teenager dealing with hormones and first loves, while also dealing with the devastation of my family being torn apart. Back then, I let those emotions seep in. Now I don't. I remember years of being sad, more years being angry, and even more years trying to forget. "I was so angry, and every time he called or sent birthday cards or something, I'd get even more pissed. But then when the communication stopped all together, and I didn't get that birthday call that I could blow up at, or rip a card to shreds, I felt even more empty." I let out a self-deprecating chuckle. "I guess I'm all over the place. Looks like not a lot has changed."

She gives me a soft smile, but she's not matching my energy with a chuckle. And then, she sets the cup down by her feet, kneels in front of me, and pulls me into what might be the greatest hug of my life. Her arms hold me, transfer a message to me that I'm okay, that I'm good enough, that none of this was my fault. My lips tremble, and I bury my head into her shoulder.

I try to stop the tears. I try so incredibly hard, but I can't. I break down, right here, in the middle of the snow-filled forest, on Colby's soft flannel shirt, and I hold on to her so tight that I think my arms may fall off. I cry the tears that I've withheld for years, I cry for the kid that was left, for the years wasted, for the memories that I buried.

And she holds me. For so long, she holds me and supports me until the tears stop.

For the first time since I was a kid, I feel the first stitch in my broken soul tug tight.

SEVENTEEN
COLBY

It's not creepy, it's not creepy... Okay, fine. It's a little creepy. But Josie is just so lovely when she sleeps. She tucks into herself like she's giving herself a hug. I swear this woman can conk out just about anytime, anyplace. When she fell asleep while streaming our show, I stayed on the couch, with our legs intertwined, and took one too many glances at her soft face.

I slither off the couch as quietly as possible, and my body immediately misses the snuggles. My legs tingle with the evaporating warmth, and now I'm standing here debating if I should slide back and sleep on the couch with her.

Sigh. I tug the blanket up to her chin, lay one more on her from the basket, flip on the night-light, then saunter down to the recording studio to start my session. I put on my headphones and hit record.

For the past three nights, Josie's fallen asleep on the couch way before I'm even tired. Although today we were outside chopping wood for almost two hours, plus the emotional release she had probably contributed to the fatigue. I saw something in her break when she talked about her father. The pain was real, and raw, and I wanted so badly to take it away. It reminded me a bit of how I broke down after Amelia, the moment when the denial fog lifted, and reality sank in, and it felt like my insides were being crushed.

It's been four full days since Josie got stranded here, and to outsiders, that probably seems like nothing. A blip in their daily life, an interruption before things go back to normal. But for me, it's shaken up the world that I know, the one that I cultivated like a vault around me. And I'm not sure I want to go back to the world I knew before I met Josie.

This closeness, this bond I'm feeling to Josie probably isn't rational. I hear my inner "Ruby voice" as if someone were to write my show with this exact same conundrum. "Hey, Ruby, does it seem rushed that I feel like I'm falling for someone that I've only known for four days?" My overwhelming response would be, "Yes, a million percent, it's rushed." But even with the expedited timeline, my reality is not changing. *Fuck.* I am totally, unequivocally, *fearfully*, falling for Josie.

Okay, so technically it's been more than a week, not four days. And even more technically I met her a year ago, and she occupied my brain for quite a while back then, so does that count for something? And I keep reminding myself that she is now the human I've had the most contact with, *collectively*, for years. I need to stop falling into the societal rules on the *amount* of time you spend together with someone being the only factor that determines how much you should feel.

And also *falling* is a pretty intense term. But the truth is, I like her. *A lot.*

The office chairs squeaks as I adjust myself and readjust my headphones to record in my journal. "I don't know, Amelia. Am I overthinking this? I remember what it was like to have friends. I'm not totally obtuse. I just didn't realize how much I missed sharing space with someone. But this... I don't know. Feels different." I rub Kona's ears where she's nestled at my feet. "Okay, okay. I'll stop watching her sleep. I swear I wasn't there that long. Just like a moment too long. I promise I have some self-awareness even if back in the day you'd tease me that I didn't."

I continue recording into the journal. "But there's something about having Josie here. I like taking care of someone other than Kona. Maybe I missed my calling and should have gone into the medical field, or some sort of caretaking field. Every meal, every blanket, teaching her how to crochet, even with some of the most colorful swear words I've ever heard—who knew *fuck nugget diamond butt plug* could come out of a mouth so many times—it's all filling me, bit by bit. It's like my insides were hollow, an empty bucket with traces of past liquid, and every day since she's been here, it's finally holding some water. Does this even make sense?"

I turn off the Amelia recording and pull up the questions I need to answer on my show. Even though I'm normally diligent about keeping my recording schedule, I can push it off for a little bit and run an "encore" episode from a few years ago. However, according to both the news and the Minnesota Department of Transportation, the roads are terrible, and even though the snow seems to have slowed, it's going to take at least a day or two to clear the main roads. Once it's cleared, *then* I need to attach the snow scraper to my Jeep, plow the drive, and try to pull Josie's car out of the ditch.

Getting too far behind on my recording schedule will not bode well for me after Josie leaves. So, even though I'm sleepy, I pull up question one and read.

Oh yeah. Crap. A few weeks ago, when I pre-vetted this question, I thought it'd be easy. Reading it now, a tension builds in my chest, because everything has changed. Having Josie here is shifting my mindset, and I'm not sure my answer today is the same as it would've been last week.

I clear my throat, channel my inner Amelia, and hit record. "Hey, everyone! Welcome to the *Love 'Em or Leave 'Em* podcast. I'm your host, Ruby Reanne..." I finish my intro and then read the question. "This next question comes from Nedrah in South Carolina. Nedrah says, 'Hey, Ruby. I've been dating this amazing guy for just a few weeks now...'" I continue reading the statement, but my mind is trailing a little bit, and my voice is slipping from my "Amelia friendly" to my baseline.

Come on. I hit pause to re-record, something that I rarely, rarely do. I shake my head, rub Kona's fur, and take off my headphones to make sure I don't hear Josie walking around. I push out an exhale, start again, and reread Nedrah's question from the top. The last line is the one that gets me. "'So, Ruby, I guess my question is, how do you know when it's love or just infatuation? Sincerely, Nedrah.'"

I hit stop. I'm not qualified to answer this one. If I'm being honest, I haven't really been qualified to answer a lot of these questions I've been sent throughout the years. And what I had planned a few weeks ago in my head now doesn't feel right.

Originally, I was going to talk about the tingles, how I felt when I first met Amelia, how the urge to kiss her and be with her every second of the day morphed into a beautiful combination of maintaining my own identity, and honoring my own needs, while having her needs become equally as important.

But tonight, it doesn't come to me the way it normally does. Tonight, I don't want fictional Ruby to talk about an Amelia who's no longer here. I slide off my headphones, and tiptoe back to my room.

A few hours later, a cry-moan sound rustles me from my sleep. I bolt upright so quickly I get a head rush. *Josie?* Kona's head cocks at the side of my bed and she watches me scurry from the room. Outside the bathroom, I tap my knuckle against the door. "Josie? Are you okay?"

"No..." She whimpers and cracks open the door with a sheepish smile. She's standing with one arm looped like a sling in the sports bra she fell asleep with on. "I'm broken."

"Oh no," I say, trying really hard not to laugh at the dejected image. "What happened?"

"I had the failed idea of trying to remove my death-trap sports bra when I should cut it off, instead. Can someone please explain why the inventors of these things made them so freaking tight?"

She unslings her wedged arm from the fabric constraint and drops it to her side with a wince. "And then you can explain why chopping wood yesterday clearly destroyed each and every one of my muscles, and a few that I didn't know actually existed."

"You're sore, huh?"

"That is the understatement of the year," she says. "I don't know how you do it."

I can't help but grin at the compliment. "Well, I've had years of building up to this, and you went pretty hard yesterday." I step back to assess if she's actually injured, but my gaze catches on the smooth, pale belly... the ample plush cleavage peeking from the tight fabric... the way her frustration is making the creamy slope of her neck flush with red. I blink away and keep my eyes focused on the wall behind her. A much safer spot. "Do you need help?"

"God, I'm seriously pathetic. I was thinking about just cutting it off and calling it good," she says with a laugh. "No, I think I'll be fine."

Oh thank God. I don't know what has gotten into me, but the idea of touching her bare skin is making places warm that should not be warming. I need to move myself as far away from her as I can until I calm down. "Okay. Holler if you need."

I retreat to the safety of my living room, from where a moment later I hear, "Um, Colby? Yep. Definitely need your help."

Inside the small bathroom, the air turns intimate. Josie smells nice, even before her shower, like dreamy sleep and woman. The soap remnants from her shower last night linger on her skin, and even though it's the same kind I'm using, it somehow smells more delicate, more feminine, on her. My nose seeks out the comfort of her scent, but I stop myself.

She turns her back to me, facing the wall, and I start to tug on the strap. "Christ, what is this made out of? Spandex stitched inside a wetsuit?" I say with a chuckle, because oof, my heart is thudding in my ears, and I need to keep talking. *Do not touch her any more than necessary. Maintain your cool.* My fingers drag against the strap, and I lick the corner of my lip. Thank God she's facing the wall, not the mirror, and can't see me.

Yes, I've seen the fireplace cast a glow over Josie's naked body, felt her smooth bare skin, and even though my fingers are itching to do it again, I force myself to tackle this sports bra straitjacket removal as clinically as possible. When I grip the fabric and lift from the back, tugging up to her neck, I see her throat roll with a swallow. Her fingers touch mine, soft, and a heavy moment passes. "Thank you," she says as she clears her throat. "I can take it from here."

Something in me is as disappointed as I am relieved. I nod and step outside the bathroom door. The moment it clicks, I press my forehead against the wooden frame, pull in a deep breath, and debate about knocking.

EIGHTEEN

JOSIE

Did Colby feel that? The surge that went through my skin when she touched me? Yes, I was in pain, but she was so delicate, taking long, smooth strokes, and making me feel so comfortable and not embarrassed even though this is super freaking embarrassing. I *seriously* need to work out more. My muscles are dehydrated and angry, and feel like someone's roasting them over a fire.

But now, after sharing this moment with Colby, there's more embers burning than just the ones in my deltoids.

Shit.

The heat from the shower water does little to ease my muscles, and even less to soothe my mind. Something is shifting between me and Colby. Something tangible, that's both heavy and light. An electric current that hums in the air, mixed with a comfortability like this has always been our state of being—living in this house, snuggling on the couch, playing with Kona. It's reality nested inside of a fantasy, and it's warm and tingly, as much as it's pretty damn terrifying.

My body is marginally better from the shower. I step out from the bathroom and *whoa...* Something hearty, like bacon or sausage, funnels through the air, and I instantly salivate. *God, she's a good cook.* Yesterday Colby made crepes for breakfast. Freaking crepes.

She was not joking that first day that she's fully prepared and stockpiled with goodies in case an apocalypse happens. Is it terrible for me to wish for an apocalypse? Probably.

I grab my one fresh pair of underwear, scoop up my other pair and the devil bra to throw in the wash, and toss on the new clothes that Colby left out for me last night. When I slip on her shirt, I sniff the collar. When I leave here, I might see if I can take one of her shirts home with me. They feel good on my body, they're cozy, they carry her scent...

Everything feels like it's becoming a routine. The clothes, the laundry, the eating together, playing with Kona, washing dishes. A casual, easy, seamless routine. And I love it.

I don't think I ever realized that maybe I needed a little bit of a break from my frantic after-hours life. Nothing about my world was routine. I think I've been pushing for anything that's *not* routine. Drumming classes, Pilates, art... these hits of dopamine I was seeking to find something new, to give me a spark, to find my passion, bled into all aspects of my life.

And not only did I need a break from that hustle, I think I needed a break from my job. I love working at the clinic, truly. Being with the animals touches a piece of me that helps me as much as it helps the animals. But I don't even remember the last time I took more than a weekend off. My mind has shifted somehow, relaxed in a way, and it feels like this purgatory-style hunt is reaching the end.

I'm still nervous that I'm leaving the staff shorthanded, though. I've been checking in every day with Leo, who assures me that things are fine and, with the blustery weather, most people have cancelled their appointments.

Colby, on the other hand, does not seem to have that same fear. She hasn't even so much as pulled up a laptop since I've been here, at least not that I've seen. I still don't understand the nature of freelance work. Maybe she has one of those jobs where she has an assignment and has until the end of the month to complete.

Braless—and will probably remain as such because I am never

wearing a sports bra again—I follow my nose down to where Colby is standing over the oven, stirring. "Hey, do you need some help?"

She'll say no. She's said no for the last fifteen meals. I'm keeping this as a running tab of everything I owe her. Food, cooking time, utilities... probably even some therapy sessions thrown in there, too.

"Nope, I'm good," she says and flips the bacon.

I remove Kona's cone of shame and stroke her fur before I wash it. "Just one more week, baby girl, and you can take this thing off forever."

"She will be so excited. Poor thing. That has to be so miserable." Colby gives Kona a small piece of bacon from her palm and sets down a bowl of scrambled eggs in front of her.

No lie. Kona eats better than me most days.

At the table, Colby hands me a plate. I really do feel bad about not getting my own food, but after eating over a dozen meals here, I realize that she likes cooking and serving. It's a bit of a foreign concept to me, but every time she sets down a plate, her soft gaze focuses on me until I take a bite.

"So, I'm thinking if you want, we can go in the hot tub later," Colby says and scoots up her chair. "Might be good for your limbs."

"Oh God, I was hoping you would say that."

"*Josie.* If you want to go in the tub, you need to just say something." She hands me the salt, and I hand her the ketchup—gross—for her eggs.

I take a huge bite and grin into the food. "I'm already putting you out so much. Look at you. You're housing me, feeding me. I'm using your washer every day. The list goes on."

Colby reaches her hand out and puts it on top of mine. And she leaves it. She's trying to transfer a message, a warm one, firm one, and I'm so close to absorbing. "You are *not* putting me out. At all..." Her eyes dip to the table. "I really love having you here."

Oh, that tone. Okay, I feel that tone, the sincerity, all the way down to my toes. When was the last time I felt like someone really wanted me somewhere? Leo loves me, yes, but I'm a perpetual third wheel. My family is too scattered. My past relationships since Zoey were limited, at best. Even at the end with me and Zoey, I didn't feel like she *loved* having me there. It was more of us going through the motions. "Are you sure I'm not cramping your style?"

Colby tilts her head back and forth like she's contemplating. "Well, I've had to stop myself from having full-on conversations with Kona because apparently in the outside world, people perceive that as odd. Who knew?" She grins and slices into her eggs. "But really. I think I didn't know how much I was missing human contact, you know. It's been wonderful."

There is something so genuinely kind and open about Colby that I also forget that this—having people in her space, in her home, in her life—is way out of the norm, too. "You really went balls to the wall with the whole reclusive thing, huh?"

Colby giggles. "I really did. I thought for so long that this is what I needed."

Something in my stomach tingles. "And what do you think now?"

A long pause stretches between us. A pink hue flushes her face, and she looks at her plate. "Now I think I'm getting ready for something more."

My gaze drops to her mouth. I say to myself it's to look at her smile, but I think that it's more. Dammit. I *know* it's more than to just look at her smile. When I sweep my gaze back up, our eyes lock. It's a blip, really, a fleeting moment. But whatever this is, it's an extension of what happened in the bathroom, and a small flock of butterflies release in my belly.

After breakfast, I wash the dishes while Colby takes Kona outside. I'm feeling something but can't pinpoint exactly what it is. I'm prickly and restless, but not for an activity. More for some alone time, which is rare. Whatever it is, though, it's gnawing at me, hard, and when Colby returns, I ask to borrow some gear.

As I finish up the dishes, Colby gets everything out for me. Snow pants, insulated jacket, gloves. She lays them out, organized, neatly, and I swear she wants to attach a note to the top with a bow or something. I can't help it. I *love* it. The thoughtfulness, even with the way she sets a pile of clothes on a bench, gets me right in the heart.

Outside, I blink against the sun. The snow has stopped completely, and the only accumulation in the air is the fog releasing with my breath. It's so tranquil, so quiet, the only sounds are the whistle of a soft wind, and the crack of branches succumbing under the weight of the snow.

With the walking stick gripped in my palm, I trudge through the path. My breath turns heavy, my heartbeat kicks up, my mind begins to free. The sun splinters through the woods, crackling against the snow like a diamond kaleidoscope, and I stop for a moment to take it all in. The beauty is astounding. How have I lived here my whole life, right outside of Duluth, in one of the most gorgeous parts of the country, and never once noticed the way the sunbeams sparkle against the snowflakes? Did I notice this when I was little and forgot? Or have I really shunned this entire nature-loving part of myself as I grew up?

The tree branches are wide and open, stretching like they're ready to give me the hug that I need, the hug that I've been missing for years. God, I used to love being outdoors so much. Visions of me jumping in the lakes on a blistering hot summer day, skipping rocks, building snowmen, and crunching into a heaping pile of burnt orange and red leaves fill my mind.

And then it all stopped. In a snap, I swapped running outdoors with sitting in my room, hating that I felt small and invisible, but not knowing what to do to stop it.

"Minnows are the best for walleye, why?" My dad would ask me this—or a variation of this question depending on what we were fishing for—during one of his many outdoor lessons.

I see myself, my blond hair, my gap-toothed smile, my favorite rain boots with the cherries on them, casting out my fishing pole next to my dad on the dock. "Because it acts like what it would in the real world."

My boots crunch into the snow. Each breath I take I let the

memories flood me without kicking them away. I allow myself to drown, even though I hate it, even though I want to run, but I need it. Something in me is screaming at me to allow the memories to consume me. Just this once, to submerge myself into the past.

Hot tears burn behind my eyelids and trickle down as I think of long moments of quiet between me and my dad as he'd set up a tent. The way I'd hand him the mallet to pound the stakes into the ground, and he'd say things like I had so much potential, that if I set my mind to something, I could do anything. "A president or a princess, Josie-bear. You get to decide."

The tears fall stronger now as I picture him and me ice fishing in the dead of winter, the hollow winds outside. I remember me not understanding how the ice wouldn't crack underneath our tires as we drove out on the lake with our truck, how the ice fishing camper with the propane fire wouldn't melt the ice beneath us and send us to our impending death.

Fuck! It hurts so bad, these memories, these feelings, but I keep going.

My chin trembles and a choking sob releases as I remember us hiking to Gooseberry Falls, the way the power of the water blew my pigtails back and my dad would point out the different types of rock. My tears fall, hard and heavy, as I keep pushing through the snow, keep stabbing my walking stick into the earth, keep thinking of camping trips and the magic of making s'mores around a fire.

The air is stinging my lungs, but I don't want to go back to Colby's. I want to be here, in the outdoors, in the place that I used to love so much. When my dad left, I wanted to strip that part of me and never return. Even though he maybe didn't mean to, he stole my love for nature when he abandoned us all.

"Why did you leave?" I scream into the woods, and the voice echoes back to me. "We didn't fucking do anything wrong!" Our lives could've been so different. Were we not good enough? Was *I* not good enough?

Fuck my dad. I let him take so much from me. My self-worth. My trust. My *heart*. The tears flow now, dripping underneath my chin, and for every sob, something in me breaks. There's an ice pick hitting over and over into this frozen wall I've built. *I was just a kid!* I didn't deserve for my dad to leave, to be raised by an overworked, stressed, exhausted mom, didn't deserve to be made to feel like I wasn't enough, or too much and couldn't be handled. The pick cracks and cracks and cracks, the sobs invade my body, my shoulders shake with each step.

I grab a stick and whip it into the tree, thinking of the school concerts he didn't go to, and the Christmases that he didn't show up to. I throw another, then another, then another. The prom that he missed, and my graduation, and me moving into dorms, and teaching me how to change my tires. The pick hitting my inner wall finally cracks through. I drop to my knees, bury my head in my hands and let the pieces fall. It floods out of me, cathartic, drowning me behind the sobs. I'm trying to catch my breath, my much-needed breaths, the breaths that I've waited twenty goddamn years to pull in, but I can't.

He cannot define me anymore, his absence cannot hold me back. I've let it control me for all these years, locking a piece of me away that deserves to be free. I refuse to give him any more power, I refuse to keep myself locked in this cage of sadness while wishing that my childhood was different. For so many years, I've held this in. A beaker, bubbling with a cover on, needing someone to pop off the top and let me overflow with grief and anger and longing. I've needed to let myself sit with all of my feelings. I've never been good with that before, and as uncomfortable and gut-wrenching as it is, it's liberating. I can breathe. For the first time in forever, I can breathe.

My sobs slow, finally, the tears turn cold against my cheeks, but body aches, and it's the best I've felt in years. I stay like this for God knows how long. Until my shakes stop, until my breath evens, until I officially let go. I'm lost so far in a trance, a beautiful, needed, all-consuming trance.

So much so that I don't notice what's standing in front of me.

NINETEEN
COLBY

Josie left a while ago for her solo walk, and I sneak into the recording room. Something is happening here between us. Something deeper than I expected and I need some time to process. I'm really not sure if I'm ready for something, but I'm definitely much more open to the idea. All I know is that I really, genuinely like having Josie here. And when she goes home, I'm going to miss her. *A lot.*

But I need to be smart about this and settle my sporadic thoughts. It's like I've known Josie for years. There's a comfortability with her that's hard to describe. It's easy, light, normalized somehow. But I need to think, slow down, and gather myself because right now, my body is urging me one way, hard. My brain another. And my heart... is all over the place.

The very last thing I want to do is hurt Josie. Or myself.

I crack the window to pull in some cool, fresh air and check the cameras I have set up on the perimeter of the property (which is more for wildlife than a murderous zombie). *Good.* Josie's far enough away that I can squeeze in a quick journal entry and get some of these things off my chest.

I slide into the chair at the desk and hit record on my laptop. "I really like her," I say. "She's funny, and smart, and so kind. I see how she is with Kona, and it just melts my heart, you know? Sure, it's her job in the outside world, but it's not her job here, at my place. And yet, she does it without any complaints. Would I be this nice to someone else's dog? Maybe? Of course, I would never hurt a pet or anything, but I am not sure I would be this caring."

I shift the chair further under the desk and shiver under the air streaming from the cracked window. "The first few days of having Josie here, I was so off. It was jarring, having someone in my home. Not that I minded, of course, but being alone for six years and then being essentially trapped with someone was a huge shift. I didn't talk a lot, which I know is my standard operating mode. But now it's completely switched. It's like something in me splintered, and all of these things that were stuffed inside for so long begged to get out. Sometimes I feel like I'm talking too much. Like Josie is this cushion that I'm dumping everything that I've held in for years onto, and she just absorbs it all. And Josie, who's normally a total chatter bug, now seems more thoughtful. Quiet, but not like the kind of quiet that makes me think she's sad. She's more... pensive, I guess?"

Is this normal? Is this what happens when two people who are so stuck into their daily routine have something that shakes them up and forces them to look inside? "The weather app showed this morning that roads should be all cleared by tomorrow or the next day. And honestly, when I read that, my heart sank. Can you believe that? I'm not ready for her to go."

This is what's really confusing me. I genuinely don't want Josie to leave. I don't want to go back to watching TV alone, or making meals for myself, or crocheting without a cranky, frustrated partner. Will she come back sometime out here to visit? The friendship that we started before this, will it remain and maybe keep growing, or slowly wilt? Being cocooned in my house like this, it's easy to think things won't change. But once the security blanket is ripped off, I'd be silly to think that they'll stay the same.

I prop my elbows on the desk and rest my forehead in my palms. "I don't know, Amelia... What should I do here? Nothing?

Something? And *shit*. I *really* want to kiss her again. But this time, I want to kiss her because I want to kiss her, not because I'm filling some void. But what if I'm *still* filling that void, but I'm not recognizing it? How do I know when it's right?" I sigh a shaky breath. "It really does feel different, though. The first night when we slept together, there was this ache in me, and I just wanted it filled so fucking bad. I just needed it gone, for even a moment. But now... it's not to cover up something. It's to explore." I bite the inside of my cheek, pulling back a smile. "It's funny, I feel like I need to write into my own show and ask 'Ruby' this question."

I tap stop on the recording and wait. I've been journaling like this for years, and Amelia always talks back to me. Of course, she doesn't *really* talk back. But I always know what she'd say if she were here. All these years, I've imagined the way her nose scrunches when she says something cute, or the dramatic eye roll when I definitely *don't* say something cute, or the way that she'd whisper and tell me what I need to hear.

But for the first time since I started recording these sessions, I'm met with silence.

A hefty sigh leaves my mouth, and I dig through my emails. Questions pour in from listeners and I scan them to see if anything jumps at me. It's shocking how many couples, straight, gay, platonic, experience similar issues—annoyance at a messy partner, feeling unheard in a relationship, angry that the one invites people over without a fair warning.

It seems at the core of relationship problems is communication. Sure, sometimes people are just assholes. But really, people just want their partners to be respectful and truthful. I press my thumbs into my forehead and exhale. *Sigh.* Josie is not my partner. And yes, I feel really close to her, closer than I've felt with anyone since Amelia. And it's not like I've forgotten that I haven't told her that I'm Ruby Reanne, the one who gave her terrible advice and encouraged her to rip her heart open to her ex and be humiliated. Obviously. But I still don't know if I have to tell her about my show.

She hasn't asked about my job, not much anyway, and it's not like I've flat-out lied to her.

And no matter how close we're getting, I don't *want* to tell her about my podcast. The show is something that I hold closest to my heart, a secret that's just for me, a little piece of my identity, even though the identity is a facade. I'm not ready to tell her.

But why? Why, if I feel so close to her, am I not opening up to her about this entire other side of my life?

"Don't make me say this," I say to Kona, who looks up with a very uninterested eye. Besides the fact that I'm not ready to share, what happens if I do share this side of me with her? And what happens if it's something she deems unforgivable, if she blames me for her and Zoey not getting back together, and she *leaves*. Not only leaves the house, but *leaves* leaves. My life. Our friendship. Right now, after just dipping my toes back into the social waters, I'm not ready for the first friend I've made to vanish. Maybe it's selfish. And maybe it's okay to keep this piece to myself. Sure, we've shared a lot, but it's only been a week. There's got to be a ton of things that we don't know about each other.

Right?

Kona lifts her body up, with a whimper. "You're getting used to having her around, too, huh?" I say and rub the top of her head under the cone. "Don't worry. I know she's been gone for a long time, but she'll be back soon. She just went for a walk." The whimper grows. And grows some more. Kona dashes—as quickly as she can currently—and barks at the window.

"What's the matter?" I ask. "Do you have to go to the bathroom?"

The barking turns furious for my typically mellow dog, and the hair on my neck stands up. Something's not right. A tree on the verge of falling? My roof collapsing? Are my fire alarms not working? I leave the room as Kona hobbles next to me, still barking at the window.

At the kitchen I look outside. The sun is bright, the wind settled, the snow barely moving. I crack the door open to listen if there is something else happening that I'm not noticing, but Kona's so agitated that I quickly shut it. "What's going on, girl?"

I grab my phone from my pocket and pull up the security app. Way in the distance where my camera barely pans, Josie's standing frozen. What's she looking at? I tap the other camera feed, pinch to scroll, scanning the dense snow, the trees dragging with accumulation, the foot stamp path that Josie made on her hike. "What in the..." My heart flies into my throat. Oh *shit*.

"Oh no. *No, no, no...*" I leap from my spot so fast that I knock into a chair and it slams into the hardwood floors with a sickening thud. My pulse rages as I spring to the entryway, shove my feet in boots, and grab my shotgun from the wall. I shove a couple of rounds in the chamber, sling it over my back, not even bothering with a jacket or hat, and sprint outside.

The winter air smacks me as I rush outside without proper gear and bolt to the shed. My heart hammers in my chest as I grab my keys and hop on my snowmobile. My mouth dry, my hands wet, my body alert, I grip the wheel and tear down my property.

Go, go, go! I scream internally at the snowmobile as I push it to max speed. My pulse thunders against my chest.

For everything holy in this world, I have to get to Josie in time.

TWENTY

JOSIE

Oh my fucking God.

I'm only one minute past having the most cathartic, rejuvenating, soul-opening experience where I shed my past with my dad and opened up my heart, and now, *this*. Right here, out in the woods, God knows how far away from Colby's home, definitely within charging distance, is a bear.

And it's absolutely beautiful.

A magnificent, gorgeous, majestic creature, with its huge broad chest, and dark, glossy black fur, and a deep, pointed snout, and my breath hitches.

Not only is it beautiful, it's *terrifying*.

Every survival instinct screams at me. Fight, flee, freeze. I'm currently in the middle of all of them, and my limbs don't know if they should follow my brain. Yes, I work in a vet hospital, but we don't treat *bears*. I've never seen one up close except for when I was a kid and went to the zoo. My mouth goes dry. In my head, I hear my dad's voice, talking about the importance of bear spray, and how if you ever encounter one, to not play dead unless they attack, and *for God's sake, never, ever run*.

Okay, okay, I won't play dead. And thank God my feet are cemented into the snow, preventing my body from doing what it wants and sprinting as fast as I can back to the safety of Colby's house. But I definitely don't have any bear spray, and I might be fast, but I'm pretty sure I can't outrun a bear.

I pat my pockets and swallow the boulder lodged in my throat. Yep. I left my cell phone again, charging on the nightstand. *Shit, shit, shit.* Beads of sweat prickle on my neck. Do I move? Stay here? I'm frozen. Rendered completely useless.

It's okay, it's okay, it hasn't seen me. The bear's going to turn the other way and find its mom, or maybe this is the mom... it's so huge I can't tell... and then I'll calmly walk back to the house, and later I'll have a good story to tell Colby. Yep, I'm good—*shit*. Oh my God, it sees me. My chest is so tight I don't think it's getting in air. *Stay calm, avoid eye contact.* This is what I do at the clinic when working with animals with higher levels of aggression. I assume I can apply this to the bear, right? *Oh God, oh God.* The knot in my stomach is so fierce that I really can't breathe.

I turn my head to not make eye contact but keep the outline of its body in my peripherals. He's curious. That's all. He doesn't want to eat me. He doesn't want to attack. Everything I know about bears doesn't calm me the way it should. *Because it's a fucking bear!* Jesus Christ, is this how I go out? Honestly, that would just be my luck. I've made the mental breakthrough that I've needed since I was twelve, finally feel like I just dipped my toes into the well of becoming a whole, complete, better person, and then I get mauled to death?

Okay, okay, think. I'm supposed to open my jacket, make myself big, and walk away backwards. But that seems super counterintuitive. The very last thing I want to do is wave my hands above my head like I'm waving them over for a meet and greet. Did any of the people who gave this advice ever actually encounter a bear? Or encounter one in snow higher than most children?

And aren't bears supposed to be freaking hibernating right now? Sure, it's April and this storm is a true freak of nature, but still...

Beads of sweat prickle at my forehead, at the base of my neck, and I'd whip off my scarf and hat right now, but who knows what the hell would trigger this animal. God, it's so gorgeous, but... nope. I never need to see another one in person for the rest of my life.

A faint zipping sound echoes through the valley. A snowmobiler? Do I wave them down? Will the sound freak the animal out? Should I try to warn them?

My body starts to tremble, but I breathe through the shakes. The bear is still watching me, probably sizing me up, definitely wondering if I'd make a good post-hibernation snack. I grip my walking stick in my hand, praying to God I don't have to use it against this incredible creature, and move backwards. One step. I stab the walking stick into the snow. Two steps. Stab again. Three steps.

The zipping sounds of what is definitely a snowmobile get closer and my breath locks. I cock my head toward the sound, but in this vast, open field, it's nearly impossible to know where it's originating from. Is it Colby? Someone else?

Like so many things in my life that seem to be at extremes, this is both the most terrifying and one of the most beautiful moments I've ever experienced. Yes, I'm scared. I've never been so incredibly scared in all my life.

But also... I believe in myself that I can handle this situation. I keep my gaze not directly on the bear, but to the side where I can monitor. Stab into the ground, step again. The bear stays where it's at, thank God. It's not charging, or moving, or growling. Yet.

I'm still absolutely terrified. If the bear roars, I'm going to pass out.

Stab, step. Stab, step. The snowmobile is getting closer, and when I shift my gaze from the bear to up the hill, my heart certifiably leaps from my chest. Colby, in a haze of snow whipping from the blades on her snowmobile, clad in her sweatshirt and boots, tears through the woods like a thirty-something-year-old Katniss Everdeen, a shotgun attached on her back instead of a bow. And everything, *literally everything* in me crumbles. She pulls a sharp, controlled turn with snow spraying like a firehouse; her face is so serious, so heated, so determined, and *so fucking hot.* "Get on! Watch the gun."

I throw myself on the back and hold on to her with everything in me, while also leaning away from the gun, which is almost as terrifying as the bear. Let's pray to God it takes a hefty trigger pull to release the bullet. As Colby tears up the hill, I turn back only once to see the bear running in the opposite direction.

My breath doesn't fully return until we reach the shed. Colby kills the engine, and I know I need to slide off first, but my shaking limbs can barely peel themselves from the sled. When I finally stand, the adrenaline hits me and I start shaking like I was just pulled from a frozen lake.

Colby doesn't ask. She just pulls me into her arms and squeezes. She squeezes so hard that I lose my breath again, and it's the best feeling in the world.

I don't have any tears left in me from earlier, but if I did, I'm sure they'd fall. Instead, I let my legs wobble, my head fall, and my chest collapse. She rubs my head, strokes my arms, whispers that I'm safe, that I'm okay, that she's got me.

When I pull back, she searches my eyes. "Let's go inside, okay? I'll make some tea."

My lips are trembling too hard to form any words. I nod instead and am grateful when she holds my hand the entire way, like she knows that right now, I don't have the strength to carry myself on my own.

After I take all my gear off at the entry, Colby wordlessly wraps me in a blanket, tosses another log on the fire, and pats the couch for me to sit. A bear. *A fucking bear.* I cannot believe that happened. Did that actually just happen? Did I make it up in my head? I swear it's like I watched a movie of it happening to someone else, although my shakes confirm that it did, in fact, happen to me.

Over the sound of cabinets opening, and water filling a tea kettle, my pulse slowly stops thundering in my veins. *Yep, that really all just happened.* My walk, the beginning of me letting go of the pain from my father, the bear, and Colby.

My God, Colby. The image of the way she looked racing in to rescue me will never leave me. I hope. God, she's beautiful. Her typically kind, gentle face flushed with determination, her eyes fiercely narrowed, the gun strapped to her like some action hero, ready to defend, ready to save.

I've never thought of myself as a damsel who needs saving. Never once. But holy shit, I dare anyone in the world to be in a situation like that, have a phenomenally hot woman slide in like some professional snowmobile NASCAR driver, pull you away from danger, and not have all sorts of tantalizing thoughts rush through you.

A few minutes later, footsteps sound behind me, and I glance over my shoulder.

"Here." Colby hands me a mug and slides onto the couch. "You doing a little better?"

I'm doing both the best and worst of my life right now, and my brain is exhausted. Not that I was facing death, not *really* anyway, but right now, I'm filled with so much gratitude and I don't know where to channel the energy. "Yes, thank you." And just when I thought they were done, a few surprising tears trickle down. I swipe the annoying liquid from my face, irritated the adrenaline letdown is coming out through my eyes. "God, this is so embarrassing."

"What, crying?"

"Yes, no, I don't know." I blow into the mug and take a tentative sip. "Crying. Having you rescue me, yet again. I swear you must think I'm totally helpless."

"No, I actually don't." Colby dunks her tea bag in the mug and sips. "Can we talk about who's rescuing who here? You saved my ass at the clinic, you saved me out here with Kona..."

This gives me more relief than I probably deserve. I give her a soft smile and focus on the flickering flames. The chill has finally left my body, and my limbs have stopped trembling, but I replay the moment on a loop. "Were you going to shoot the bear?"

Colby shakes her head. "No. I mean, that wasn't the plan. I should have brought my bear spray, I just kind of panicked in the moment. I was going to do a warning shot and hope it ran away."

An exhale releases. "Good." Sure, I didn't want to be bear food, but technically, the animal was in its home, and I was the intruder. It didn't deserve to die. "My God, that bear was beautiful. I've never seen anything like it."

"It really was," Colby says with a grin. "And *big*."

"Holy shit, so freaking big." The tea is finally cool enough for me to wrap my palms around the mug. I take another sip of the warm cinnamon, and the heat trails down my throat. "How did you know I was in trouble?"

Colby reaches down and pets Kona's fur. "Actually, Kona started barking like crazy. I don't even know how she knew, but I swear she's the most intuitive dog on the planet. So, I checked the security camera, and well, there it was."

"Has that ever happened to you before?"

Colby shakes her head. "I mean, I've seen them on the camera feed, only maybe once or twice over the years. It's pretty rare. I'm sure it was terrifying for you. It was for me, and I was just a bystander. But my God, kind of incredible, right? Such majestic creatures."

I nod and look back at the fire. Yes, it really was. But you know what else is incredible? This. Sitting here, with this beautiful woman, my heart open, my body alive. Colby presses her pretty mouth onto the mug again as she stares into the fireplace. The flame flickers in her eyes, highlighting that beautiful amber, and Christ, I want to kiss her so bad. Yes, rescue syndrome a little bit, sure. But for so many more reasons than that. It doesn't feel like a pattern that I'm falling into this time. It's because she's a good person. It's because she thinks of others first, and not herself, and I'm going to say it... it's also because she's hot as hell. Seriously. I shift in my seat and push away all of the heat that's seeping into my bones and settling on my center.

After the tea is finished, Colby rises and grabs the mugs. "Do you need anything?"

Is there seriously a more selfless person in existence?

"You know..." I say, lifting my brow, trying to push away the tingles that are threatening to totally invade me. "I'd really love to try out the hot tub now."

A long moment passes. So long that I am not sure if I said something wrong. I glance at Colby and study her face. And absolutely cannot decode the look she gives me back.

TWENTY-ONE
COLBY

When I first moved into this place, I bought the hot tub almost immediately. It's a luxury that I love and still don't take for granted. Growing up in Florida, we had a pool, but not a hot tub. Except for the really hot summer days, several times a week, I slide into it until my skin shrivels. But I've never once sat in the hot tub with someone else. And the idea of being in the tub with Josie is moving so many things in me that I'm frozen in place.

I lean my head toward Josie, who's tugged off the blanket from her shoulders and tossed it on the couch. "Sorry, what?" I ask.

"Do you have an extra suit?"

"Um no." I twist my mouth. "I, um, well, I live alone and my closest neighbors are these pine trees. I'll just get it set up for you, and then you can hop in with privacy."

"Don't you want to go in, too?" she asks with what I think is actual innocence in her voice, but she's kidding right? Maybe she didn't catch the intention with the words about privacy and not needing a suit. "You were outside without a coat."

"I mean... yeah, but, you know..." Right now, I'd love nothing more than to sit in the tub with Josie. But I'm not completely naive, and honestly, I'm not sure I can trust myself. Every second I'm with her, it's getting harder and harder to push away this deep attraction, this fierce magnetic pull I'm feeling. And today, when I thought she was in danger, seeing the bear, thinking of how she was out there, all alone, scared... I still can't shake it. So yeah, being naked in a hot tub with Josie is not a good idea. "The whole no-swimsuit thing..."

Josie cocks her head. "Seriously? We're adults. And, well, I hate to point out the obvious that we're both so clearly avoiding, but we've already seen each other naked. It'll be fine. Doesn't it have bubbles and stuff?"

I mean, she has a point. A really good one. I've been to women-only spas before, gyms, I played sports where we had to shower after. I've seen a ton of women naked in a setting like that. But as much as I'm trying to fight this, I *want* to see Josie naked again. And *that* is a problem.

"Oh yeah, um, good point." I say, my voice unnaturally high. Why am I nervous? I shouldn't be nervous. God dammit, now I'm nervous.

"No pressure, for real," Josie says, following me into the kitchen. "If you don't want to do this, we can totally take turns. That's not a problem."

"Nope, I've already made this twenty times weirder than it needed to be." My face is hot. And my chest. And other parts, which I am totally ignoring. "I may not have swimsuits, but I do have two robes. Be right back."

I dash away before I do or say anything even more awkward. Twenty minutes later, we're both bundled up in a robe—Josie in the winter one, me in the summer one, and I'm really, really trying not to let my teeth clatter as we heave off the top. Well, as *I* heave off the top as Josie's arms are still practically useless from chopping wood yesterday.

And then she drops her robe. Just like that. Free and open, and I turn my back, as casual as I can, trying to be respectful and not freaking ogle like I want to. She's just so beautiful. The way her pale skin highlights the rose tattoos, the way her curves drape her body.

Do not look.

When Josie sinks into the tub, the moan that is elicited from that pretty mouth of hers is something that I'm not sure I've ever been able to elicit from a woman. It's probably weird to be jealous of a heated tub, right? Asking for a friend.

"Oh my God, this is *heaven*..." Josie rests her head on the back of the tub and for a fleeting moment I wonder if the chlorine will mix with her cotton candy pink hair and she'll leave here a dusty brunette. I vow right now to tell her it's beautiful even if she emerges looking like swamp water straight from the Florida Everglades. When I tug on the robe tie, Josie closes her eyes and slides a few inches away. I'm not sure if I should feel respected or offended.

The water slides up and over my skin, the heat contrasting with the cool air, and yes, I'm in here almost every day, but it's the equivalent of the first coffee sip of the morning. "Mmmm... this does feel nice."

"Are we in any danger of Yogi Bear returning?" Josie asks.

Thank God for bubbles. Not that I'd look, of course. But Josie is here, within touching distance, *naked*. And I'm not going to lie... it's tempting. "No. I really don't think so," I say, flicking at the iridescent bubbles in the water and taking peeks at Josie's cheeks pinking from the heat. The water sloshes against that long, lean neck, making her skin glisten, darkening those sexy-as-hell rose tattoos...

My God. Stop. I turn away.

"Tell me about the tattoos," I say, staring up at the gazebo roof and definitely not the way the water is glistening across her chest.

Josie lifts her arms out of the water like she's inspecting the ink. "I started when I was eighteen. Well, technically, sixteen. With a sewing needle and pen ink."

"You *didn't*," I say, but the look she gives me is showing that she's absolutely not kidding. I hold back my urge to shudder. "God, that sounds..."

"Unsanitary? Painful? All of the above?" Josie smiles. She

smiles a lot, but there's something about that small gap in her front teeth, the wet skin, the flushed cheeks... She has one of the greatest smiles that I've ever seen. I think I'll do almost anything to keep seeing that smile. "Yeah, not the smartest moment of my life. Hence all the cover-up I started doing once I turned eighteen and could get a legal tattoo."

I like to think of myself as pretty tough. I live in the woods. I have a shotgun. I chop wood. But voluntarily sticking needles into my skin is a hard pass. As we keep chatting about tattoos and rebellious teen things—me sneaking out to drink beer with friends pales in comparison to some of Josie's shenanigans—she lowers herself under the water and digs her thumbs into her shoulder.

"How's your arm?" I say, overheating just a tad but knowing that I don't have the freedom to lift any higher without exposure. *Even though I kind of want to lift higher...*

"Hurts," she says with a laugh.

Maybe she needs my hands working out that tight muscle. It's always easier to have someone else rub the muscles than yourself. But I shouldn't. Right? Not with all these tingles and zaps running through me.

But maybe I'm overthinking this. Because really, I'm just helping out a friend. Someone who's in pain. It's what I would do for anyone else in this situation. It has nothing to do with me having this nearly feral need to touch her again, to see if I remember the smoothness of that skin, to get close and make her feel good. "Want me to rub your shoulders?"

She bounces her eyebrow with a quick giggle. "Have you ever heard what eighty-five percent of shoulder rubs lead to?"

Dammit. She's too adorable. "Well, let's just say this will be the fifteen percent that break the mold." Because we can't. I think. Not because I don't want to. But because, holy hell, I think I want to.

I float over to her and sit behind her, and *shit*. Maybe this wasn't a good idea. Maybe me being so close to her naked body was actually one of the worst ideas I've ever had. *Shake it off. Be good.*

I'm just going to go ahead and tackle this like physical therapy. Like if I were a chiropractor or massage therapist or some sort of medical personnel. Not someone who is nearly firing on all cylinders and, even with the cool air hitting my face, unable to cool myself down.

My hands glide across her neck, her shoulders, rubbing into her back. It was so quick and frantic when we first slept together that maybe I didn't realize how perfect her skin is. The intricate rose tattoo and vines weaving down her arm are silky underneath my touch.

"This feels really nice," Josie murmurs.

Through the sound of the hot tub jets, I can barely hear the honeyed tone, but I do. And it's enough to nearly tip me over the edge. It feels nice for me, too. *Too nice.* My thumbs press into her, kneading in small circles. I watch the steam rise from her skin, the water droplets trickle down her neck, then down her spine, and I want so badly to lean in and push my lips into her neck. Just once. One little taste, and I think I'd be satisfied.

Our naked bodies seem to float together. She's between my legs, but I'm keeping myself away, as much as humanly possible, as her neck lobs and my heartbeat rises. As I continue to rub, and Josie's body melts beneath my touch, my thoughts bounce between a lust haze and focus. This, *Josie,* is no longer a needed distraction. I want to kiss her. I want her back in my mouth. I want to touch her and make her feel good. Slow this time. Nothing rushed, nothing frantic, no feelings of regret.

My palms slide down the round of her shoulder, the biceps area, and back up. She's silent, but her breathing is getting heavier. My thumbs trail down her spine, and she lifts to give me access. I want to reach around, cup her, feel her thighs in my grip. My mouth is watering and my pulse is raging against my ears. My God, I want Josie. All of her. Now.

I indulge in the vision of me pulling her into me, my fingers grazing her belly, lowering to her center. I picture my lips pressing against her neck, my hands cupping her breast, the sounds she'd make as my fingers dance over her. My breath turns hot, wet, anxious. I want this. *I want this so fucking much.*

I freeze, drop my hands, and push myself back. "Oh shoot. I think I heard Kona." I lie, and she knows it. Josie glances at me with flushed cheeks and half-opened eyes and nods. She puts her back to me, and I practically sprint from the tub and head inside.

TWENTY-TWO

JOSIE

What the hell am I doing?

I'm staring at myself in the bathroom mirror as I brush my teeth, unable to let go what happened in the hot tub and it's been *hours*. We came in, we showered, we cooked and finished dinner. We worked on crocheting our scarves, we watched a show, and I *still* can't let it go. God, Colby's fingers are magic. Yes, my shoulders feel better, of course. I mean, how could they not? But does Colby have any idea the amount of physical restraint it took for me to not turn around, pull her into my lap, and taste that sweet Cupid's bow mouth again?

Something has changed. This time together, the air, the quiet. It's been less than a week, but I am not the same person I was when I first came here and got stuck in the snow. Sure, I haven't *totally* changed and there's so much to work on, but I know that something in me has lifted. I'm lighter. More settled. Not filled with this incessant need to keep moving until I drop.

At the sink, I spit out the toothpaste and swish my mouth out, and when I come out of the room, Colby is standing in the hall with a freshly washed face, wearing pajama bottoms and a cotton shirt. Her long chestnut hair is cascading down her shoulders, and I swear this woman can wear just about anything and she'd be the most beautiful woman in the room. Flannel, jacket, Henley, cotton pjs. It doesn't matter.

I want to take a moment to absorb it all. But the look on her face is something I haven't seen since I've been here, and it makes me stop in my tracks. I swallow back the nerves in my throat. "Everything okay?"

Her gaze sweeps her clasped hands and she nods. When she pulls her head back up, she gives me a smile. "Yeah. I, um, I just saw on the news that everything should be cleared by tomorrow morning. So, after we get up, I can get the scraper on the Jeep and clear the driveway, then pull your car from the ditch."

A sickening thud hits my chest. *It's over.* This time, this moment, this honeymoon period where I shut out the outside world, learned things about myself that I never knew, relaxed in a way that I didn't know was possible, is gone.

And so is my time with Colby. Someone who I've very quickly grown to care for, someone who I want in my life, someone who I really, really don't want to leave. It's all done.

Of course I knew that it was all going to end at some point. We live in Minnesota. The weather might be somewhat unpredictable, but I wasn't delusional enough to think that we'd be stuck here for months. The sun was always going to come, the snowplows were always going to clear, the snow was always going to stop. And our time together was always going to end.

And yet, I held on to this hope that it would last just a few days longer. I swallow back the urge to cry and push out a smile. "Ah... that's great. You will be so happy to get rid of me. Wow." I scratch at the back of my neck and avoid her gaze, because if she sees me, she will see through my bullshit. She's already done enough. I can't exactly ask her to keep housing me indefinitely. "It'll feel nice to be back in my bed."

None of this is a lie, but it's also not all the truth. Sure, being back in a bed would be nice, even though Colby has offered her bed to me every single night. But this place has grown on me, and the idea of going back to my tiny apartment on the third floor of a semi-decent complex isn't as nice as being surrounded by acres and acres of trees, the coolest dog in the world, and the woman that I really, really like.

Colby clears her throat. "I was thinking, if it's not weird... Do you want to sleep in the bed with me tonight?" There's a flush to her cheeks, one that makes my cheeks match. "Nothing like... *you know*. Just friends. Like a sleepover from when we were kids?"

She's shifting the weight in between her feet, and I feel every silent emotion. *In the bed. With Colby. In Colby's bed.* But she marked out her boundary line, which I respect. And it's probably a good thing that she clarified, especially with the way my body is still tingling from that massage this morning. Because seriously, how does she have such gifted hands? The way that she worked my shoulder made me think all day about the way she could work other areas.

Seriously, snap out of it.

A smile spreads. "A sleepover, huh?" I say. "That means that you'll either have to get out the Ouija board or tell ghost stories. We can flip a coin and decide."

"Hell to the absolute no on that," Colby says with a laugh, clearly relieved I didn't make her request awkward. "You forget that you get to leave to go back to the safety of your un-haunted apartment, and I'll be stuck here with whatever demons we summoned. And sadly, I'm fresh out of holy water."

"Okay, that's totally fair." I giggle. "Yeah, sleeping in a bed sounds nice. I'm going to grab my pillow."

Holy shit. I'm going to sleep in the bed with Colby. Keep hands to self, be respectful, do not, under any circumstances, do exactly what you want to do.

After I grab my pillow, I stand in the living room and take a few deep breaths. I need to calm my insides, because I'm terrified that I am going to do something really stupid and mess this up.

But the moment I crawl into the bed with Colby, every hesitation I felt about this being awkward or weird, or even deeply sexual, evaporates. I should've known. Her bed is so plush. She has so many layers of blankets that it feels like I'm in a velvet cocoon. Kona settles with a scrape of the cone and a heavy thud against the floor by Colby as I roll onto my back and clasp my hands under my head. "Oh, you have an amazing skylight. And... wait... you have glow-in-the-dark stars? This surprises me."

"The glow-in-the-dark stars?" Colby asks as she wiggles lower and tucks the blankets up to her chin. "Why?"

I stare at the hundreds of stars lined across her ceiling. "I don't know. I guess there's something so innocent about it," I say. "Like what a kid would have in their room. And you are so..."

"Not innocent?" She chuckles. "Really. Tell me all your true feelings. No reason to hold back now."

"Stop." I laugh and slide down further on the pillow until our shoulders are touching. Her body sinks like it let out a sigh when we touch. I stare at the stars, the real ones from the skylight and the fake ones on her ceiling, and try to soak this moment in. My last night here. Maybe even forever.

We're silent for a while. Comfortable. Quiet.

And then we talk. *For hours.* Through heavy yawns, Colby tells me about growing up near the ocean and how much she misses it, but how Lake Superior and the smooth beach rocks up here are so phenomenal that they fill that void. I tell her about my family, go through each of my siblings, talk about my mom. We talk about the difference between being an only child and one of six, and I say just because I was surrounded by people, it didn't make me any less lonely. And then I tell her about my solo walk in the woods today where I started making the peace I desperately needed with my dad, with myself on my dad's absence, and how for the first time in my life I feel simultaneously lighter and whole.

Turns out that Colby loves to hold and I love being held, and somehow during all these words, we seamlessly intertwine. She spoons me like we've done this a million times. I settle into her, comfortable, relaxed, satiated by the warmth.

A few things happen tonight.

One, we don't have sex. We don't even kiss. Not a peck, not a brush of lips on the top of the head, not a hand.

Two, I feel safer than I have in a long time. Maybe even ever.

And three, I realize that I'm developing true, deep, serious feelings.

I just need to figure out what I'm going to do about it.

TWENTY-THREE

COLBY

When I wake up, Josie is gone from the room, but her clean skin scent lingers in the air. My arms immediately wish she was back here. I'm a cuddler. I've always been a cuddler. But much like everything, I thought this piece of me had died along with Amelia.

Clearly, though, it didn't.

I remember years ago recording an episode about the importance of skin-on-skin not only for babies, but for adults, too. That it lowers heart rates, reduces stress, releases that much-needed oxytocin so the couple can bond. So sure, I knew the logistics and remembered the way I felt snuggling with Amelia. But I had *no* idea how much I'd missed physical touch.

We'd grown so close, so quickly, but I didn't know if I'd be comfortable sharing a bed. But the moment Josie lay down and inched towards me, it felt like I put on my favorite cozy sweatshirt after the first chill in the fall air, but the scent was different. Familiar and foreign all at once. Legs entwined, heartbeat to heartbeat, never breaking contact even as we rolled and adjusted. The tingles of it being new, but like I was never meant to sleep any other way.

Something shifted last night. Josie stopped feeling like a guest. She felt like *home*.

When I look outside, my heart sinks. There is no more snow coming down, the roads are supposed to be clear, and there's no reason that Josie can't go back home. She has a life, and a job, and I need to get back to recording my podcast, so I still have a job. I should be happy, getting back to routine. What we've had here this week isn't real life. It isn't sustainable. But yet, there's an ache, starting low in my chest, building at an uncomfortably speedy rate and spreading through my body. I'm not ready for her to leave.

"It's a big day," I say to Kona and rub her fur. "We're gonna have Josie take a look at your wound, and if everything's good, I think you can ditch the cone of shame for good in just a few short days."

Kona cocks her head. But when I release her from this plastic monstrosity, she'll understand. I drag myself from the bed, tug up the covers, and take a moment to sniff Josie's pillow. Well, it's official. I'm not going to change the sheets for a few days once she leaves. I'm going to hug the pillow, pretend it's her, and wait for the smell to naturally fade.

Another scent fills the air, not unpleasant, but one that I can't totally identify. Kind of doughy maybe, but not like baked goods. *Hmmm.* I make my way down to the kitchen with Kona trotting next to me. At the stove, Josie's stirring a wooden spoon over a big pot, and my breath locks in my throat. Messy, wet pink hair from the shower, cherry-laden scrubs on her body. There's a finality in seeing her in scrubs. If any indication exists that today is the last day of her staying with me, Josie not wearing my clothes is it.

"Morning, sunshine," she says.

I peek over her shoulder and try *so hard*, yet fail miserably, to not scrunch my nose at the mushy, and very, *very* gray contents. "What... do we have in there?"

"Do not even give me that look," she says, even though she can't see my face. "You'll like it. I think." She gives me a quick hip bump and I retreat to the corner to fill up Kona's food. "Yesterday on my walk, I remembered when me and my dad went camping, he'd make oatmeal in this huge pot over the fire, and I got so hungry for it. I hope you don't mind I raided your fridge. And pantry. And basically used the last of the sugar."

God, I'm going to miss this so damn much. Most likely not this meal, per se. But *this*. Having Josie here, navigating around each other in the kitchen, having her watch me cook, watching her hand-wash dishes. *Making me smile.*

"I don't mind at all," I say. "Can't wait." I actually can wait. I'm a little terrified.

As she continues cooking and I continue pretending that I'm thrilled to eat whatever she's got stirring, I squat next to Kona and peek at the incision. "I think we're getting close to taking the cone off. Before you leave, can you take a look and let me know what you think?"

The words drag out of me harder than I thought they would. I need to get a grip. Josie's leaving, and that's that. It doesn't mean I'll never see her again. Of course I will. I just... Who knows how often? When I come into town for my weekly cupcake run? Or if she comes out here? We'll probably go back to our text-message-only friendship, even though I know in my heart I want more.

Holy shit. I know in my heart I want more. I want to be more than friends with Josie, and everything in this moment crashes into me. She's what I've been missing all these years. And even though Amelia will never be replaced, this might be a moment for a new start, a fresh new beginning, with someone else, who fills different needs.

Josie is quiet at the stove, but glances over her shoulder at me. "Yeah, of course I'll check out Kona's leg. When you finally take off that cone, you'll have to send a video. It'll be damn near ceremonial."

Send a video. I need air.

Outside, I walk Kona around the house as she sniffs out a spot to go to the bathroom. It's sunny out, almost blindingly bright as the beams ricochet against the blanket of white, but it feels gloomy. The silence that I once craved, that once I needed to breathe, I no longer need. Now, it carries the threat of impending loneliness.

A dark void starts in my chest. *I don't want Josie to leave.*

Inside, Josie has two fresh cups of coffee nestled up to two heaping bowls of oatmeal, with what looks like every nut I owned sprinkled on top. I vow right here and now no matter what it tastes like, I'm going to eat the entire thing with a smile on my face.

Here goes nothing. I lift the spoon to my mouth and... *oh thank God*. "Yum. This is delicious. You guys made this over a fire?"

"Yep. And thank you. Such comfort food, too, right? Carbs, sugar, and cream. What's not to love?" She says it with a smile, but I can tell she feels the heaviness of the situation, too. The oatmeal is good, but not enough to warrant the long bouts of silence as we both stare out the window and keep eating. Finally, she sighs. "Ugh. Don't make me go back to work. Can you and Kona just kidnap me or something? Keep me hostage? She can be the guard dog, you can make up fun little ransom notes, I can take a picture of me with my wrists bound..."

"I can go to prison... sign custody of Kona over to you." I chuckle, then pull in my lips. Because really, besides prison time, I'm kind of loving this idea. "It's going to be quiet without you here."

She scoops a heaping pile of oatmeal onto her spoon. "I snore, don't I? Be honest."

I laugh at her accusatory look. "You don't," I say and take a sip of coffee. "You're actually quite peaceful when you sleep."

When I say that, the air shifts. Our eyes lock, so many unspoken words lingering between us, and maybe I should just open up. Maybe I should tell her that I don't want her to leave. That this last week has been the best I've had since my wife died. That for the first time in six years, I didn't think of heartache or trauma or feel this burn in my chest that's haunted me since Amelia passed. Josie has cracked open this layer and her sunshine poured in, and I'm absolutely not ready to let any of this go.

Why can't I just tell her? Fear of rejection? That she doesn't think the same? That I'll push away a friendship that means almost as much to me as potentially being together? Whatever the reasoning is, I'm blocked from blurting it out but pray that she'll say something.

Josie lays her hand on me. "Thank you for letting me stay here."

When I rest mine on top of hers, I fight back the urge to lift it to my lips. God, I hate this so freaking much. Why can't I just say something? Anything? "Anytime. Seriously." I squeeze her hand and go back to eating. "We do need to talk about when you're returning because we still have four episodes left of *Killing Eve*, and I won't feel right finishing those without you."

A smile crosses Josie's face. "Deal."

After breakfast, Josie and I head outside to start the process of digging out her car from the mound of snow it's buried under. Much to my dismay, it goes much quicker and smoother than I'd hoped. This entire time, I've held on to a delusion that maybe her car was permanently stuck and she'd have to stay here for another month. Or maybe the mini-plow wouldn't hook up properly to the Jeep and she wouldn't make it down the path. Or maybe when I was done with the path, we'd discover that the county roads hadn't been plowed yet, even though I was almost sure I heard the scrape of metal on pavement echo through the forest last night.

But nope. The Jeep tugged the car out almost effortlessly. As Josie shoveled the patio, the mini-plow tore into the pathway and we finished almost at the same time. And when I got to the end of the street, MnDOT had plowed so perfectly that I saw concrete.

There's officially nothing keeping her here. No reason for another popcorn night, or more hot tub moments, or more snuggles in my bed. Why, why, *why* the hell did I not invite her to sleep in my bed right away? One night of snuggling and I want more. So much more.

Back inside, Josie shoves her minimal items into her gym bag, and my neck grows hot. Just say it! *Tell her you don't want her to leave. Tell her that you've developed feelings. Tell her you're scared, and you don't know what this looks like, but you're both worth it to figure it out, if she wants to.*

And that's the key. How would I know? Every show I've ever done on the podcast about being brave and putting yourself out there, and just admitting your feelings, is coming back to bite me square in the ass because this is an absolutely terrifying place to be. The threat of rejection, laced with the threat of losing a deeply developing friendship, is making my gut turn. So, no. I can't ask her to stay. My heart cannot take it if she doesn't want to.

Josie folds an already folded blanket lying on the couch and pats the pillow. She bends down and rubs Kona's fur and whispers some things about being a good dog, and making sure to take care of me, and other sweet stuff that I can't hear because my heart is pounding so hard in my head that it's drowning everything else out. *Don't go. Don't go. Please don't go.*

"Well, I should probably head out," she says and tugs on her coat.

Tears prickle at the back of my eyelids. "I suppose that makes sense. Back to the grind, huh?" I sound like an idiot, but I don't know what else to say.

She reaches her arm out and gives me a hug. It's a nice hug, warm, but it's not enough. I pull her into me, hard. Her body sinks against mine, her hands clutch at my back, her heartbeat thunders against my chest. We stay like this for a long time. Longer than friends. Longer than people who shared space for a week. Longer than people who may have only met a few weeks ago but seem to know more about each other than anyone else.

"Why does this feel like a goodbye?" Josie whispers into my ear.

I don't say anything, because I feel that, too. This tug to keep her here but knowing that it's not logical, that we're probably in some sort of post-snowstorm fog and reality will step in soon. I step back because if I hold her any longer, I'm going to explode. "It's not a goodbye. It's a see you soon, okay?" My eyes drop to her cherry pink mouth, and *God*, I want to kiss her again so bad. Not out of desperation, not out of a ploy to keep her here, not out of anything but simply wanting to kiss Josie.

She slings her gym bag over her shoulder and makes her way outside. At the porch, I tug my sweater around me with Kona at my side, still in denial, still thinking she is going to stop and rush back into my arms, and say she wants to stay. I keep this delusion as I wave, as she starts her car, as she makes her way down the drive.

And when I shut the door to my house, I'm met with the silence of what just happened. I pace the house, I step into the recording studio, I look at my laptop. It's too quiet. It's way too fucking quiet. The solitude is deafening, covering me from head to toe, a dark isolation that's shaking me to my core.

It's only been ten minutes, but I can't stand it. I want her back here, in my arms, filling my space with me, making me smile.

I pick up my phone and my thumbs fly off a text before I can reason with them to stop.

COLBY

I wish you were still here.

The three dots pull up immediately.

JOSIE

I never left.

TWENTY-FOUR

COLBY

I race to the front door with my heart thundering in my chest as Josie pulls up to a stop. She slams the door, and marches to me. She's determined, serious, smiling, the pink in her hair matching the flush in her cheeks. Her look mirrors my insides and carries the weight of a million unsaid words. All the hope, the fear, the desire, the trust. She runs up to the porch, throws her arms around me, and crushes her lips against mine. The kiss steals my breath. I stumble back a few inches with my mouth warm and hungry, and so fucking grateful.

She came back.

When she pulls back, her eyes search mine, and a sheepish grin fills her face. "I only made it to the end of the driveway."

"I'm so glad," I say, squeezing her hand. "Let's go back inside."

She interlaces her fingers in mine. Inside, we're quiet. Through soft smiles, I kick off my shoes, she removes her boots and hangs up her coat. When she turns around, I cup her face in my hands and look into those beautiful, soulful, inviting brown eyes. The eyes that not only captured me, but opened something in me.

I pull her into me again, and press my lips onto her sweet, luscious mouth. When she parts my mouth with her tongue and gently swipes against mine, I swear my knees almost buckle. My breath increases as quickly as my pulse as I lean her into the wall, and she tugs me against her. God, her lips are everything. The first night, it was so frantic that kissing took a back seat to everything else, and I didn't realize how soft her lips were, how plush and delicious. I push my leg in between hers, my knee gently grazing against her core, covered with the minimal fabric of her pink scrubs. A soft moan escapes her lips, the exact sound I've been chasing while she's been here, and I want more.

Footsteps patter our way and thunk right next to us. We break the kiss and both look at Kona lying next to the couch on her doggie bed. I grin at Josie, then glance at Kona. "Sorry, girl. You're going to have to stay out here for a while." What I want to do, what I'm pretty sure Josie wants to do, Kona cannot see.

Without another word, I grip Josie's hand and walk her down to the bedroom, closing the door behind us. The urgency of that first night is gone. The frenetic nature, the clawing at the skin, the intoxicating heat. Everything is slow, warm, intentional. I can feel my pulse rise against my ears, my stomach fluttering with anticipation.

Josie's fingers reach up, and she drags my sweater down my shoulders. She lifts my chin, kisses behind my ear, down my neck. Her lips are so soft, gentle, grazing with the slightest of touches, yet it shoots a charged electricity through my body. I lean into the touch, and when she pulls back, I immediately want more. "Do we need to talk about anything first?" she says.

"No," I say. All week we've talked. We've gotten out everything that needs to be said. Now, I'm ready. *I am so, so ready.* "This feels different." Last time was a means to forget. This time, it's to connect.

"It does," she says, biting on the corner of her lip. "Thank you for letting me come back."

"Thank you for being here."

I move to kiss her again and melt against her full mouth, that cute gap in her teeth, her beautifully soft and firm lips. Her fingertips grip the bottom of my shirt and she helps me toss it off. My heart is pounding as her mouth moves to my cleavage, as she plants kisses on the top of my breasts, as one hand slides to cup my ass.

I lift her out of her scrub shirt, up high and over her arms, and let my gaze linger on her black bra, the way the fabric pulls against her, how silky her skin looks. God, she's so beautiful. Her curves, her fullness, she drips with sexiness without even realizing it. "No sports bra, huh?"

She grins and shakes her head. "Never again."

Our mouths connect. Kissing, tugging, licking. Her lips moving against mine. She guides me to the bed, and we lie down, taking our time. This is happening. This is all happening and it is sweet, and calm, and hot, and real. Everything is grounded in reality. As we turn to our sides, and she drapes her leg over me, and I tug her into me as close as I can, I take in everything. The sweet smell of her skin. The fabric of her scrubs rustling against my legs. Our bra-covered chests brushing against each other.

Goose bumps skitter up my arms and down my neck with every touch. Our mouths lock. My pulse pounds in my chest, and urgency grows in my body. I need to feel more of her, to see her, to taste her.

I turn and slide her beneath me. God, her skin is so smooth, so perfect. I trail my mouth across her jawline, kiss the column of her neck, her clavicle, the rose tattoo at her shoulder, her cleavage. I put my mouth over the fabric on the bra and give it a sharp suck, and Josie moans against me and wiggles her hips. "Everything feels so good," she murmurs.

When I slide my tongue down her bare belly, her stomach quivers beneath me. "Are you okay with all of this? Tell me if you want to stop," I say as I trail kisses to her hip.

"Don't stop," she says with a wet, heavy breath. "For the love of everything, please don't stop."

These are the exact words I was hoping for. Fingertips rake through my hair, tickle my shoulders, dig into me when I reach a very sensitive spot below her navel that I'm desperate to explore even more.

Everything about this moment feels right. Solid. Perfect. I tug down her pants and take in the sight of her beautiful pale legs, of the way that the lace of her underwear rests against her skin, of the goose bumps that rise on her thighs. My palms slide up and down her legs and the heat from her powder-soft skin seeps into my hands. Nothing is rushed. The craving in my mouth, in my fingers, in my body, is so strong, yet so... settled. We have all the time in the world. Josie is here with me, *really* here with me, and this is exactly where I want to be.

She sits up and wraps her legs around me, capturing my mouth again. We each unclasp our bras and toss them to the side, and the moment mine is off, her eyes drop, heavy lidded and filled with so much lust I feel it in my toes. She touches me like she wants to memorize everything, like she never wants to let go, then her mouth moves closer, and *mmmm*... Her tongue moves across my nipple, and when she pulls me into her mouth, I clasp my hands behind her neck and moan against her ear.

"You're so beautiful, Colby..." she whispers against my skin as she licks, and sucks, and kisses.

My mind only flutters to Amelia once, a quick blip to allow my brain to acknowledge that this is the first time being touched by a woman since her—the couch escapade barely counts—and it's okay. It's time. I'm ready.

Josie's hands reach the top of my pajama bottoms and she dips her hand inside my pants. "Is it okay if we take these off?" she asks as she brushes her lips against my neck.

"Yes. I'm ready for everything," I say as I shimmy out of them, and when she hooks her fingers around my underwear and tugs them off, I swear I almost stop breathing. My cells, my skin, everything is alive, dancing, anticipating, and my knees start to quiver.

"Me too," she says as she trails kisses. Down my breasts. To my stomach. To my thighs... my hips... and *oh God*... right there.

I press my back into the mattress and moan as her mouth moves around me, delicate yet expertly like she already knows me, what I need, what is making the tingles stronger. Heat rushes to my core and spreads, and when she dips a finger inside me, I nearly whimper.

"Oh, Colby. You're so perfect, so beautiful." My heartbeat kicks up, more, higher, then starts thundering in my chest. I don't want this to end, but this tension, this longing, this deep connect I'm feeling is building the ache in my body at a fast and furious rate.

Her lips and tongue move along with her hands and I'm so close. "Yes, so good, Josie... Shit... it's so good..." I say, my hands reaching for her head, for my pillow, for my sheets. My body starts to tremble, deep in my core, in my legs, in my stomach, as she keeps the most perfect pressure, the most perfect consistency. I'm almost embarrassed that I'm coming too quickly, but I'm letting myself go to the sensations, to the feelings of being with Josie, to this deep connection we're creating with every touch, every moan, every kiss.

The tension is building. My heart thuds, my mouth waters, so close, *so very close*, my body starts to tremble, and I'm moaning and murmuring so loud, but I can't stop because everything feels so fucking good. Her tongue moves, sweet, perfect, delicious, and my core clenches. "*Yes... mmmm... right there.*" The orgasm tears through me, long, shuddering, releasing, and I blink away spotted stars. My heart is thudding so loud in my chest that I think she hears it from where she's resting at my side. Once I stop, she shimmies back up, lies on my chest, and wraps her arms around me.

I have an urge to cry, but it's different than last time. Last time I cried with regret. This time, the tears springing to my eyes are filled with hope.

I twirl her soft pink hair in my fingers for a few moments, absorb the heat of her body against mine, and let myself catch my breath. And once I do, I guide Josie to her back, trail kisses down her body, and show her how much she means to me.

TWENTY-FIVE
JOSIE

At some point, I really do need to go back home. I don't have a plant that I need to water or anything, but I do have to work in the morning. But lying here, cradled in Colby's arms, after round three of the day, I don't want to move. I'm gummy and limby, and boneless in the best way possible.

I roll over and plop one hand under my head, lace my fingers in her hair with the other, and absorb a drowsy Colby lying back on the pillow. I kiss her arm, her hand, each fingertip, and drag the pads of my fingers across her skin. "I have to go."

"Negative," she says with a smile. "Five more minutes." Colby sits up, and tugs the blankets up to her neck, which she shouldn't do. That woman should walk around naked all the time.

I love that I never made it out of here this morning to my house. I can't believe that eight hours ago, or so—who even knows at this point—I started driving down Colby's pathway to return home for the first time since getting stuck, and I'm still here. *In bed. With Colby.* My heart and body are so warm and full that I'm not sure how much of this is a physical afterglow or an emotional one.

We lie there for a while longer until we take a shower together, and I get dressed. I'm not sure what this all means, but we've bonded. I feel like I know Colby, on every level that I need to know someone. And yes, there's so much to discover and work through, but I'm convinced that I'm not the same person I was when I first met her. Something in me has fundamentally shifted, and I cannot wait to see what the future holds.

"I don't want you to leave, but it's getting dark and you haven't driven in town yet since the storm. What if the roads are slippery?" Colby says, slinking up next to me as I tug on my sweatshirt, and presses her lips to my neck.

Goose bumps skitter through me. Eight hours later, and I swear I want to hop right back into the bed. "You know I was born and raised in Minnesota, right? I promise I'll be fine."

"I'm in denial that you're leaving," Colby says as she escorts me towards the front door. "I'm going to text you in a few minutes and see if you'll turn back around. It worked this morning. Maybe it will work again."

Everything in me is begging me to stay. What if I walk out of here and this magic spell breaks? What if I return to my apartment, and my job, and everything reverts to the way it was before? Colby and me go back to being friends. My need to search for something fires back up. The hole in my heart opens back up.

For the first time since Zoey, being with Colby feels right. Like actually *right*. But we're still in a fog, and I'm terrified that in the real world that fog will lift. A heavy sigh leaves me. "*Trust me*, I don't want to leave, either."

Colby's gaze scans mine and she grabs my hand. "Oh no, I'm just kidding. I mean, I'm *not* kidding. You could totally stay here, but we're good, right?"

"Yeah, yeah, we're good. I just... If this is what I think it is"—I wave between us, swallowing back all the nerves that seem to be at a tipping point—"I want to be smart about it, you know? I've jumped in headfirst so many times, and I don't want to ruin this—our friendship, or our time together, anything." *And the sex. I'm going to say it. Holy shit, I don't want to ruin the phenomenal sex.*

"I feel the same. And I—" She swallows and tucks a long dark lock behind her ear. "I want to see what it grows into, and I don't want to put a ton of pressure on whatever this is. But I like you. A lot. And I like our friendship. And I want to do that" —she casts her gaze to the bedroom and back up at me, chewing on the bottom of her lip—"again and again."

My heart flutters. My legs are shaking from the daylong activities, but one more word and I may drag her back in there, cavewoman style. "Me too." I pull her face into mine and softly kiss her pinked, swollen lips. "But for tonight, I think it's a good idea that I go home, sleep in my bed, go to work tomorrow. And you should go back to your freelance editing stuff that you do, that you'll actually have to explain to me more in depth sometime."

Colby's cheeks warm, and it feels like the energy shifted. Is she worried that I'm *leaving* leaving? I'm not. This between us feels good. Stable. *Healthy.* We're on the cusp of something amazing. I'm not going anywhere.

I pull Colby in for a hug and breathe in her scent one last time. "I'll call you later, okay?"

From the front door, she waves to me with Kona standing dutifully at her side. I keep one eye on the snowy path in front of me, and one eye in the rearview mirror, until Colby and Kona disappear. Even when I hit the country road, my smile still hasn't faded.

Beep, beep, beep. I tap off the alarm and blink up at my bedroom ceiling. Someone tell me again why I thought I should sleep in my own bed, at my own place, when I had the most beautiful woman in the world, with a way better bed than me, and the coolest dog next to Lucky Charms, offering me a different place. This is one of the least bright things I've done, and let's be real, I did a lot of dumb shit in my teens.

Two hours later, when I stroll into work with coffee in one hand, my purse in the other, and the widest grin that Leo has probably ever seen on me, he rightfully glances up from the computer screen with scrunched eyes. "Well, hello, you. You look like you've been on vacation."

He has no idea.

"I feel like I haven't seen you forever," he says, rolling his chair back. "I can't believe you were stuck for a week."

"*I know*." I toss my keys into my purse and sip my coffee, which is not as good as the one Colby makes. Oh, what I would give to be eating eggs and bacon at Colby's table, looking outside at that beautiful forest, and sneaking Kona chunks of cheese under the table. "I feel like a completely different person."

"Yep, yep," he says, strumming his fingers and staying silent for so long I feel like tossing a pen at his head.

"What?" I say, but dammit. I can't hide the grin. And maybe I shouldn't. Colby makes me smile. But even more than that, *I* make myself smile. I handled a week in near isolation, alone with my thoughts, worked through so much stuff, and came out the other side happier and healthier.

"Something is *really* different about you."

Everything is different about me. "Honestly, a lot of stuff happened this past week that needed to happen for years. I processed so much pent-up shit. I swear it was like I was at a mindfulness retreat or something."

He cocks his eyebrow. "*And?*"

Well, darn my cheeks blushing. I slide my chair up to the desk, log on to the computer, and absolutely avoid my cousin's ultra-invasive gaze. "*And*... Colby and I bonded. We spent so much time just talking and existing in the same space. She's kind of amazing."

"Wow," Leo says and slides his chair up to the desk. "You're not your typical weirdly giddy self when you meet someone. You look—"

"Grounded." Which is not only the only term I can think of that accurately describes what's happened to my insides, it's a state of being I wasn't actually sure I'd ever achieve. And my God, it feels *nice*.

"Grounded. Yes. Good word," he says. "Okay, tell me everything that happened. Except for... you know." He scrunches his nose and this time I actually do throw a pen at him. "Just be prepared the next time when we go out, Emma will want a play-by-play of everything you're telling me now, so you're going to have to repeat yourself. You know my girlfriend... she lives for details. So, start with the day you got stuck out there."

I suppress a grin. Leo blames the need for intel on his girlfriend, but he's more gossipy than a prayer circle.

Where do I even begin? More snow than I've ever seen—which is saying a lot since we live in Minnesota. Breaking every muscle in my body by chopping wood. A freaking bear. The hottest woman alive saving me from said bear. Falling hard for someone in a pretty short, intense amount of time. Feeling supported and cared for more than I ever have before. The list is pretty endless.

I don't want to compare Zoey and Colby. It's not fair to either of the women. But Zoey and I were so deeply independent in our relationship. We supported each other, of course, but not like what I've seen with Colby. It feels so different. More mature somehow. More equally dependent. I have to laugh-cringe that I took that stupid podcast's advice last year and tried to win Zoey back. Honestly, I don't know what I was thinking. And had that ridiculous advice worked, I would have never met Colby.

But even more than the disastrous event last year with Zoey, there were a lot of things in the past that make me wonder what I was thinking. Decisions I made that were not in my best interests. Starting with pushing myself so hard to get distracted, to run, from myself and my memories, when really, I just needed to stop, learn, accept.

Is it possible to find myself in a week? Probably not under normal circumstances. But I suppose those who go on wellness retreats and spiritual journeys do it in less time than that. I think I just finally discovered what it is that I'm looking for, and it's not a thing, or a person. What I was looking for was a release, a shedding of my past skin, of renewal.

And I finally got it.

In between clients, I tell Leo as much as I'm comfortable with. Does he really need to know that yesterday was some of the best sex I've ever experienced in my life? Nope. But I can share how cathartic it was to know that I genuinely don't need to give my dad any more of my mental energy, but also that it's okay if I do. I'm not running from it anymore, I'm not pretending it didn't happen, I'm not pushing away any memories. If some pop up, I'll work through them.

The hardest thing for me to articulate, because I know how it will sound to an outsider, is that everything has changed. And I never want them to go back to the way they were before.

TWENTY-SIX
COLBY

The bakery bell jingles against the glass and even before the warm whoosh of baked goods scent floats to my nose, I salivate. I have never related more to Pavlov's dog than I do at this very moment.

Zoey looks up from behind the display case and pushes her chunky frames back up her nose. "Hey, Colby!" she says, waving. "Did you survive the winter storm?"

Um. Yes. Not only survived it but absolutely praying for another one. Maybe it could last for a month next time, or a year. Something that would keep Josie at my place, wrapped in my arms, naked in my bed. Enough time where we can test out the hot tub, and shower, and next to the fireplace and... "I did," I say with a smile. "I can't believe how intense it was. And in April, for Pete's sake, huh?"

She can read it on my face, I'm sure of it. She knows I spent the week with her ex-girlfriend, the best week I've had in six years, and she's going to completely bust me. Not that I have anything to hide, at all, but there is the tiniest bit of me that feels like I might be stepping on some toes.

"You getting your usual?" Zoey asks, already grabbing the tongs.

I pull my lips into my mouth. Yes, I love routine. I live for routine. And I'm pretty sure that Zoey knows this. After coming here for six years, with the exception of last week, I rarely deviate. "Actually, why don't you do a variety pack. Six things, whatever you think I might like."

Zoey's brows lift beneath her frames. "Oh gosh, wow. Okay, let me think... Shaking things up, huh? *Again.* It's like a whole new you." She holds the tongs over the bakery items and finally adds a few macaroons, cookies, and a scone. She glances at me with a sheepish grin. "And... if you're sharing this with Josie, you might want to go with the pistachio cream cupcake."

Well, she called it out. No more avoiding the conversation. If I were back in my hometown of Fort Lauderdale, I wouldn't even have a conversation. I'd simply find a new bakery, no matter how much I like Zoey, and probably never see her again. But small-town Minnesota is different. Even as much of a hermit I was (am), it's inevitable that I'd run into Zoey somewhere in town. And besides, from a purely sugar-addicted self-preservation stance, there is no chance I'm letting anything get in the way of me and her baked goods.

I nod at the pistachio cream cupcake suggestion, and she adds it to the box. "Is this weird?" *God, I hope it's not weird.*

My fears disappear with her smile. "Not at all. At least not for me," she says as she tapes up the box and carries it to the register. "Are you two..."

I chew the inside of my lip, and God, there is no way she doesn't read the smile that I'm trying to hide. "I'm not really sure what we are. But I know that I like her." *A lot.*

"I am so happy for the both of you," she says as she blows her black fringe back from her face and rings up the items. "You two are such great people, who both deserve all the happiness. I'm so glad you found your way to each other, however that looks."

Zoey is good with this, I'm good with this, I don't need to seek out a different bakery... I hand her my credit card and breathe out a sigh of relief. "How are you and Quinn?"

"Amazing, actually." She holds up her left hand and twinkles her fingers.

"Ah, Zoey! It's beautiful," I say, peeking at the emerald cut ring. "Congratulations. When's the date? How's the wedding planning going?"

"September," she says. "And thank you. We're *so* excited. Between us, the wedding planning has been interesting." She laughs. "Kind of the easiest thing in the world. We're going to do it at Quinn's tree farm, her sister-in-law Morgan already has a binder the size of a wedding cake filled with every detail, her sister, Frankie, is taking pictures... I'm just sort of stepping back, nodding, and smiling. I swear after running my own business all these years, it's blissful, letting everyone else take the reins."

After we chat a little bit more, I tell her I need to get home and back to Kona, since this is the first time she's been alone, and refrain from saying something super awkward like I'm glad I have her blessing to move forward with Josie.

Because every second that passes, every breath I'm breathing, every freaking heartbeat, I know this is what I want. To move forward. With Josie.

One the way home, I stop at the light when I feel my phone vibrate.

JOSIE

Sleeping alone last night was the worst. I'm absolutely taking you up on the offer to come back to your place for the night.

If I thought that smelling baked goods turned me into Pavlov's dog, it pales in comparison to the flutters that run rampant in my stomach and beeline to my core from this one single message. I didn't like waking up this morning and not having Josie in the house. Sure, she's only slept in my bed once, but now that I've had it, I want it again.

With Amelia, I was never codependent. We had such independent lives, work, friends. Sometimes we even took weekend trips without each other. So, it takes me a moment to process if all these new sensations are codependency or not, but it's not. It's simply knowing that I prefer having Josie here than not having her here. And something about that feels wonderful.

Back at home, Kona is clearly less worried about me leaving her than I was. She peeks up from her nap, more annoyed that I woke her up than anything, then closes her eyes again to continue her mid-morning snooze. I fill up my water bottle, then head to the recording studio.

I have to record at least two episodes this week to make up for what I missed, and there are a ton of unread emails and DMs to my account. Which is fine. I'm allowed to take a week off just like anyone else. Just because I haven't taken any time off since I've started this show, I don't think my listeners would think any differently of me if I do.

The headphones feel different today than last week. Heavier maybe? Almost uncomfortable. I take them off, adjust the height, and finally set them to my side. I tap on the list of emails I had earmarked a while ago for this next recording. A husband convinced the wife likes the dog more (might be true), a burned-out mom feeling the husband might like video games more (also might be true), work flirting going too far, a wife that's becoming a little obsessed with the sapphic romance books she's reading and comparing her own wife to the ones on the page.

Oof. There's a lot to go through. I swallow and slide on my headphones. "Hey there! Welcome to *Love 'Em or Leave 'Em*, I'm your host, Ruby Reanne." My voice cracks, sounding unnaturally off-key. Something doesn't feel right. I hit stop on the recording, take a sip of water, shake out my limbs, and try again.

And I fail, once again, to sound like the Ruby Reanne that I've cultivated. *Shit.*

I know what it is. Although I still stick by my thought process that this is my private creative space, that I don't owe anyone my real name, that I say at the beginning of my show that I have no professional credentials whatsoever in the relationship department, there's a layer of deception happening here. But... shouldn't people be listening for entertainment? I mean, honestly. When I listen to podcasts made by the Brené Browns of the world, I take their advice to heart because they're researchers with credentials and letters behind their name. When I listen to other shows whose hosts are actors, football players, or comedians, I know it's entertainment. So really, others should be looking at my podcast with the same critical eye, and I can't help it if they're not.

Right?

And along those same lines, I still don't know if I need to tell Josie about it. Do authors with pen names tell their partners? Not that Josie is my partner... yet... I don't think... but are you really obligated to share something like this? I honestly don't know. I'm trying to think of my own advice—my Colby advice, not my Ruby advice, and I'm coming up blank. God, if she never heard of the show, it'd be so much easier. And if she never followed some terrible advice from the show and got humiliated, this would really be a hell of a lot easier.

So, am I not telling her because this is my private life, and I'm keeping it as such? Or because I didn't tell her before, and I let her open up to me, and didn't stop her when she told me how this show pushed her into a humiliating situation? Or am I not telling her because I'm scared that I messed something up for her, and she'll be mad?

I take off my headphones and retie my ponytail. I'm trying to justify all of this in my head, but really, I think I know deep down that I need to come clean. But we *just* started this relationship, and God, I don't want to do something to screw it up. I'm getting the tiniest slice of happiness pie after all this time, and the very, very last thing I want to do is have it end prematurely.

She's happy. I'm happy. It's not fair for me to ruin this for her because I feel the need to clear my conscience. *Right? Right.*

I clasp my fingers on the nape of my skull and tap. Everything changed yesterday with Josie. I want to go down this path, see where it leads me, where it leads *us*, and take a chance on something both terrifying and potentially wonderful.

But there's something I need to do first. Something that I've needed to do for a long time but didn't have the strength. My breath feels tight against my throat as I pull back on my headphones and move to my journal.

"Hey, Amelia," I say into the recording. "Well, Josie and I…" I trail off. Yes, again, I know that I'm just speaking into a recording, and not actually to Amelia, but she doesn't need all of the details. "Anyway, she's so wonderful, you know? When you died, I really didn't think there would be anyone else. I was prepared to spend my life alone. I spent six years of my life, just knowing that my fate was sealed the day you died, and it would be me, alone in my grief, in my solitude, until I joined you in the afterlife. And now… I think this is the start of something really amazing with Josie, and everything that I've thought since that day in the hospital has shifted."

My lips tremble and stinging tears well behind my eyes. I swipe at a few that trickle down my cheek and swallow. My chest is hurting at the same rate it's healing. The rips in my heart that I've carried all these years feel like they're finally suturing.

The image of Amelia's face starts to pixelate and haze. I close my eyes and picture myself hugging her at the ocean. The waves crash around us, the seagulls fly high, and I'm squeezing Amelia as tight as I can. She's hugging me back, her mouth at my ear. "It's okay, Colby. Time to let me go. I'm okay, and you're okay."

I sob into my hands and speak into the recording. I'm terrified of truly letting this piece of me go, but I need to. It's no longer fair for me to hang on to Amelia, and it's not fair to anyone I may want to be with to have her ghost lingering over us.

I'm crying so hard now that I hear Kona patter down the hall and stand outside the door. I cry for my wife who's gone, for the relief that her memory stayed with me for so long, for the freedom I feel knowing that I am finally at peace with what happened.

The air in my lungs sputters with the sobs, but my chest lifts with the release. "I need to let you go, Amelia. You've been with me this whole time, and I'm going to miss you. Fuck, I'm going to miss you so much. You were my first love, the one that captured and held my heart, and you will always have a piece of me."

Tears stream down my face and I swipe them off my chin. Everything in me knows that this is time. A closing of a door while a new one opens. "Thank you for being there with me while I hung on to you, but I'm ready now. This will be my last recording to you." My chin trembles and I pull in air until my sobs stop and my heartbeat evens.

"I love you. I will *always* love you," I say into the laptop. "But now I'm ready to love someone else. Goodbye, Amelia."

TWENTY-SEVEN

JOSIE

These blankets are everything. Truly. I need to ask Colby where she bought them, because I need them for my place. Although, that might be a waste since it's been three weeks since I slept at my own place. I can't believe a month has passed since I was first stranded here, and *I know, I know*, it sounds like a cliché, but every single day it keeps getting better.

I grin at a rosy-cheeked, heavily sleeping, *fucking beautiful* Colby and snuggle into her. That first day when I came back here, the moment her lips met mine, everything felt right. Everything still feels right. I'm not in some infatuation haze. I'm in deep admiration of the woman that Colby is, the way she has opened up to me, and the safety and trust I feel when I'm around her. If I could stay like this forever, I think I would.

Lips press into the top of my head, and a moment later, Colby shifts and wraps her warm legs around me. My God, can this woman cuddle. It's so yummy I never want to sleep any other way. "Hey, you," I say, blinking up. "Did I wake you?"

Of course I did. I think I'm single-handedly adjusting Colby's sleep schedule to meet mine. I feel kind of bad that for years she's slept in late, and now she sees me off when I go to work. At night, I've told her she can stay up even though I have to go to sleep to be ready for work in the morning. But she just gives me a look and says, "Absolutely not," and climbs into the bed with me and snuggles.

Okay, we do other things first, and *then* we snuggle.

"No, you didn't wake me," she says sleepily. "I was just about to get up."

"You're a terrible liar," I say, grinning, wiggling my ass tighter into her lap.

"Even though it's Sunday, we can skip the confessional and head straight for the hot tub." Colby kisses my neck, and just like the hundred times she's kissed me this last month, my skin erupts with tingles. "What do you think?"

"Mmm... I love the sound of that," I say. "Coffee first, though. And then a walk if you're okay with that?"

"You never have to ask. I'm *always* okay with that," Colby says as she slowly slides out of bed. "I love that you take your walkabouts."

I do, too. As much as possible, in almost any weather, I walk Colby's property. On the weekends, sometimes Colby and Kona join, but most often I like to go by myself, often for hours until my hungry belly nudges me back to Colby's. Of all the things that were missing in my life, my connection to nature was one of the biggest. Every time I'm out here, in the open land, I learn a little bit more about myself.

Once we get out of bed, Colby goes into the shower while I take Kona outside for a quick walk and potty break. This girl is healing so well that soon enough I feel like she'll want to take a jog with me. Once I bring her back to the house, I grab a few snacks and the bear spray and head out for my hike.

The air is still a little crisp, but it carries a hint of the warmth to come. Everything smells green. Invigorating. From the moss-filled trees to the way the earth squishes beneath my feet to the buds on branches that just a month ago were weighed down with snow, it feels like spring is finally here.

I fill my lungs, my nose stinging with the sharp air, and start walking down the path. I'm intentional at first, taking in the sounds of the birds chirping, the twigs snapping under my feet, the whistling of the breeze against the pines, until my mind relaxes. It's my favorite part of my hike—the moment when I realize that time has passed and I have no idea what I've been thinking about. These moments are the most cathartic for me, healing bits and pieces step by step. I nearly make it to the creek when I reach back in my bag and... *crap*. Before I even unzip, I know that I left my water bottle sitting on the kitchen counter. Ugh. I'm only half a mile away, so I turn around and head back to the house to grab it.

Inside, it's quiet. No Colby, no Kona, no sounds emitting from anywhere. "Colby?" I call out. *So odd*. Did they go on their own walk? I grab my water bottle off the counter, when I hear a noise coming from Colby's office. I move to the door and knock. "Colby?"

Shuffling sounds behind the door, and a moment later, she cracks it open. "Hey," she says with a blush to her cheeks. "Everything okay?"

"*Ooh*... the elusive office. I've always been curious what's behind this mystery door." I glance behind Colby to get a better look. Is she trying to block me from seeing behind her? She's hesitating, and I get the distinct feeling that I'm invading on her private space. She's a little bit of a clean freak and maybe this is messy. Does she think I'd care if it was messy? Oh, I love learning everything about her, including a closeted messy space. Honestly, I should probably back away since she's blocking me, but after a moment, she steps back and opens the door wide.

Wow. This place looks like a recording studio. There's black foam boards all over the walls and ceiling, a microphone attached to a boom arm, two huge monitors, and two laptops. "Dang. This looks like I just stepped into a hacker movie. Are you a spy? Those monitors are bigger than my TV." I'm exaggerating, of course, but they are pretty damn big. "You do all your editing in here?"

Her throat rolls with a swallow and she nods. "Yep."

Did the room just get a little warmer, the air a little thicker, or am I imagining things? "I seriously thought that you never let me in here because it held a wall of highchairs that held life-size dolls or something." I scan her wide desk, the dark leather office chair, the Post-it notes strewn across the screen. "Are you working today? Sorry, I didn't know. I can leave you be."

She waves her hands, and I swear it looks like she's avoiding my eyes. "No, no, it's fine. I was just cleaning up some things since I thought you were taking a longer walk." Her cheeks flame and she shifts on her feet, and it's so painfully obvious that she doesn't want me here. I try to push away the ickiness. Maybe this is the way I'd be if she suddenly showed up at my work unexpected. I'm not sure what editing all entails, but it might be one of those jobs where if you break the flow, it takes you twenty minutes to get back into the swing of things.

Ugh. I totally messed up her flow.

"Is everything okay?" she asks as she stuffs her hands into her front hoodie pocket. "Why did you come back early?"

Now I'm feeling my cheeks heat. We're still going through the getting-to-know-everything-about-you phase. I'll have to add this to my list to tell her that if she needs quiet time to edit, she just needs to shoot me a text, so I don't go stomping around the kitchen and ruin her vibe. "Yep, everything's good. Just forgot my water and didn't want to drink from the creek, which, if I remember correctly, you told me was not a good thing to do."

She grins. "Yes, dear God, please don't." She gives me a kiss and a pat on the ass, and I instantly feel better. "I'll finish this up and be ready for the hot tub by the time you get back."

I end up walking for almost two hours and only drag myself back to the house when my limbs are in danger of falling off. When I return, I'm famished. Which apparently is perfect, because the moment I step into the house, I'm not sure what hits me first—the sound of a sizzling skillet or the mouthwatering smell of butter, lemon, and basil.

"Mmmm..." I say, coming up behind Colby—who's whisking away at the stove—and kiss her neck. "What do you have going on here?"

She leans back into my touch, but keeps stirring. "I was hungry for lemon basil chicken pasta."

"You were hungry for my favorite meal?" I laugh. "God, you're amazing. And I would totally take advantage of you right now and show you exactly *how* amazing you are, but I'm a sweaty mess, so will have to wait. I'm going to hop in the shower."

She chuckles and adds a dash of pepper to the pan. "I will gladly take a post-shower rain check. Take your time. Lunch will be ready when you get out."

I pat Kona's head on the way down to the bathroom, strip my clothes, and hop into the shower. The heated stream beats down on my limbs, and I take my time doing a full loofah scrub. Among all the things that Colby has shown me, the African net loofah might just be my favorite. I start to rinse off when the bathroom door opens, and a moment later a naked Colby steps in behind me.

"*Mmmm...*" I say as my eyes close and she wraps her arms around me. "This is a nice surprise."

Her hands splay across my stomach, and she presses her lips against my shoulders and back.

"Are you going to burn the lunch?" I whisper, kind of not caring in this moment if the lunch is burned because, Christ, her hands are magical. She slides up, cups my breasts, and gently plays with my nipples in the absolute exact way that makes me melt.

Her lips meet the back of my ear. "I would never make a rookie mistake like that," she whispers, keeping one hand on my breast, and sliding the other lower to my center. "I removed it all from the heat."

I turn over, meeting my lips with hers. I will never, ever get sick of kissing this mouth. She holds me tight, kisses me deeply, gently pushing her tongue against mine. God, this woman. How did I get so lucky? I thought when Zoey and I were done that I'd never meet anyone else that I considered "my person."

I was wrong.

Colby slides her leg between mine and props it up on the shower bench, guiding me to rock against the wet, smooth skin. My pulse grows with the friction of my core against her knee, and her fingers circling me. The steam from the shower, my heavy breaths, and my moans saturate the air. She latches on to my nipple while holding my ass steady, and keeps gliding me back and forth. Urgency builds in my body, turning into a fever, and soon, I shake and collapse against her, my chest rising and lowering against hers.

This whole month, these walks, being in here now as Colby is holding me and coaxing me through my orgasm is almost too much. I cup her cheeks and press my mouth against hers, overtaken with feelings and emotions and gratitude. There are so many things uncertain in this world, but I know one thing is true.

Colby is the one who makes me sing.

TWENTY-EIGHT

COLBY

Fuck.

As I lie here with Josie wrapped in my arms, her legs tangled in mine, her breaths sleepy and heavy, I stare at the glow-in-the-dark stars on my ceiling. The guilt is officially killing me. She's asked about my job before—of course because that's what normal, healthy couples do—and I keep avoiding telling her the truth. I make enough vague comments to ease my conscience, using words like "editing" and "it's so boring if I told you the details you'd keel over" and "I basically just answer emails." But I know in my heart that this is not truthful, and I need to put a stop to the dishonesty.

Earlier today when Josie stepped into my office, I almost had a panic attack on the spot. I completely froze. I teetered between telling her the truth, and making up some insane story about working for someone famous and having to sign an NDA. Thankfully, she was in the middle of her walk and left before I had a chance to do something really stupid and make up an even bigger lie.

This is eating me alive. I've opened up to Josie about every-thing, but this show is the final thing keeping me tethered to the life I once had, and I'm sure, deep down, Josie can feel this. *I* can feel this. The only reason I was even in the recording studio is because I'm so behind schedule and was hoping I could cram in a short episode during her walk. During the day, when Josie's at work, I've been sitting down to record and choke. My entire motto of "keeping things real" for this podcast is that I do minimal editing, and rarely censor myself. This formula has worked incredibly well, not only allowing me to build my audience, but allowing me to feed those hungry listeners by cranking out a few episodes a week.

But now, it's taking me days to record even one episode because I can't stand the way I sound. I end up breaking my golden rule and re-recording over and over until I get it right. Since Josie came into my life, I can only stomach answering one question at a time. The listeners are chiming in, noticing I've cut the shows to half the length and asking why I'm using so many encore episodes. And listeners are like toddlers—if you don't keep them constantly stimulated, they will quickly burn out and move to the next show. Once that happens, it'll only be a very short amount of time before my sponsors start pulling out and I lose my ad dollars.

The bed shakes as Josie rolls to her side, and I fight the urge to snuggle up next to her. I want to, I always freaking want to, but I need to think about what I'm doing, and if I snuggle, my mind will get lost in her scent, in her soft hair tickling my chest, in the warmth of her skin, and not in the decision I need to make.

I should just open up and tell her the truth. I trust her with my secret, of course. She won't tell anyone about my real identity, I'm sure of it. But what I *don't* trust is what she might say about me withholding this secret from her during our time together. I'm not naive. I understand our relationship is in its infancy, and pretty fragile. If I tell her the truth, are we strong enough to survive? But if I don't... what's the alternative? I just lie to her for the rest of my life? I blink at the ceiling and release a slow exhale. I pride myself on being logical and calm, and I'm absolutely spinning.

God, I don't want to do this, but I don't know what to do. I flip the pillow to the other side to cool my head, and finally, around 3:00 a.m., with my eyes burning with fatigue, I slide out from the bed, grab a robe, and tiptoe down to the office. It's so late, even Kona stays in the room rather than following me. I really don't know what to do, but I know that I need to get this off my chest and sleep is out of the question.

The office door clicks softly behind me. I grab a light blanket from the basket next to the office chair and drape it over my lap. I haven't done a digital journal since I said goodbye to Amelia, and I need something to help me sort out the chaos in my brain. Tonight —this morning—whatever time it is, I keep my headphones off so I can hear if Josie approaches.

My fingers hover over the laptop. I take a breath and tap record.

"Hey. I don't know who I'm addressing this recording to anymore since it's not Amelia, but it feels weird to address it to myself. So, for now, I guess I'll just pretend this is whatever entity that might be out there, helping to guide me." I rub the back of my neck. "I'm so lost as to what to do. After all these years, I've found the person who has opened me up to the idea of a future. A *real* future. I've fallen for Josie in such a beautiful, deep way, and I'm so fucking scared it's going to end. I need to tell her about the show. *Of course* I need to tell her. But will she understand why I kept this from her? How do I really explain the reasons why I withheld this massive part of my life? The idea that she'll be upset with me, or worse, makes my stomach knot so hard I feel like I'm going to puke. I never, ever thought that I'd find anyone I care about again after Amelia, and now that I have, I can't bear the idea of it being stripped from me again."

I keep talking for the next hour into the journal, contemplating just letting the entire podcast go and finding a different job. The show used to bring me joy. Or, at minimum, used to dull the pain of losing Amelia enough where I equated it with joy. But it's not filling me anymore. I never once thought of it as a job, even though it's pretty lucrative. But now it absolutely feels like a job.

Although I said that my show and advice was there for entertainment purposes only—and I still hold on to that belief—there's a part of me that did hope I was helping people. But honestly, who the hell am I to think that? Even though some listeners follow up with thank-you emails for my advice, I don't know what I'm doing. I don't think I've known what I'm doing for a long time. What I know, however, is that I'm living a lie, and even as hard as it may be, I need to come clean.

I stay in the recording studio until my eyes can no longer hold open, until the morning sun breaks through the windows, until all of the words are out of my body. The journaling helps, as it always does, and it's so clear what I need to do. I close the office door, step down the hall, and crawl back into bed.

When I tug the covers over me, Josie rolls over and rests her head against my chest. "Is everything okay?" she asks with a raspy, sleep-filled voice.

I kiss her head and breathe in her warm scent, but stay silent. What am I supposed to say? Continue lying and say everything is fine? Tell her no, and wrestle her out of sleep? Potentially crush her first thing on a Sunday morning, and pray that she doesn't leave me?

My heart thuds in my chest and I blink at the glow-in-the-dark stars, praying that the clarity I received in the office was wrong, and I don't, in fact, need to tell her the truth. But when I don't say anything for so long, Josie lifts herself from the cuddle position, props on her elbows, and searches my eyes.

She can see it on my face, I'm sure, because a moment passes, then two, when she lifts herself to sitting and tugs the blanket up to her chest. The morning sun illuminates her from the window. Pillowed sleep lines crease on her rosy cheeks, and she tugs her lower lip into her mouth. "Colby, what is it? What's wrong?"

I want to tell her everything, but I don't know where to start. I don't even know how to start.

"Did I do something wrong?" she says, her morning voice cracking.

The nerves catch in my throat and the only thing I can do is shake my head. Finally, I suck in a breath. "No. God, no," I finally say. God, I don't want to do this. Please, please can a storm crackle through the home? Can the floor open up and suck me into the cellar? The air in the room has vanished and left nothing but ash. I swallow back needles pricking in my throat and close my eyes. I have to do this now. There's no more waiting, no more hiding.

"Josie..." I whisper as I tug my hand out of her reach. "There's something I need to tell you."

TWENTY-NINE

COLBY

Josie's wide, expectant, beautiful brown eyes are looking into mine after I just said there was something I needed to tell her. And then followed that bombshell up by remaining totally silent. My stomach is so tight I think I'm going to throw up. I'm looking at those pale cheeks still flushed with sleep, the blankets tucked around her naked body, and when I open my mouth up to speak, I freeze.

"What is it?" she asks, stroking her thumb against my hand. "Whatever it is, you can tell me. I'm here, okay?"

God, this is so fucking hard. Why does she have to be so wonderful? This would be a hell of a lot easier if she were a snappy, terrible human. I exhale a shaky breath and twist the corner of the bedsheet in my palm. "When Amelia died, I was so broken. I couldn't accept that she was gone, that I'd never talk to her again, or listen to her voice or hear her stories. And... I needed a way to connect with her. I wanted to find a passion... a hobby... something that helped me forget that she was gone."

Josie nods, her eyes filled with understanding and confusion. "Okay? I completely understand that. You lost your wife so suddenly that it makes sense that you'd seek out something to ease that pain. I didn't lose my wife, and I still tried every hobby in the world to replace the spark I was missing."

Right. Okay, this is good. My chest settles. Maybe she can relate my need to do this podcast to how she described spending years searching for hobbies to fill the void of her father leaving the family. "So, I searched and searched, and tried different things, and just wasn't finding anything that made me keep her spirit alive." I swallow and go back to twisting the blanket. "And, well, have you heard of how some writers have pen names?"

Her eyebrows scrunch together. "Ah… yes, of course."

She looks confused. Never mind the fact that it's six in the morning, she's only been awake for a few moments, and everything coming from my mouth is nothing how I intended. "Why do you think they would do that?"

She hesitates for a long moment. "This is a really weird line of questioning." She yawns into her shoulder and snugs the sheet a little tighter across her chest. "I suppose that they want to be private. Maybe it helps them be more creative? Or maybe their name is Mary Smith or something, and they think, I don't know, Genevieve Gold McQueen sounds better on a cover. Why?"

I should tell her that I'm delirious with lack of sleep, don't know what I'm saying, and we should just crawl back under the sheets and go back to sleep, because I don't want to do this. *My God*, I don't want to do this. My hand shakes as I tuck a piece of hair behind my ear. "I, um, in my day job, I actually use a fake name. For most all those reasons. I mean, I think Colby Jackson is a perfectly fine name, but I need some anonymity to be able to… spark… a certain level of creativity and freedom."

Josie cocks her head, then slowly nods. "When you say you are a 'digital editor,'" she says, air quoting the words *digital editor* that I've used before, "does that mean you make sex videos or something? Just so you know, there is no judgment here. Seriously. You do whatever makes you happy."

The breath that leaves my body feels like the first full one I've taken for weeks. Yes, *of course*. Josie is one of the most easygoing, nonjudgmental, open-minded women I have ever met. I don't know why I didn't latch on to this right away. God, this woman is amazing. "No, no videos," I say with a quick grin. "But I do make content."

"No way. Like what?" she says. "Feet videos? You do have freakishly cute toes, and I'm not even a toe person. I bet you could make a ton of money off of those babies."

And now, I'm back to feeling like I want a crater to suck me in whole. I'm just stalling at this point and need to come out and say it. My insides are raging, my pulse so loud in my head that I feel like I can't hear anything. "I make a podcast. I'm, uh, I *host* a podcast."

Josie's face flushes. A moment passes, then two, as she cocks her head. "That's so cool! Why wouldn't you just tell me that? Honestly. I used to love podcasts, I mean before that whole shitshow scenario. Whatever, doesn't even matter. Even if it is like a bunch of fandom *Star Trek* people, I wouldn't care. You know that right? This right here"—she draws a box around herself—"is a judgment-free zone. Unless it is about the dolls. Because those are seriously freaky. Actually, nope. You know what? Even *with* the dolls, you do you. I want to listen to it! What's the name of the show?"

I can't look at her. I can't look at her face, at her eyes, at the innocence that is surely flushing her cheeks right now, because she doesn't get it. I've withheld so much from her. She has opened up about everything, and I didn't come out and tell her that last year, I caused her to go through the deepest humiliation she's felt in her adult life. My chin trembles. Tears well behind my eyes, and I blink them away.

"Oh shit. Colby? Seriously. You can tell me anything." She tugs my hands from the death grip they are currently wrapped in on the bedsheet and squeezes. "It's okay. Really."

I gnaw on the inside of my cheek, then lower my chin. "I host the *Love 'Em or Leave 'Em* show."

A quick smile, almost like she's going to giggle, forms. I see it all pass through her sweet face. The way her eyes dash between mine. The way she's smiling, the way she clearly thinks I'm joking. One moment, two, then three follow when her smile drops and she gulps. She shakes her head. "No. No, that's not true... There's no... You? *You're* Ruby Reanne?"

I swallow back all the shame and fear that's been building in me. My chest feels like an elephant is sitting on it, my neck feels like a boot's pressed against it. I can't breathe. The air is so thick and heavy that I feel like I'm going to choke. *Please don't leave.* "I'm Ruby Reanne. I mean, it's more like a character I play, but..." I swallow a boulder lodged deep in my throat. "But yes. That's me. Ruby's... me."

Josie drops her hand, slow at first. Hesitant. Then she rips it away, pushes herself back from me, and levels a gaze. She's silent. She's so freakishly, eerily, *sickly* silent that my face and body inflame. I need her to say something. Now, anything. Yell, snap, laugh, ask questions. *Something.*

"I've never told anyone this," I say, wanting to reach out and touch her but refrain. My stomach hurts, my chest hurts, my heart hurts. The way she's looking at me—squinted eyes, dropped mouth, the sleepy blush in her cheeks morphing to a dark red, makes me want to duck my head under the covers and never look up. "So, I don't want you to think that other people knew, or something, and I only didn't tell you. It's this entirely private side of mine that literally no one knows about. I started it—"

A sharp gasp leaves her lips. "Oh my God, *your wife, Amelia.*" She brings a hand to her mouth. "You... talk about Amelia."

Shit, shit, shit. "I do. I, ugh, it's like it's me, but it's not..." Ruby's relationship with "Amelia" is the basis of my show, but it's not the *real* Amelia. Ruby isn't real, either. It seems so very clear in my head, but I stammer trying to explain it to Josie. "I channel her, kind of, I guess. That personality on there is hers, not mine, so I'm Ruby, but Ruby is actually Amelia, and—"

"You talk *all the time* about Amelia. About your marriage, how amazing it is, how she's the perfect wife, how you are the imperfect wife but try to make her happy..."

The words are coming out in spurts, and she moves as far away on the bed as she can go. And I can't deny what she's saying, or pretend that she has it wrong, because she's right. And even if I wanted to play it off, or pretend I haven't spent the last six years talking about Amelia on every show, she could do an easy search and know that I lied. Again.

Josie is gnawing on her cheek so hard that I'm worried she's going to draw blood. Her eyes bore into mine, and I feel that heat on my face spread to my chest. "Have you recorded shows since we've been together?"

I'm going to pass out. "Yes."

Her eyebrows cinch together. "And do you still talk about your wife, Amelia? Do you still talk like you're married to her?"

There is officially no air left in this room. I hook my finger against the robe collar and tug on the noose. The way she is asking me this, like she's both furious but holding on to a linger of hope, makes my gut plummet. The show's always been a show, a characterization, fiction. But there's no way to explain this in a way that doesn't sound truly awful.

"Yes." I say this barely above a whisper, and now that the words have been released, I can only imagine the level of betrayal Josie must be feeling. The way we've bonded, the way she's shared everything with me about her past, and her father, and her relationships. The way we share our bodies, and hearts, there's no way to justify the fact that I've withheld this from her.

"I think... I think I need to leave." Josie stands from the bed, dragging the sheet with her and holding it around her body.

Panic floods my system. "Wait. Hang on. Please just hear me out for a second." She can't leave. We have to talk this out. If she leaves, she may never come back, and I cannot entertain a world where that happens. "I've kept this private for a reason. And honestly, I think it's okay. A lot of people use stage names, fake names..."

"Stop." She's not harsh, but firm, and the tone cuts through the air. "This is not about using a stage name. I already thought Ruby Reanne was a stage name. I don't know anyone with the last name Reanne." Her nostrils flare as she takes a sharp breath. "This is *so* much more. And... I think you know it." She keeps herself covered with the sheet as she grabs a sweatshirt from the chair. "You help like a million people, Colby. *A million*. Your fan base is huge. You are... Your show... Everything is based on authenticity."

She's not wrong. I've spent years cultivating a persona based on truth and authenticity. And everything is a lie. I twist my fingers around the pillow as Josie grabs underwear and pants from a drawer.

"I know, I know..." *Wait*. Why is she putting on her clothes? She's not *really* leaving, right? She just said that because this is a shock and maybe she doesn't want to have this conversation naked, but she can't leave. At the end of the day, this is a podcast, and what we have is so much deeper, and she can't fucking leave. *Please*. "But I also say I'm not a doctor, or therapist, or anything. I give that warning in the beginning—"

"No one gives a shit if you're a doctor or not. That's not why they listen to you." She tugs socks on then runs her fingers in her hair. The look on her face is one that I never want to see again. The accusation, the hurt, the anger. It's emitting from her like a toxic fog. I stand to reach out for her, then sit back down under her glare. "That first night I was here, and I told you about me writing to the show, and the humiliation I felt when I followed Ruby's advice and chased after Zoey like some lost child—that was you. The entire time, that was you."

Prickles of sweat beat at the back of my neck. "I know, I know, and I just wasn't ready to tell anyone that this was me." Can she understand this? I hope? Please? I can barely meet her gaze. "I am so sorry if the advice I gave led to..."

"Stop. Please." Her chin trembles. She grips the edge of the dresser and keeps her eyes on the floor for so long that I'm not sure if we are done talking, or I should keep explaining my side, or if I should throw myself at her knees and beg for forgiveness. "That night. When I was here. I told you about the show and you fucked me anyways."

My head snaps at the harsh words. No, I mean, yes, we did, but it wasn't like that. That night, everything just happened, right? Emotions were high, and we were both searching for something, and it's not like I intentionally deceived her. She didn't ask me that night if I had a podcast or was Ruby Reanne or...

I stand to meet her, but she holds up her hand to stop me.

"You have let me come here for a month, told me how much you cared, shared your bed. We hug and talk about family, and I told you about my dad and my fears and insecurities, and the way that I never felt like I was enough." Tears well behind those eyelids, and I swear I will do literally *anything* to take them away. Lie, cheat, beg, anything. "And you haven't once even tried to tell me about this? I asked about your job, and you gave me some bullshit 'editing' line. I walked into your goddamn office, and you still didn't tell me. Never once did you think I was worthy enough to hear the truth." The tears trickle down, and she wipes them with her sleeve. "I literally feel sick."

And now I feel sick. She spins and storms out of the room. I follow her from the bedroom with Kona right at my heels as she makes her way to the living room. Oh my God, she's leaving. *No, no, no, she can't leave.* If she leaves, she won't come back, and I cannot handle her not coming back. I just found this again—a person, a deep connection, someone who makes me feel *this*—and I can't give it up. Maybe this is just an argument. Maybe this is how couples work through their differences. Dear God, please, please don't let her walk out of that door.

"Josie, I am so sorry. This show is something that is so deeply private to me. No one in the world knows. *No one.* Not my family, not my bank, no one." I want to block her hand from reaching for her purse and digging out her keys, but I don't. "Please try to understand from my perspective."

"I *am* trying. I really am. Even though it makes me sick about that first night, I can even sort of understand why you didn't say anything." She shoves her feet into her shoes and continues to swipe off trickling tears. "Keeping some things private is okay. Of course you don't have to share everything. But you are flat-out lying to and deceiving *so* many people." She tugs her trembling lips into her mouth. "You lied to *me*."

Oh God, oh God, shit. "I know I have. But it's not real, obviously. I... It's like a character, you know? A lot of people have characters that they play in media like this."

Her eyes are showing me that she absolutely doesn't care and totally recognizes that I'm grasping onto any straw I can. "It's not as easy as that, Colby. And you know it. You can't just wave something like this away. A million people are affected by your words. And not only that... you are talking about *her*. You spend like half your show talking about your wife. How do you think that makes me feel?"

Flames spread on my chest and up to my cheeks. "Please don't be jealous of Amelia," I say. "I love what you and I have—"

The heated glare she tosses me is almost too much for me to handle, and I immediately want to suck the words back in. "This is not *jealousy*, Colby. This is *deception*. Plain and simple."

"But—"

"Amelia sounds wonderful. If she were here, I bet we'd be friends," Josie says, reaching for her coat. "This is not me being some insecure girlfriend who can't handle that you were married. This is not me being in denial that you won't mourn your wife for the rest of your life. This is about you actively pretending during the day that you are married to her while sleeping with me at night."

Those words are so sharp, so painful, that if feels like she slapped me. And the worst part is, I know she's not wrong. I want to tell her she's wrong, or misconstruing everything, or being illogical about the situation. But I can't. She's not yelling, she's not fighting. She's angry, yes, but she's also calm, which is terrifying. Calm means logical. Calm means she's thinking clearly. Calm means she knows exactly what she's saying. "This is *way* more than just sex."

Josie pulls in a breath and shrugs on her coat. "For me, too. Obviously. I thought the relationship that we're building could be my future. I didn't see this ending."

Shit. No. Did she just say that she didn't see this *ending*? She doesn't mean actually ending, right? Maybe ending today? Ending for the moment while she clears her head. Ending for the day until she comes back tonight and I cook her dinner and she climbs into my bed and rests her head on my chest.

"I need to go," she says as she squats down by Kona and rubs her hand behind her ear. The way she's rubbing Kona, the way she's looking into her eyes and telling her to be a good girl, looks like a goodbye. Like an *actual* goodbye, and my chest literally feels like it's being split in half with an axe.

"Don't go, Josie, please," I say. When she stands and moves to the door, I put my palm on her arm. Hot, stinging tears build behind my eyelids and I bat them back. "This is my livelihood. Please, see this from my perspective."

"The thing is, I *am* looking at it from your perspective. But are you seeing it from mine? It feels like everything here has been a lie." Her trembling hand rests on the door handle, and she swipes back the tears again. "You've made me feel so worthless. You did not value me, or us, enough to be honest. You've had a million opportunities to tell me the truth, and you still chose not to."

When she opens the door, I consider throwing myself in front of her on the porch to stop her but instead follow her down the path to her car. The tears are flying from me now, dribbling down my cheek, but I don't stop them. "Josie, *please*."

At the car, she opens the door, and she gives me a look like maybe she has more to say, but she doesn't. When she cracks open the door, I reach for her one more time, desperate, hoping that the sensation of my hand on her arm will somehow be enough to make her stay. "Are you coming back?"

She anchors her lips between her teeth for a long moment and casts her gaze to the earth. When she looks back up, her eyes are filled with so much uncertainty and regret that I feel myself break. "Honestly, I don't know."

The car door slams, the engine starts, and soon the only sound I hear is the crunch of gravel underneath her tires. When she reaches the end of the path, I drop to my knees and bawl into my hands.

THIRTY

JOSIE

For a week, I ignore all of Colby's calls and text messages. I just can't deal with them. My brain is rumbling, trying so hard to process everything, but the wheels and chaos keep spinning. Nothing is any clearer than the day I left her house. My heart still hurts, my thoughts are jumbled, and I miss her to the deepest part of my core.

That first day she messaged and called multiple times, and I didn't respond. The next day, she sent a few messages. And then for a week, one single message a day letting me know that she wasn't going anywhere and was here if or when I wanted to talk. Three days ago, I sent her a text and asked if she would stop contacting me and she did. Just like that.

Seventy-two hours later, not one single word. And I hate the silence as much as I hated the messages.

With my legs tucked underneath me on my couch, I reread the last one she sent me before I asked for space. Again.

I swear I'm not playing games, but now I wish she would message me once more, so I know that she didn't forget about me. Because I sure as hell haven't forgotten about her.

I said I need space, and I know I should take space, but deep down, it's not *space* I'm wanting. I want to transport back to the time when I didn't know Colby lied.

My father lied. For six months, he carried on an affair, lied, and left. And of course, there's an underlying fear that I'm reliving my childhood trauma here. I don't need a therapist to tell me that I'm drawing parallels between my father's affair and Colby's deception. But it feels kind of justified. Colby hid the truth, she lied about how she spends her time, she pretends to be someone she's not for hours a day while I'm sitting at work, completely clueless.

And not only that, she talks about *a wife*. She actively talks about *a freaking wife* that she adores and does anything she can to make that woman happy. She uses examples of their relationship to teach and guide other people on how to be a better partner. And yes, I know we just started dating, and I'm not comparing myself to Amelia, but it still really fucking hurts.

During the time Colby talked about Amelia, did she think about me at all? Did she completely put me out of her brain like I was nothing? Worthless? Maybe she compartmentalizes. She said that Ruby Reanne was a character, and I get that. When actors are on set and kissing other actors, they probably don't think of their spouse back home. But my guess is that the actor's partner knows *exactly* what the hell they're doing.

And I had no idea. Every single day since I met her, I had absolutely no idea that Colby leads this secret life.

My dad had a whole other life. During the day he did whatever with that woman. At night, he hung out with the family and took me fishing, and showed me how to build fires, and I had absolutely no clue. No one did. He seemed happy. Colby seemed happy. And reconciling the similarities in those two scenarios is too much.

Since everything happened with Colby, it seems I spend all my time simply thinking. In the exam rooms, I smile at the kittens getting spayed, and the dogs getting their wellness check, and yet I'm inundated with thoughts. I bring in lab reports from a pet chicken with a terrible bronchial issue, and follow up with post-op calls, and walk through deworming medication. And yet, I can't seem to gather my thoughts enough to make any sort of decision.

I'm still upset, I'm still hurt, and I still think what Colby did was wrong. The question is, can I forgive her? Honestly, probably. What she's done isn't *unforgivable*. But can I both forgive her and allow space in my heart for us to repair our relationship? That, I don't know.

I need to process. I thought sitting in my apartment might help. I'm not running from a quiet space and forcing my brain to seek out stimuli to forget, but still, the quiet in these four uninspiring walls is not working. The longer I sit here, the more my brain rattles with scattered, nearly incoherent thoughts, the further away I get from any clarity I need. I want to be taking my walk on Colby's property, my new happy place, but that's not a smart plan for many reasons. But I do need to get out of here.

I flip my legs off the couch, throw on my tennis shoes, and grab my keys. Thirty minutes later, I roll up to a public parking space at one of the Lake Superior beaches and get out of the car.

The air is springy, carrying the trace scent of budding trees and the fresh mineral from the lake. My brain needs to fully process, and this is the place to do it. I walk the graveled, rocky path down to the lake and stare out at the endless water. The wind is a bit higher today than yesterday, making the lake roar with crashing waves that turn into the white noise I'm craving.

Along my walk, I pick up smooth rocks from the shore and shove them into my jacket pocket. My shoes squish into the sand as I travel the beach and I keep hiking until I find a huge piece of driftwood that I can sit on. It's cold, but crisp and rejuvenating, and after several long, biting lungfuls of air, my brain slowly starts to organize.

I dig a handful of rocks from my pocket and toss them into the water, mesmerized by the way the waves swallow them whole. My heartbeat slows and steadies, the muddled thoughts start to take on their own lane. Once the rocks are all tossed, I begin breaking twigs against my thighs and toss them into the water, too, one by one.

I don't want to let go of what Colby and I have. I really don't. After Zoey, I didn't think I'd ever find another woman that I could fully open myself up to like this. Sure, along the way to find Colby, I fell hard and fast for all the others, but I know in my soul that this is different. From the beginning, everything with Colby has felt different. Stable, warm, genuine. Until now. And the idea of letting this go, breaking my heart, and trying to move on again, makes my gut turn on itself.

And yet, I can't just call Colby and tell her that it's all okay. Because it's not. Do I understand why she uses a stage name? Of course I do. That is the easiest piece of this entire situation to grasp. I imagine that a lot of people in her business have some sort of stage name. But lying to me all this time and talking about Amelia like she was alive and still married to her... That, I just can't let go.

On the way home, I do something that I really don't want to do, but I need to in order to get my final piece of clarity. I pull up one of her episodes since we've been together. And then I keep driving, past my apartment, and pull up another. The episodes are shorter than what I remember, some of them encores, but it's still her. I keep driving, down the highway, listening to episode after episode, begging for this not to be reality.

She talks about Amelia in every single one.

This is not jealousy. This is me on the sidelines, feeling every sense of abandonment I felt since I was twelve years old. This is me, feeling invisible and not worthy. But now I know that I am worthy. I know in my heart that I deserve more.

And so, even though I can feel the heaviness in my heart, even though my eyes are dried and aching from crying, even though I wish it could be different, I've made my decision. I need to talk to Colby.

And let her know that we are done.

THIRTY-ONE

COLBY

By week two without Josie, I am even more miserable than the day she left. Which I didn't even think was possible. The day that Josie drove off my driveway, I don't even know how long I sat on the ground, sobbing into my hands. It was only Kona's barking from inside the house that dragged me up from my knees and back inside.

I fucked up. I *really* fucked up. And I might be considered one of the top ten relationship experts in America according to whomever the hell does these podcast surveys, but I don't have any clue how to fix this. I keep pretending that I'm a listener who wrote in, and what I would say to them, but no matter how hard I try, I can't formulate any new "Ruby" thoughts.

As I brew my second water kettle of the day, for the millionth tea of the week I'm consuming, I stare out the window at the sunshine and try to bring some in to lift my funk. But I know that even buckets of vitamin D won't erase the monstrosity inside my heart. This pain is raw, and deep, and real, and I don't know what to do with it. I'm trying to respect Josie's wishes, since she clearly doesn't want to talk to me. I'm trying not to call her every second of the day, but I really, *really* thought that we'd have talked by now.

And the fact that we haven't is making this hole in my heart gape wider by the second.

I slide open the patio door and take a seat on the swinging bench as Kona runs around the yard. I'm not sure if her leg was still bothering her, or she was missing Josie as much as me, but it took until yesterday for Kona to seem like she was fully back into the swing of things.

Billows of steam rise from the mug. I dunk the tea bag as I watch Kona terrorize a squirrel that's run up a tree. I'm breathing in so hard, trying to fill my lungs with cleansing breaths, but it's useless.

With every moment that Josie's gone, I think maybe my life will fall back into the routine I had before Josie entered my world. That somehow, this post-breakup moment will prove that I was in a haze, and not centered in reality, and maybe I misconstrued my feelings after Amelia. But I didn't. I'm not in a haze. Josie *is* my new reality. And I'm not ready for us to be done.

And yes, this situation is a little reminiscent of losing Amelia, and I can't pretend that the parallels don't exist. Sure, I've only known Josie for a short time, and I was with Amelia for years. And of course, Josie hasn't died, and we weren't married. But Josie represented a future, one that I thought I'd never have again, and having that hope stripped away from me, because of something I did, is almost too much to bear. Everything in me feels empty. Vacant. And it's not the same, it will never be the same, but it feels so similar to the fog I was in after Amelia died. I'm wandering around the house, washing dishes that I didn't use, sitting in front of the TV but not seeing what's on it, pulling out rows and rows of stitches from my blanket that I crocheted in the wrong pattern and didn't realize.

The heated tea slides down my throat, and I push my legs into the ground to swing the bench. The squeak of the chains, Kona's barking, and the faint sounds of the highway miles away are the only sounds around us. Plenty of empty space for me to think. Which I really don't want to do anymore.

"Ready to go inside, girl?" I ask Kona, who blatantly ignores me. I think she's pissed at me, too.

Ugh.

I didn't mean to hurt Josie, of course. But the silence has allowed me to do some terrible self-reflection this last week, and face some harsh truths. I think I was trying to protect myself. And part of that is okay. *Part.* I knowingly kept this persona a secret, *just in case.* Everything with Amelia blind-sided me so hard that I was left spinning. And I didn't want to be left spinning with Josie.

But what wasn't okay was building this relationship with Josie, having her trust me enough to open up the deepest part of herself, all the while knowing that I was holding back.

"Come on, girl," I say, pushing myself from the swinging bench. "Let's get a treat."

Kona finally pays attention to me at that five-letter word and follows me inside.

Once I give her a chunk of cheese, I cross the house and step into the recording booth. It has now been six weeks without a full, real episode—ever since Josie stepped into my life and changed everything. My mini-episodes and encore episodes are the only thing that have kept me afloat. But she's not here, and I am, and unless I really don't want this job anymore, I need to record.

I slide the headphones onto my ears and take a breath. "Welcome to the *Love 'Em or Leave 'Em* podcast, I'm your host, Ruby —" My voice cracks and I drop my head into my hands. I can't do this. I absolutely cannot do this. The woman I care about left me in the infancy of our relationship because of my deception on this show. I can't go back to my job, at least the way that I had it before.

My whole house feels suffocating. Even though we were just outside, I grab the leash and whistle. "Come on, girl. Wanna go for a walk?" My body may not feel like it, but I add the spring to my voice that makes Kona wag her puffy tail and dart towards me.

The temperature is nearly sixty-two today, which is almost my all-time favorite weather. Back in Florida, I would've had a sweatshirt on. Today, I tie my flannel around my waist just in case, but am pretty confident my T-shirt will be just fine once I get moving.

The smells of pine and cedar waft to my nose, and I suck in such a large breath that I start coughing. The earth is wet under my feet, the leaves are fully in bloom, rejuvenation and the promise of more greenery lingers in the air. I love this property. The space has always provided me with the comfort I need, the silence that somehow made me feel whole.

The forest bathes me in lush greens and browns. I follow the path down towards the creek, the same path that Josie loved walking, and pray that it gives me the clarity I need to move forward. I understand more than anyone how Josie was able to reconnect with nature, and it gave her the strength to release so many of the demons from her past.

And there is no doubt that keeping my identity hidden, that lying to her about the show, brought up the terrible memories of how her father lied and deceived Josie and her family. I want to reach out to her, tell her that I understand the hurt and anger, and apologize again, but I know that my words will fall flat.

Kona is wildly sniffing a trail and even though it's Dog Ownership 101 to not let her lead, I do. She drags me through the woods, searching just like me, but where she's following a scent searching for the animal, I'm trying to follow a life path, searching for answers.

What *am* I going to do? Not just Josie, but everything. My life. My career. Myself. What am I going to do? And even deeper than *what*, who? Who am I? Do I really know? Maybe everything has led me to this moment, to the point where the universe is making me rediscover myself.

For so long, I was Amelia's wife. *That* was my identity. And then I was the grieving widow. But now... who? Who is Colby Jackson, and what is the imprint that I want to leave on the world? Is it really about relationships? Entertainment? Something totally different?

By the time I reach the end of the property, I both have more clarity and less than when I started, if that's even possible. I know that I need to make some changes because the Colby I always thought I was, I don't know anymore. And there are pieces that I don't like. But what those changes are, I have no idea.

Down at the end of the property where the creek is, I take a seat on the ground and Kona plops down next to me. The sun tucks itself into the clouds, and I stare at the water sloshing against the rocks until it feels like a trance. I throw in a rock, and watch as the water ripples out in tiny circles to the edge of the shore. I inhale the coppery scent from the water over and over until I'm dizzy. Kona and I stay here for so long, resting on the ground, listening to the birds, that my butt almost becomes numb from sitting. I think. I feel. I *listen*.

I love Amelia. I always will love Amelia. But I also really, really care about Josie. I want the chance to love her. And I refuse to go down without a fight. And then, as the sun breaks through the clouds, and my butt is officially numb, and all the chaotic thoughts in my brain have ironed out, the clarity that I've been searching for appears. I know exactly what I have to do.

"Come on, girl," I say to Kona, waking her up from her sleep and gripping her leash in my palm. "Let's go get Josie back."

But it's more than just trying to get Josie back. I need this final chapter of my life closed for me. Yes, I want to make amends with Josie, almost more than anything. I miss her, I'm miserable without her, and I think she and I have a real shot at something amazing. But ultimately, this is for me. Time to reclaim my identity.

Back at the house, I refill Kona's water bowl and step inside my recording booth. My heart is pounding. Partly from the hours-long hike we took. Partly from nerves. And partly from excitement, because I know what I'm about to do is something that I should have done a long, long time ago.

I pull up my laptop and hit record.

THIRTY-TWO

JOSIE

The doomscrolling has reached a truly unhealthy level. It's been exactly two weeks since everything happened at Colby's place, and I'm struggling to not fall back into my old patterns and stuffing my time with every available activity as I can, even though the urge to not be alone with my thoughts is heavy. I miss Colby. I miss Kona. I don't want us to be done, but what can I do? I've been taking long, quiet walks every day, forcing myself to not lose this part of me no matter the level of devastation I feel, but during each walk, no matter how much I wish my pain would subside, it doesn't.

Everything hurts.

Colby hasn't reached out for a week, and damn her for being so respectful. Not a single word for seven days and even though I know that is what I asked for, I'm not sure it's what I want. This void in my heart is growing, and I *hate* it.

I scroll to yet another Reel. My phone pings with an incoming message and my breath catches in my throat when I see Colby's name on the screen. I swipe it open so fast that I worry I might have accidently deleted it.

COLBY

> I know you asked for space, and I promise I'm trying to give it to you. I sent you an email, and not sure how often you check that and just wanted you to know it's there for when you're ready to read it. I hope you are well. I miss you.

My fingers shake above the mail app. Do I want to open this? I don't think I do. I thought I already made the decision that I need to end things with Colby, but what if this email is *Colby* ending things with *me*? Panic seizes me and it shouldn't, right? Isn't this what I want? I am not the type of person who needs to break up with the other one first. I remember in high school, and then with Zoey, even when I knew our relationship was over, being terrified of initiating "the talk." I always thought it'd be easier to be on the receiving end. These last two weeks, that was the only explanation I gave myself as to why I didn't reach out and officially end things with Colby—because I wanted her to have the agency to end things with me, first. It sounded like a kind thing to do, but it wasn't. It was self-preservation. Somehow, I thought by her ending things with me, it would magically hurt less.

But who am I kidding? This *all* hurts. Ending it with her fucking hurts. Knowing she lied hurts. Not seeing her every day hurts. Not giving Kona scratches behind her ears hurts. I don't think I want to open the email. Whatever is in there is going to tear my heart wide open, and I'm not sure I'm strong enough to officially know what we had is over.

I don't know what possesses me to click on the email. Maybe an obligation to how kind Colby was during our time together. Maybe an obligation to me. Maybe curiosity. Whatever it is, I slide back into my couch and tap open the email.

Hey, Josie.

I tried to think of a million things I could do to apologize, or explain things, or try and share my side of the story. Not to get you to change your mind, but so I could hopefully provide a little peace or closure if that's what you may need. I know I do. I tried to get it out that day, but my thoughts were scattered, my guilt high, and my defense mechanisms even higher. It's funny. I feel like when it's just me and a mic, I can communicate easily. Without that crutch, it seems impossible.

I blink away from the screen. Do I want to keep reading? My mouth is parched, my throat feels like a sob is locked inside, my hands are sweating. I tug my blanket up to my waist and continue.

After Amelia died, I started a digital journal where I spoke to her almost every night. And I thought the best way to tell you what I was going through from the day I re-met you at the clinic is to actually show you what I was going through. I appreciate you, our friendship, our relation-ship, and I miss you. I miss you so fucking much it hurts. But I also completely respect your need for space.

My lips tremble and I close my eyes. Do I want space? Why does space feel so terrible? I swallow and continue reading.

At midnight, I'm dropping an unedited show. I would love if you could listen in, whenever you are ready. I miss you, but I understand your need for processing. So, after this, I won't contact you anymore. Please know that this is out of the deepest respect for you, and not some punishment or withdrawal. For whatever it's worth, thank you for sharing yourself with me for this last month. I feel so honored that you trusted me enough to give yourself to me and will regret forever that I didn't do the same. I can truly say this last month has been some of the best time of my life.

Colby

A choked sob releases with the message, and I breathe out a shaky breath. The attachment is huge. Whatever is contained in these files is the make-or-break decision for me. The real-life *Love 'Em or Leave 'Em*. The next move is squarely in my hands, and I cannot be that person that drags Colby around anymore while I decide what to do with the rest of my life. I need to cut it off altogether, or go back to her, and this decision happens now.

The zip file contains what looks like maybe twenty or so recordings. I stare at the screen like I'm contemplating whether to open or not, but I know I can't *not* open it. I don't hate Colby. And I don't hate myself. I think whatever we have is worth fighting for, but I don't know if I can get past the lying, even if what we have is worth it. Either way, both she and I deserve me taking a listen.

I take a quick sip of water, and hit play.

"Good morning, Amelia." Colby's voice sounds over the phone, and my chest immediately tightens. "I know it's been a few days, and I have a ton of things to catch you up on. So, my girl Kona is in pain. The procedure was so incredibly scary, and I wished you could've been there with me. When I took her into the clinic, I *saw* you. I mean, not you, obviously, but in a snap, I was right back to that hospital room. I was sitting on your bed pre-surgery, teasing you for being so generous to tear your rotator cuff so I could finally pitch a season in the softball league. I swear, it's like I could see you giggling back at me, convincing me I didn't suck as bad as I did, I could hear the doctor give us instructions for post-op, I could smell that almond scent of yours in your hair when I kissed your forehead. I swear, *I was right fucking there*, not in this Minnesota small-town vet clinic."

My heart immediately hurts listening to this. I remember this like it was yesterday. It wasn't even two months ago, and even though it feels like a lifetime has passed since that day, the image is still crystal clear.

"But something kind of crazy happened... I think I met a friend?" Colby's voice continues, and I hear that tone in hers, the one I've become familiar with over the last month, the one that has the trace bit of hope to it. "Well, maybe not friend since I basically screamed at her right in the middle of where she was working. But a good person. She came over here that night and helped me with Kona, and when she left, I gave her a hug."

A short chuckle escapes my mouth. My God. That day is buried into my mind, and I'll never forget it. It feels like a thousand years ago and yet I see everything. The hooded sweatshirt she was wearing, the way she stomped up to the desk so many times, the way that I thought she was a bit of an overzealous pet owner, until I understood that she was equating Kona's procedure with the one that claimed her wife. And then... Kona. *I get it.* Kona is the Lucky Charms of my adulthood. Even though I always thought I was never responsible enough to be a dog owner, I know that at its core, I never wanted to be hurt the way I was by losing Lucky Charms.

I miss Kona. I miss Colby.

I go back to listening.

"At your funeral, so many people hugged me, touched me, and I just couldn't. I equated the hugs with the loss, and I never wanted to hug anyone again. And I haven't. Not once. But then I hugged Josie, and I don't know... It felt nice. Different somehow. Can there be hope attached to a hug? Is that too new age, and all 'the universe is speaking to you' or whatever crap that you used to talk about? You know, when I'd nod and smile, and pretend I understood what reading auras and seven chakras meant? And later that night we had a few text message exchanges... and well... I think you'd really like her."

My heart swells. From day one, Colby was telling her dead wife about me. I was *worthy* of being talked about with Amelia.

I continue listening.

For hours and hours, until my eyes are groggy with fatigue, until I've paced my apartment from room to room, until I've gone from the couch, to the bed, to the table and back again. I listen to Colby tell Amelia all about me, about her struggling feelings, of being terrified to open herself up. And then tears fall down my face when she tells Amelia goodbye. I can hear it in Colby's voice. The way she cracks but is also setting herself free. There's this part of me, the friend part that is so proud of Colby that she fought through her fears to let go, and there's this other part of me that is so honored, so warm, so filled inside my soul that she let her wife go not only for herself, but for me.

I am worthy. I am enough.

It's nearly midnight by the time I finish the journal entries, and I dash to pull up the podcast app and click on the show. I stare at the screen, hitting refresh over and over until it finally pops up. And when it does, everything in me freezes.

I tap play.

THIRTY-THREE

COLBY

The headphones seem heavier today somehow. Kona is at my side, protecting me, keeping me strong. I love my girl, and am so glad she is by my side, but even if she weren't, I know this is what I have to do. This right here will affect my show as well as my life. But it is long overdue.

"Hey, everyone. Welcome to the *Love 'Em or Leave 'Em* podcast. I wanted to record a special show today, one that should have been recorded a while ago. Honestly, maybe even from the beginning. This show will be unedited, unscripted, and completely from the heart. Please feel free to skip forward through the heavy sighs and deep breaths."

I take a shaky sip of water and clear my throat.

"The question today comes from Colby Jackson from Spring Harbors, Minnesota. 'Dear Ruby, for years, I've been carrying on what some may call a double life. There was never any ill will intended, but there are people who got hurt in the process. People that I care about so deeply, good people, people who don't deserve this. And there are also others that I don't know personally but may feel betrayed. What should I do?'"

I breathe through the turning in my stomach. "Well, friends, I am Colby Jackson. Yes, you heard that right. My name is Colby

Jackson, not Ruby Reanne. For those of you who don't think this is a big deal, that this is just a name change, this goes much deeper than that."

My hands are trembling. I've just done what I've been terrified to do all of these years—shown my real identity. I've been hiding behind these headphones, double monitor, and microphone for years while running from the pain of loss.

I twist my hands in my lap and continue.

"I was married for seven incredible years to my wife, Amelia. Six years ago, Amelia died suddenly, and it shattered my world. The pain was so sudden, so crushing, so deeply devastating, and I didn't know how to channel it. So, I started this podcast as a way to keep her memory alive. The personality you hear on this show is not mine. Amelia was lively, and fun, and funny. Colby is intro-verted, quiet, and honestly sometimes kind of boring."

The room isn't hot and yet sweat needles at the back of my neck. I pick up a notebook and fan my face.

"The stories I've told about Amelia are not true. And the ones that were true were so heavily anecdotal and stretched for truth that they barely count. I'd read these messages from you all, think of how Amelia would respond to them if she were here, and then I recorded what I thought would be her answers. In my mind, I justi-fied that it was for your entertainment, and that I tell you all that I'm not a therapist, but deep down, I know damn well this was all for me. To numb myself. It became a sort of addiction to step into this fantasy space. I took you all, unknowing victims, along for the ride."

Kona shuffles at my feet and I rub behind her ears until my heartbeat slows.

"For those of you who have put your trust into me, to help navi-gate your relationships, I am *so* sorry. I have hurt you and broken your trust, and I truly am sorry."

My lips tremble and I take a deep breath.

"A while ago, I met a woman. An *incredible* woman. The type of woman that people hope to exist, pretend exists, but she's so pure and good that you don't actually think she's real. She's fearless, fun, and opened me up in a way that I didn't think possible. This woman gave me hope. Actual hope. After all these years of feeling utterly hopeless, she made me think that maybe there is an alternative universe out there, that maybe my dreams didn't die along with Amelia. And in this process, I have lied to and hurt her as well."

This feels both so terrible and terrifying, and also the most freeing thing I've ever done. I am officially diving into the ice-cold waters of the deep end and hoping that I will float to the top. Who knows what will happen after this, but one thing is for sure: I will get to live authentically, and on my own terms, the way I tout about in every episode. And this time, it's for *me*. I am authentically living for Colby Jackson—dog mom, widow, friend, human. Not Ruby Reanne.

"So, friends, as of right now, this is the final episode of the *Love 'Em or Leave 'Em* podcast, at least as hosted by Ruby Reanne and in the format that we've come to know over the years. I need to take some time and reassess; I need to hear from you, my incredible listeners, address your concerns, and see if this is something that you still want to listen to. If I come back, I will come back as me— the real Colby, the authentic one, who is struggling through my own heartache while apologizing for the pain I've caused to my loved ones. I am no longer interested in living a lie or living in the past. I am ready to live, truthfully, in reality."

I push through the forming tears and sigh.

"And to the one I hurt. You know who you are, but to protect your privacy, I am not using your name. Just know that, even if you never speak to me again, I am so grateful we met. You unlocked a piece of me that I thought was gone forever and gave me the greatest gift I could have imagined—you allowed me to dream again. I will always be indebted to you."

My heart is splitting, and the tears are flowing, thick and fat and rolling down my cheeks, but everything in me knows that this was the right thing to do. This is much deeper than trying to win my girlfriend back or apologizing after a fight. This is saying a sorry to my listeners, to the people who trusted me, and believing that whatever happens after this, I will be okay. I'm praying to God that it is enough for Josie.

Because I know right now, it's enough for me.

"All right all, I am signing off today. Maybe forever. It's been a wonderful ride, and thank you for being on this journey with me. I will miss you all. Colby."

THIRTY-FOUR

COLBY

The sunbeams pour into the skylight and even though this is normally the time I'd tug on my sleeping mask and go back to bed for a few hours, I don't. Oddly, last night after I sent the recordings to Josie, and then recorded and uploaded my final episode, I thought I'd toss and turn all night, waiting to see a response.

But something totally unexpected happened.

I fell asleep immediately.

I roll over in the bed and check my phone to see if Josie has replied, and my heart sinks that she didn't. It's okay, though. Of course, I'm heartbroken and had grand visions of her driving here in the middle of night to crawl into bed with me and profess her love, but I also know that isn't reality. I'm not even sure if she saw the email, much less listened to all the recordings or the show. And, to be true to my word, I won't contact her again and find out. She drew her boundary line, and I need to accept it, even though my heart is shattered.

"Come on, girl. Let's go potty." I slide out of the bed, throw on a sweatshirt over my pajamas, and stuff my feet into sandals.

Oh, the joy of sandals. Well, technically Crocs, because they're more practical in this terrain, but sock-less shoes after a long winter is pretty damn dreamy. With Memorial Day weekend right around the corner, the weather is absolutely glorious. That perfect mix of warmth with no humidity, verging on shorts and T-shirt weather, is my favorite.

The hot tub is bubbling over, and today, after breakfast, I'm going in. After everything that happened with Josie, I haven't stepped in the tub. Even though I went all these years tubbing solo, once I had her in it, it didn't feel the same to go back to it alone. But today is a new day. Today, I will sit in the tub, and breathe in the nature, and think about what I'm going to do with the rest of my life.

Because I *did it*. I told the world who I was. I came clean, and I feel so incredibly free. I thought that I would be overcome with anxiety. That I'd fret about my livelihood, that I'd have to take on a job in finance again, that maybe I'd even have to sell my beloved home and move elsewhere. I thought that I'd be worried about the backlash and what people would say, and hateful comments about being a fraud.

But even though my chest aches for Josie, I feel nothing but freedom. What may have originally started out as a grand gesture, quickly changed. This was not about me trying to win Josie back. This was me officially shedding the very last piece of the protective shield I've armored myself with since Amelia died.

I dig my foot into a large stone stuck into the ground, and when it releases from the marsh, I rub off the dirt with my palm and hold it to the light to try and determine what type of rock it is. It's beautiful, a color that I'm not sure I've seen before out here. Maybe this will be my new thing—rock collecting. I love agate hunting, and I live in Minnesota, dammit. The geology is spectacular. Time for me to discover more. About this area, about *me*.

Because yes, I am a widow. But you know what? I am so much more. Being a widow can no longer be my sole identity. I am also a dog mom, and a podcast host, and a damn good cook. I'm a daughter and a sister who desperately needs to reconnect with her family. I am a lover of books and crocheting and watching really terrible reality TV. I am an unashamed lover of cupcakes, and hater of edamame (no matter how much soy sauce or butter I add). I'm a lover of living in the woods, and chopping wood, of nature, and of naps.

I am more than just a person with a dead wife.

I am a survivor.

The air is so rejuvenating. Is there any other better time in Northern Minnesota than late May? The summer on the cusp of breaking through. The winter already gone and forgotten. The smell of lilac trees and pine, the rush of the rivers, the creeks at their peak from all the snow runoff. My mood has lifted, but there's a lingering pinch in my heart. I have no idea what Josie will say, if anything.

Kona and I are almost halfway home from our afternoon walk when she starts barking wildly. My chest freezes for a moment, and I pat my pocket to confirm the bear spray is ready and loaded. When I look around, though, there's no bear. But Kona is a hell of a lot more intuitive than I am, and my hair stands on edge. "It's okay, girl," I say, patting her on the side. We walk a little more, and Kona starts tugging me upwards, with her fat, floppy tail wagging.

My heart leaps. *Maybe? Could it be?* I scan the woods, turn in a full three-sixty, squint and see nothing. Oh... there. A bunny hops out from his hiding place and scurries across the path. My heart drops. Cute of course, but by some miracle (delusion, perhaps?) I thought Josie would be here. She's probably working today, back from her lunch break, logging in a pet chicken with a raspy cough. Or she's squatting down in her favorite pink cherry scrubs, rubbing an animal on the back while calming the owner and assuring them their loved one is in good hands.

The earth crunches below my hiking books as I walk a few more steps, up the hill, and I stop. Kona is barking and wagging her tail, and my heart thuds against my chest. Am I dreaming? Is this the product of me feeling this incredible relief that my mind is manifesting all of my hopes and dreams, and seeing what else I can handle?

Because at the top of the hill stands Josie. My heart leaps into my chest, drums against the column of my neck, and I freeze. Kona absolutely cannot hold back her excitement, and before she tears my arm off, I release the leash. With her tongue flapping, and tail wagging, she runs.

And so do I.

I don't take my eyes off her. I want to make sure I'm not dreaming, make sure this isn't a mirage, elicited by the golden sun cutting through the dense forest and the feelings of hopefulness that have overtaken me.

As the earth crunches beneath my boots and Josie sharpens into focus, she drops her gaze from mine and squats next to Kona, absorbing all of Kona's doggie kisses and scratching behind her ears. The hope running through my heart is electric and warm, but also tight. I don't know what Josie's going to say. Is this a goodbye forever, or let's stick with being friends, or let's dive in together and shoot for something wonderful?

Whatever it is, I'm braced and ready for it.

By the time I reach the top of the hill, I'm sort of regretting running because all I can mutter out is a heavy-breathed, "Hey."

Josie rises from squatting, with a soft grin, and pushes back a swipe of her soft pink-blond hair. "Hey," she says, digging the tip of her toe into the mossy ground.

It's only been two weeks, almost a quarter of the total time that I've known her, but I swear I didn't remember how beautiful she was. I don't have any pictures of her, and I thought I distorted the beauty in my mind. That somehow the little gap in her front teeth was not as endearing, her pale cheekbones blushed with pink wasn't quite as sweet, that her Bambi-brown eyes didn't catch the light the way that they did.

But I was wrong. She's even more beautiful.

"Do you want to sit down?" I ask, pointing to the patio set. When she nods, I follow her to the covered area, sink into the cushioned chairs, and stuff my shaky hands underneath my legs while I wait for her to speak.

Her gaze sweeps mine and she nibbles at the corner of her lip. "I listened to the journal, and the podcast."

My heart is still kicking against my chest from the run up the hill, but now it's leaped and stuck in my throat. The moment of truth has arrived. My stomach is turning so much that I feel nearly sick. Sending my journal was the most vulnerable thing I've ever done. It's my diary, my innermost thoughts, it's *me*. All of me.

"I want you to know that I didn't do that for some manipulation tactic. I just... I knew that you deserved all of the truth, and this was the way to give it to you." My face is beating so red that it feels like a blood vessel will explode. "Please know that I will completely respect your decision. If you want to never talk to me again, just say so. Of course I will be heartbroken, more than you probably know, but it's okay. Or if you want to be friends, even better. I would love to be your friend. You can come here whenever you want, you can visit Kona, you can take your walks and chop wood and we can snuggle—or not—while watching shows. Really, you tell me how I can fit into your world, and I'll do it."

Josie hesitates for so long after I say this that I score all of my words to make sure I made sense. She brushes off debris from the table and watches it flutter to the ground, then takes a deep inhale. "What if I don't want to be friends?"

It's fair. It's so unbelievably fair from what I did to her. My heart drops into my stomach, and *dammit*, my eyes are turning shiny from tears. I promised myself if she came here or wanted to talk, I wouldn't cry in front of her. I bat them back and give her a sad nod. "It's okay. I understand," I say, swallowing back the choked sob. "Then I'll say, thank you for the time you've shared with me, and I'll remember you forever. You've opened something up in me that I thought was dead, and from here on, for the rest of my life, I will be forever grateful."

Her chin trembles, and that flush in her cheeks spreads. "What if I want to be more than friends?"

My heart leaps. Does she mean that? I don't want to get my hopes up, don't want to leap out of the chair and scare the hell out of her, but my legs are buzzing with energy, my arms heavy with the need to pull her into them. I catch her gaze, reading her, the hope and fear, the hesitation.

Josie stares at her hands for a long while before speaking. "You have no idea how much it meant that you spoke to Amelia's spirit about me. For so long, I've felt sort of invisible, and never thought I'd impact anyone enough to do something like that." She reaches down to rub Kona's ears, clearly adopting the same nervous coping mechanism I've had all these years. "It still really hurts that you withheld your identity, and the show, and honestly, we are going to have to spend a lot of time rebuilding that trust. But I'm game to do it... if you want to."

If I want to? Right now, I would do just about anything to keep Josie in my life. Rebuilding trust, starting at the very beginning, starting over, whatever it takes, I am all in. "Of course I want to." My heart feels so open and raw, but now is the time to lay it all out. "I want you in my life. Everything feels lighter, more acute, sharper. You bring that joy, that sparkle, that I've been missing. I will spend whatever time it takes regaining that trust."

Josie drops her hand from Kona, and brings it back to her lap, with a soft smile tugging at the corner of her mouth. "I don't want you to think this is going to be an unfair playing field or anything. I still have things to work out on my own, and I absolutely let my inherent trust issues affect me. We're both still trying to find our way and navigating what this sort of post-self-discovery world looks like for us. But there is no one else I'd rather be on this ride with than you."

And yep, my heart has officially leaped from my stomach and back into my chest. Her smile, the sincerity in her eyes, the way she's looking at me, I want to take it all in. "Really?"

Tears form behind her lashes, and she nods. "I *love* this." She waves her hand to the forest, to Kona, to me. "I love what this is and what it all represents. And I love the new me. Well, maybe it's not the *new* me, but it's just *me*. I love who I've transitioned into, who I'm still learning to become, that I'm stronger than I ever thought." She swallows and the tears slide down her cheek. "And... I love you."

The words are so soft, lobbed so tenderly but carrying so much healing weight that it feels like she's hugging me. I push away from the chair and kneel in front of her, holding her in my arms as she embraces me back. I'm lifting and breaking and healing, with her touch, with her words, and my body trembles. "You do?" I whisper, needing to hear it again, needing the confirmation that I'm not alone on this, needing to know that even though this is scary, for me, for her, that I trust we will ride along together.

She pulls back and cups my cheeks in her hands. "I do. I really love you." Her dark eyes travel mine. "I know we're going to have ups and downs, and not everything will be smooth, but you are the only person I want to do this with. We are worth figuring this all out, together."

Josie leans in, presses her soft mouth against mine, and I melt into her. The way her body feels against me, the way our hearts are pounding against each other, the way that she is stitching me back together one minute at a time, fills my soul. "I love you, too," I say and then kiss her again.

After Amelia died, I was lost. In who I was, in what I wanted to be. And I never thought I would find love again. My body fills with the type of gratitude that I've only read about in books, the type of warmth I've only seen in movies. I squeeze her into me, bury my head into her shoulders, and sigh. "How about you get trapped here for the next, I don't know... lifetime."

A soft giggle, the most beautiful sound in the world, escapes her lips. When Kona makes a huff, clearly annoyed that she is not getting any attention, we both grin and break our embrace. She lays one hand on Kona's fur, one hand on mine, and smiles.

"That sounds... heavenly."

EPILOGUE
COLBY

One year later

"Hey, everyone. Welcome to the Half-Assed Life Hacks podcast. I'm your host, Colby Jackson. Today we have a very special guest, my beautiful, smart, and *amazing* girlfriend, Josie."

"Please keep going. I'll wait," Josie says with a chuckle as she adjusts her headphones. "Hi, everyone! Glad to be here."

I'm glad she's here, too. It took Josie a bit of convincing—six months to be exact—to be on her first show. This is only the fifth one she's done, and even though she's told me over and over she can't stand to hear herself on the podcast and is worried that she sounds ridiculous, the fan letters that come in for her, begging for her to join the show, tells something totally different. Josie has that natural charm that I fell in love with last year, and it resonates over audio to the listeners as strongly as it resonates in our home.

Our home. Sometimes, I can't even. Although Josie and I had what we call a quick-start relationship, we've taken this last year at a beautiful snail's pace. After spending only a few nights a week at my place for a solid several months, she increased her visits to the point where finally, only a few months ago, she moved in permanently.

I suck up every second with her I can. I love cooking for her, and I pretend I love the dinners she makes me. We go in the hot tub every chance we get, she takes long solo walks, and I pout over the debilitating jealousy that Kona has a new favorite, no matter how many treats I give her.

"As many of you know, Josie is a vet tech, helping heal one animal at a time. Today, we are going to be talking about the best way to bathe a dog, what to do if you're alone with a bear in the woods, and the best hidden vacation spots in northwest Minnesota. And next week, we'll be following up on the series we started last month for tasty, easy recipes to get you over the long winter. And of course, we'll have a throwback to the love advice podcast, where Josie and I will each give our perspectives."

"Tip number one. Just nod, smile, and refrain from telling the other person that you're right, even when you know dang well that you are, in fact, right," Josie says with a laugh. "Now, on to bathing our fur babies. Let's face it, friends. Dogs can be stinky. Trust me, our girl Kona here can probably win some awards on that. But did you know for some dogs, bathing too much can actually be hurting your animal? We need to look at breed, coat..."

As Josie talks into the mic, glancing at her notes that I know she doesn't need because she's phenomenal at her job, I sit back and marvel at what we've become.

When I released the episode last year, outing myself and my identity, I thought I was prepared for what would happen, but I wasn't. There was *way* more backlash than I anticipated. I was the trending topic on several social media sites. I got hate messages and emails, DMs that I could barely comprehend, people leaving angry voice messages about me being a fraud, sponsors pulling from the show, and others telling me that they hated me. Even with the harshest messages, the relief I felt about being out, about Josie coming back, helped me ride that turbulent storm.

But the other thing I wasn't expecting? The love. The massive outpouring of love from all over the country. People writing in about their own experiences with loss and grief, people sending me messages of encouragement. A small army of troll defenders on social media telling people to look past the identity piece and how much value the show has brought to their life. Dozens and dozens of the people that I gave advice to on the show wrote in to tell me how I positively affected their world.

And Josie stood by me this entire time, holding me when I cried with guilt, celebrating with me as each message of encouragement came in.

And now, as she wraps up her segment, I mouth, *I love you*, and she winks and continues talking about oatmeal-based shampoos and drying times in the winter.

I don't know what the rest of my life will look like. Will I do this podcast forever? Will Josie and I get married and grow old together? What does the universe have in store? No one knows. But what I do know is that I am ready for what the world gives me, and I'm going to tackle my life, head-on, one step at a time.

A LETTER FROM THE AUTHOR

Hey there!

Thanks so much for reading *I Will Always Love You (Maybe)*. I loved having you follow Colby and Josie's journey and concluding the Meet Cute in Minnesota series. This book was the most difficult book I've ever written. Not only was it challenging on a craft level to write a rom-com that includes death, an injured animal, and individual spiritual-healing journeys, it was deeply challenging on a personal level. I am always engrossed in my stories, but I rarely cry while writing. For this book, I had to pull myself away multiple times to take a break as the tears refused to stop.

Folks often say that grief goes in waves, and they're not wrong. Writing this story helped me gain a little bit of closure on the sudden passing of my beloved father. Although this book dealt with the loss of a spouse, there are so many parallels. The shock, your life changing in an instant, being overcome with grief one moment while laughing at memories the next. It's a journey, one that most of us will eventually take, and it's gut-wrenching. But, at least for me, the pain does lessen, and writing this story helped.

On a lighter note, I am so happy to have concluded the stories of Quinn and Zoey from *Any Girl But You*, and Morgan and Frankie from *The Ex Effect*. I had so much fun creating this fictional town in Northern Minnesota, which is heavily influenced by some of my favorite areas in this state—Two Harbors, Duluth, Grand Marais, and Lutsen.

As I continue to write my sparkly, upbeat romances celebrating queer joy, I'd love to keep you posted about my new releases and bonus content. Please sign up for my newsletter, below. I promise I won't spam you or sell your info.

www.stormpublishing.co/dana-hawkins

I'd be so grateful if you liked this book and wouldn't mind leaving a review. Even a short review can make all the difference in encouraging a reader to discover my books for the first time. Thank you so much!

I consciously choose to write stories where coming out is not an "issue" and that being LGBTQIA+ is nothing to "overcome." Creating a world where my characters live in a safe, affirming, celebratory space while navigating their relationships and real-life issues fills my heart. I am keenly aware the queer community continues to live in fear and is subject to discrimination, violence, anti-inclusive legislation, and more. I write novels that create a reality I want to be a part of—a hate-free world.

Thanks again for being part of this amazing journey with me! Please stay in touch—I have so many more stories and can't wait to share them with you.

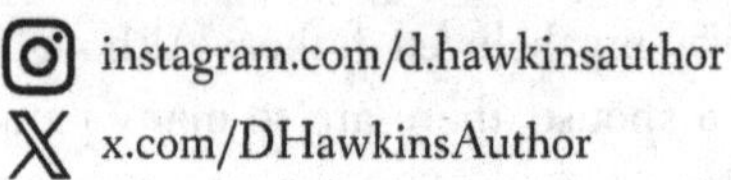

ACKNOWLEDGMENTS

To my spouse, "My Forever." I seriously love you. Thank you for everything, always.

Jennifer Gatewood. My life-long shoulder-shimmying partner! Over the years, watching our friendship grow along with our careers has been so deeply gratifying. Thank you for always being there for me and for critiquing my work. Please prepare yourself for the longest hug of all time, and perhaps a little dance, when I finally meet you in person.

S.E. Reed. What would I do without you? Your constant celebration, support, and love mean everything to me. You are the cheerleader and friend that I always dreamed of, the one standing in my corner, screaming for me louder than everyone. Thank you for always being there for me. Two years, baby! (*You know what I'm talking about.*)

To my kiddos, Tanner, Kianna, and Joey. My babies! I love you.

To Erica Dusha. Thank you for putting up with me! Still.

To Esther Dusha. Your strength always astounds me. You are a gift to this world!

To Dr. Joe Freeman. Thank you for answering so many of my health-related questions for this book! Your time and expertise are extremely valuable, and I am so grateful you were so willing to walk me through some of these details.

To Ms. N. Ah! Still the greatest teacher my children have ever had. It's been years, and they talk about you all the time. Thank you for the inspiration for the character name. ;-)

To Emily Gowers. This book was tough, and I appreciate you so much getting on multiple calls with me to guide me through everything. You are a dream partner. Six books! We've done six books together, and you have literally changed my life. Thank you for taking a chance on me.

To "Team Jenna." You all are the best!

And to my agent, Jenna Satterthwaite. Book #3 between us done. My life completely changed after we met and you offered to be in my corner. I feel like I thank you over and over, but it's still not enough. I truly hope you understand the deep impact you have on me and others. Thank you, thank you, for having me on your team!